GLASS TOWN WARS

'*Glass Town Wars* is a beautifully crafted, multilayered story with a gripping adventure at its heart. Wonderful'

MELVIN BURGESS

'Celia Rees' stories are always clever, inventive and packed with incident, and *Glass Town Wars* is particularly striking... Dazzling!'

LINDA NEWBERY

'Excellent'

AMANDA CRAIG, THE BOOKSELLER

'A conflict-drenched adventure with more than a whiff of *Game of Thrones*... The intricate and intriguing plot is driven by drama, by ancient rites of passage and by magic'

BOOKS FOR KEEPS (FIVE STARS)

'Rees's gorgeous prose unfolds a tale of intrigue, love and power... Rees effortlessly weaves in fairies, enchantment and a sinister hacker who's at the centre of the plot. Wise and sweeping, this novel will enrapture readers'

PHILIP WOMACK, LITERARY REVIEW

'Imaginative and inventive'

A DREAM OF BOOKS

'Rees takes her inspiration from the early writings of the Brontë siblings creating a compelling narrative that will find favour with teenaged readers'

THE BAY

GLASS

TOWN

WARS

CELIA

REES

Pushkin Press
71–75 Shelton Street
London WC2H 9JQ

Copyright © 2018 Celia Rees

First published by Pushkin Press in 2018
This edition first published by Pushkin Press in 2019

3 5 7 9 8 6 4 2

ISBN 13: 978-1-78269-163-1

Designed and typeset by Tetragon, London
Printed and bound by CPI Group (UK) Ltd, Croydon CR0 4YY

www.pushkinpress.com

GLASS

TOWN

WARS

*To the memory of Emily Brontë (1818–1848)
and in celebration of her bicentenary (1818–2018)*

No coward soul is mine,
No trembler in the world's storm-troubled sphere:
I see Heaven's glories shine,
And Faith shines equal, arming me from Fear.

"No Coward Soul Is Mine"
EMILY BRONTË

CHAPTER ONE

A CONJURING

NOTHING IS STRAIGHTFORWARD. Nothing is as it seems...

As in life, so in dreams.

To bring the two together, it was important to stay still, to concentrate, not to blink. It was a ritual, a kind of seance, conducted in the early hours, when the rest of the house was quiet, when the rest of the house was sleeping. She sat on the floor, the dog stretched out by her side, his thick brass collar gleaming in moonlight that was shining bright through the window and making patterns, casting sharp, blue shadows on the wall opposite.

That was where she'd seen it before.

A tower. A glass tower, glass from top to bottom, all lit and aglitter. Other lights flashed and flowed around it, red, blue and silver, like a stream diverted. In the tower was a room, all white, a white box, a white cube. Inside the cube, a boy lay on a bed, not moving, his eyes sightless. The boy was as white as the sheets tucked about him, as white as the walls that surrounded him, but he wasn't dead, neither was he dying: he lay somewhere between unknown and unknowing, alone between two states of being, machines keeping him alive, machines doing the breathing for him, machines that she did not know or

11

recognize, machines such as Mrs Shelley's doctor might have invented.

She put her hand, star shaped, against the cool, smooth glass of the window. The boy needed her help but she didn't know how to reach him, how to give it.

CHAPTER TWO

THE ECHENEIS PROJECT

MILES. Milo Mindbender. He'd taken the name from that guy in *Catch-22*. Tom should have known not to trust him but what could he do? He was lying here, as helpless as a monkey strapped to a table in a lab.

He heard him from way down the corridor, boot heels clicking on the floor. Swish of the door. Nothing wrong with his hearing; it was more acute, if anything. A displacement of the hospital air, the tang of fags and Ralph Lauren aftershave added to hospital antiseptic. They say the other senses, the ones you're left with, kick in, don't they? He'd found that to be true.

The girl stopped reading. She was a friend of his sister's, part of a rota of people who came in to talk, read, play music, even sing songs to him. Anything to try and get through. That was the idea but Tom found most of them tedious, what they did pointless; he wanted them to go away as soon as they came through the door. She was different. He couldn't remember her name—there were a lot of things he couldn't remember—but he liked it when she was here. Just her and him and the chunk, beep and chirp of the machines, as regular as heartbeats and breathing, which was what they were there to monitor and do. He liked to hear her. It gave him a peaceful feeling. He was annoyed at the disruption that Milo would bring.

Milo was tall and skinny, dressed in a black suit: slim-fit, tailored with narrow trousers, narrow lapels, over a white shirt and narrow black tie. How did Tom know that? Because that was what he always wore.

He came close, casting an eye over the machines that were keeping Tom alive. He was a whizz at electronics. Tom hoped he wouldn't fiddle with anything, or think of making a few little adjustments…

Milo walked round the bed, hands in pockets, his fingers turning over coins.

He stopped. Spun around. He always moved like that. Still, then quick and jerky. Each movement unexpected.

"Get us a coffee, love, would you?" The chink of coinage. "There's a machine down the corridor. White. Two sugars. Get one for yourself while you're at it."

"Why should I?" The girl's voice was low and even, but not because she was the mousy quiet type. There was a yawn at the back of it, as if she didn't care a whole lot.

"Because I'm asking!" Milo didn't like "No", especially from girls. "Give us a bit of guy time. Boy talk, you know?"

"They're not even sure he can hear anything," she said.

"That right? So why are you here boring the arse off him with that book?"

The book snapped shut; the chair scraped on the floor.

"I've got money, thank you," she said.

Milo pocketed his change.

The door opened. Closed.

There was just him and Milo.

"How ya doin', Big Man? Not so good, from what I hear. Natalie's doing a great job on social media—thought you'd like to know. You've got a ton of followers. I mean, *Hashtag heroinacoma* is going even better. She's even raising funds. Not sure what they're for. I've tried to get her to invest in MiloMindbender but so far, no dice. Here's the thing…" he said, coming closer. Tom could smell the smoke on his clothes, the mint on his breath. There was a rustle as he took something out of his pocket. "You're lying here not doing anything and I've got a little something that might fill those empty hours. It's real small. Practically invisible. It's called Echeneis, named after some kind of magic fish. Made from this wonder substance. Even I don't understand the science. All *you* need to know is that it works like so…" He was very near. Tom felt something go into his ear. "At least, we *think* it does." Tom heard the shrug in his voice. "We don't really know."

What is it? Tom wanted to yell at him. *What do you mean, you don't know how it works? What have you done?* But he couldn't move, couldn't even blink, and it was in there now.

Tom felt Milo step back, watching, as if he was waiting for something to happen.

"The potential is *huge*," Milo went on when nothing did. "It will take gaming to a whole new level." He carried on talking, filling the time, waiting to see what the result might be. "I mean, we've been gaming since we were little kids, right?" He laughed. "Xbox and all that. I always won."

Of course he did. He was a genuine genius. He passed A level Maths and Computing when he was twelve. He didn't play games any more—he wrote them. He was a bitcoin millionaire well on his way to becoming a real one. He ran his own software company from his garage, MiloMindbender and Associates. There were no Associates. He made a ton of money hosting sites where people buy and sell things, although he never said what exactly: "*Oh, you know, this and that.*"

"Well, here's the thing. What you've got in your ear, it's gonna make the gaming we've got right now look like old-style Atari ping-pong. You're always on the outside, right? Looking at your console, your computer, your tablet, or phone, or whatever. But what if you could be actually *inside* the game?" His voice went dreamy. "What if you could be living it? Not just hear and see but feel, smell, taste it—just like in the real world. What if it can *become* your real world? VR headsets? Nowhere near this… It will take you places, bro. Give you experiences…"

This thing in his ear, it was something to do with games and gaming. Milo's new project.

"You know? I'm almost jealous…" Milo was saying.

Almost. Not quite.

"It's, hmm, experimental. A prototype," he was saying. "Yeah. Not one hundred per cent certain what the effect might be but I figured you might as well do something useful while you're lying here." His voice lost its easy, bantering tone, and dropped to a menacing purr. "Let's face it, you've got nothing to lose, have you? Hey!" Tom heard the rustle of the shirt inside his sleeve as Milo reached across him. "I wonder what *this* does?"

Just then, the door opened.

Milo moved quickly away from the bed.

"Gotta go," he said. "Things to do."

"Your coffee?"

"Another time, maybe."

Tom started fitting.

The coffee hit the deck.

Alarms went off.

"That's *very* cool." There was a laugh from Milo as the girl ran out to get help. "I like to know how things work. See you, bro."

"You'll have to leave now," a female voice said—one of the nurses.

"No problem, darling. I'm off."

A doctor came in. Adjustments were made to this, to that, but Tom wasn't there any more. He was somewhere else entirely. Somewhere he'd never been, never seen, never known. It was something to do with Milo, he did know that. What had he done to him? And now Tom was here—wherever "here" was—how was he going to get back?

CHAPTER THREE

THE SUMMONING

THE MOON HAD GONE from the window. In the unsteady light of a candle, the drawings on the wall opposite seemed to move and flicker. The longer she stared, the more she would see, until the rest of the room became insubstantial, as easily erased as pencil on a page, and ceased to exist at all.

"Play nicely, children," Aunt would say. "Play nicely!"

They never played nicely. They fought up and down the Parsonage stairs with sticks, broom handles, anything they could find. Then, when their roaring got too much, with Tabby shouting for them to "stop their racket" and Father complaining from his study that he couldn't hear himself think; when the house became just too confining, they barrelled out and on to the moors, into the wind and the sun. Running, always running, over the hills, hiding in the deep glens, waiting, scarcely breathing, ready to leap out in ambush and renew the battle. They dammed the little streams and rills, creating lakes and seas. Finally, out of breath and tired, they would throw themselves down and lie in a circle, heads together, making kingdoms in the clouds, palaces and towers, white and shining, sunlit and glowing, or grey and glowering, ever-changing at the whim of the wind. They were making a world for the Twelve, for them to voyage and explore. The Twelve had long stepped from the box given to Branwell by Papa; they were no longer just wooden soldiers, as *they* were no longer just children. They were the Genii, creators of worlds.

They were as one then. All together. Only later did they begin to bicker and squabble over how this new world should be. The game had come back inside the house and inside the head. She and Anne, the two youngest, sided together in natural rebellion at being bossed by the older two. The game was changing in ways they didn't like, with Branwell's endless wars, battles and tiresome politics and Charlotte's obsession with handsome but cruel, cigar-smoking heroes and long-suffering, simpering heroines whom she threw together in unlikely romances.

In greatest secrecy, Emily and Anne had begun to plan their own world. It would be discovered by Parry and Ross, their soldiers from the Original Twelve. Led by Emily's character, Augusta, they would establish a new territory and call it Gondal.

Therein lies the difficulty…

The candle flame bent, as if in a sudden draught, and she knew she wasn't the only one awake in the house. It might have begun as a game that they played when they were children, but they were no longer children and this was no game. She sensed him, felt his intention, his power seeping out like the light from under his door. Charlotte, his ally, was absent, but that didn't matter. They had been scheming, conspiring, reading each other's writing, spurring each other on. Emily could feel his fury, his arrogance and ambition, sense his excitement.

They'd found out about Gondal. How? Although she wouldn't admit any such thing, Emily suspected that Anne had told Charlotte, tricked into it by her older sister's interest. Anne would have found it impossible to resist her; Charlotte was good at wheedling and cozening and finding things out. Whatever the way of it, they *knew* and, now they knew, they would use every means to prevent her from leaving. They meant to crush her for once and all, and that meant war.

Anne was too young to get involved in such bloody business. She had to be protected from the wars and fighting. Emily had set her to drawing maps and making plans, sketching the characters that she'd invented. Anne was quite happy and didn't bother Emily—well, not too much anyway. The odd "Yes, that's nice. That's good" sent her away satisfied. Emily's most common response was "I'll look at it later", but she was always sure to thank her younger sister and, for the most part, Anne went off happy in her dreams of lords and ladies, doodling their hairstyles, designing their dresses, and left Emily to fight alone.

CHAPTER FOUR
HIGH LAND RIDGE

SHE WAS STANDING HIGH UP, under a wide sky just turning towards evening, rain blowing into her face. Fir trees grew around her, their dark needles feathered with fingers of bright new leaf. The full force of the Glass Town Federation, a mustering of the Founding Twelve, was sweeping across the plain towards her like a summer storm. Her own men, Parry and Ross, were far away in the distant North, exploring the frozen regions, their ships bearded with ice as they voyaged to ultima Thule in search of the fabled North-west Passage from the Atlantic to the Pacific. Many had died in the attempt to find it, but she was sure they would succeed and enable her to escape for ever. She should have gone with them and braved the frozen ocean, the mountains of ice. Staying here, even this long, was a mistake.

A high ridge in a desolate landscape. Drear and drab, all browns and greys, and it was sluicing with rain. The narrow path was stony, fast turning into a stream as it wound between gorse bushes, low wiry clumps of heather, thin spiky rushes and tufts of coarse grass. He looked up through the water dripping in front of his eyes. Not far to go by the looks of it. He slowed. The ground was slippery and he didn't know what might be waiting over the other side. His head felt heavy, strange. He was used to his body giving him weird sensations: of being too big, or too small, or not there at all, but this was different. He put up a hand and found that he was wearing some kind of furry helmet, like a bearskin, but smaller, square, and on the side was something that felt like feathers. A sodden cockade. He looked down at himself. He was wearing a uniform with frogging across the front of it, the wire threads tarnished and rusty from the rain and dampness; under his cloak, the green wool jacket was dark and soaking, the wet seeping through, meeting the sweat from his body. He pulled his collar closer to stop cold water from trickling down his neck and to keep the moisture inside, heated by his body, so that his uniform acted like a kind of woollen wetsuit. *How do I know to do that?*

If this was a game, like Milo said, he'd have expected to be in combats—light and comfortable, breathing with the body, water repellent—sitting in an armoured car maybe, or a hummer, riding across the desert somewhere, sorting out jihadi warriors; or in an urban landscape, some kind of futuristic scene, full of dereliction, with burnt-out buildings, broken-down bridges, smashed-up carriageways strewn with corpses, bodies in ditches on either side of the road. That kind of thing.

He wasn't expecting this. He was on a horse, for Chrissakes, with boots up to his thighs, a rifle at his knee and a sabre hanging down by his side. He couldn't even ride but he was managing fine and his horse, a big bay gelding, didn't seem to mind. The horse plodded along, picking his way carefully, ears pinned back, mane streaming, enjoying the rain about as much as his rider.

Tom shook his head, attempting to get the water out of his eyes without dislodging his hat. He rode on, trying to figure out exactly who, or what, he was. Some kind of avatar, although you didn't get cold and wet in any game he knew. He'd have to tell Milo about that. Telling would not be that easy, of course. Telling would be problematic. Telling would be the difficult thing. Which was why this was happening...

The big horse shifted under him, snorting and lifting his head, his ears flicking as if sensing his rider's sudden fear.

"Woah, boy." He leant forward, patting the horse's neck, speaking into his ear. "Steady now."

The horse's name was Hector. *How do I know that?*

The path took another turn, bringing him closer to the top of the ridge. Thin streamers of mist had detached from the low-hanging cloud, wrapping themselves around a line of dark, ragged pines. It was colder up here; steam puffed from Hector's nostrils as he took the steepness of the slope. The terrain flattened near the top and the thin path broadened out into a wider track. Smooth stones shone, slick with rain. The way was marked with rounded boulders, crusted with moss and lichen and carved with strange patterns.

Hector came to a halt, whinnying and whickering and taking dainty sideways steps, as a figure came out from under the dripping branches of the trees. A young officer, slenderly built, long hair tied back with a black silk ribbon, in highly polished boots splashed to the knee guards, buff breeches spattered with mud as though he had been riding hard. He wore a tight-fitting blue jacket, the thick epaulettes fringed and crusted with silver. A sabre hung down by his side. He was holding a long brass spyglass. As Tom rode closer, something about the slight build and the stance made him think that this handsome young chap was a girl.

"You took yer time." A girl's voice with a bit of an accent, like he was in the North somewhere. It seemed that he was expected and he was late, or something. She sounded annoyed, impatience masking her anxiety. "How many men have you brought?"

Her gaze went behind him.

Tom turned in the saddle. He'd been riding at the head of a troop of men, as sodden and miserable as him. They were already dismounting, unsaddling their horses, getting ready to set up camp.

Her hawk-sharp, clear grey eyes narrowed.

"Who are you?" Her look was appraising, accusing. "Get down from the horse. Take off your headgear."

He dismounted and removed his sodden shako, tucking it under his arm. *How do I know it's called that?*

One of her men took his horse's bridle. Two more stepped forward: one big, thickset with a thatch of wheat-coloured hair; the other nearly as tall but thinner, dark and wiry. Each held a long musket armed with a bayonet edged as thin as a razor blade. They thrust their bayonets towards his belly. He put up his hands in surrender, but to whom and for what, he didn't know.

"What's yer name?" She stood back, arms folded. The point of a bayonet flicked a button from his jacket. "Did Parry or Ross send you? Are they back?"

He shrugged at questions he could not answer.

"You're not one of mine." Her eyes darkened with suspicion. "So you must be one of theirs. Can you not speak? What's your name?" she asked again, sharp and imperious. "Answer me!"

He shook his head. There was an empty space where a name should have been...

The rain was still streaming down, wet hair falling into his eyes. The strands he pushed back were black. His hand encountered thick curls. They'd shaved his head, he knew that; the stubble growing back had itched his scalp. But his hair had been fair, not black.

Brain damage—memory loss one of the symptoms—but that wasn't the reason his real name was gone.

As she stared, a name came to him.

"Tom. My name is Tom. Who are you?"

"Lady Augusta Geraldine Almeida," she said with a certain pride and flourish, like he was supposed to be impressed. "I'm in command here. You are a captain?"

"How do you know?"

"By yer epaulette."

Tom peered sideways at his shoulder. "Oh, yes. I guess."

Augusta frowned. "You don't know much, do you? You don't know your name, your rank. Who *are* you?"

Tom shrugged. He had no answer.

"Are you one of theirs?" she questioned. "Come to deceive? Come to spy?"

"Who are they?" he asked.

Augusta stared at him a long moment, then her eyes changed colour, as if she'd made her mind up about something, turning from storm-cloud dark to a lighter grey.

"Come wi' me."

She led him into a small campaign tent pitched under the trees. It smelt of damp canvas and wet grass. A huge dog lay under a folding wooden table, his smooth fur yellow and brown. He lifted his massive head from his paws at their approach and came loping from under the table, his muzzle drawn back in a snickering snarl.

"Keeper, down."

The dog subsided back on to the ground but kept an amber eye fixed on Tom and continued a low, rumbling growl.

The girl unrolled a map, smoothing it across rough wooden slats, and beckoned Tom forward.

He bent his head to look closer, sweeping back his hair to stop it dripping on to the parchment. The map was beautifully hand-drawn and coloured to show seas, countries, rivers, mountains, plains and forests, towns and villages, each place marked in small, neat black lettering. He frowned down at a country he didn't recognize, at names he'd never seen.

"We are here, see?" She pointed at a ridge marked by little, spiky dark-green fir trees. Her thin finger moved to the plain below. "They are there."

She took the long brass telescope from the table and left the tent. He followed her up through tall, dripping pines, their trunks bare and rough. Shed needles, like a silver carpet, deadened their footsteps.

When they neared the top of the ridge, she put out her hand.

"Far enough. If we're watching them, they're watching us."

Augusta crept forward stealthily and put the spyglass to her eye, twisting the long brass barrel. She beckoned him to her.

"Come on. Take a look."

Tom took the telescope, adjusted it to his own sight and trained it down on to the wide plain spread out before them. A vast army, as far as the eye can see. Smoke rising from innumerable campfires; little figures, miniaturized by distance to the size of toy soldiers, moved about, setting up camp. Teams of horses hauling cannon into position; men on horseback riding to and fro, bent on urgent business, delivering and taking messages to and from a command tent standing in the centre of the encampment: a grand pavilion panelled in red and blue, fluttering with flags and streaming with pennants.

"Looks like you're in trouble," he said.

Augusta looked at him, her eyes darkening again. Was he here to help? Or had he been sent to trick her? He'd brought men with him. Reinforcements she badly needed. To turn him away might be foolish, or worse. His men were in her camp now. The battle would be over before it had begun. She looked away, making her mind up. She would set him a test for his loyalty, his bravery, to see if he was her man or not.

"See that big tent?" She pointed.

Tom nodded.

"See them standards outside it?"

Tom nodded again, focusing on two tall military standards on an ornate golden pole, the quartered flags, flapping and snapping in the wind.

"Get them. Bring them here to me and I'll decide."

"Decide what?"

"Whether you live or die."

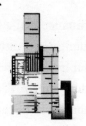

"Keeper. Sit."

The dog stayed with Augusta at the top of the ridge, settling down by her side to watch the mysterious Tom With No Name set off into the gloom of oncoming night. *Who* is *he?* She put that aside for the moment. Whoever he was, he'd brought soldiers with him. Riflemen, and she was in need of them. She'd see if he passed the test she'd set him. Her guards, Webster and Roberts, had gone with him, with strict orders to cut his throat if he showed the least sign of turning his coat. She watched them follow a snaking path down the hillside into the murk and misting rain and then moved the telescope to focus on the sprawling encampment below her.

All she wanted was to be free. She hated the city in the South; the heat; the day-and-night din from the crowded streets and the great mills and factories. The very scale of the Great Glass Town was exhausting: the wide avenues, the vast squares, the blinding glitter of soaring towers. She had grown to hate the grand palaces; the intrigues that went on within the marble walls, behind the great porticoed doors. She hated the gossip and the politics of the taverns and coffee houses. High life, low life—it didn't interest her. All the time she was there, she longed for her own country: the oak, the ash and the bonny willow tree; to be under grey skies with cold wind on her face and rain in the air. In her *own* country, living her *own* life—but even there, they would not leave her be. They had pursued her. Declared war on her. Sent the might of the Twelve against her. To take her back to Glass Town in chains if needs be. She didn't even have her commanders, Parry and Ross. They were far off in the Arctic Sea. Through them, she planned to escape for ever, but that dream was distant.

All she had now was a boy soldier who didn't seem to know his own name. He hadn't come out of any toy box, though. At least, she didn't think so... He'd better prove useful, because her forces were few while theirs were many and this was where she'd chosen to make her stand.

She had the advantage of higher ground but her men were spread thin, even with the reinforcements brought by this Captain Tom, wearing the green of a Rifle Company. Except she had no Rifle Company—neither did Ross and neither did Parry—so who *was* he? He *seemed* real enough but he'd come from nowhere. Not hers. Not *theirs*, either. She would bet on it. They were clever but not that clever. They couldn't conjure from nothing. He was brave, this soldier boy. He'd not flinched from the bayonets. And resourceful. He'd taken up her challenge without a word. He'd studied the camp and made careful preparations. He could be useful, and beggars cannot choose. She watched on, intrigued, wondering what he would do.

He'd swapped his uniform for homespun. He pulled the dark cloak round him, hood up against the weather. His mule, laden with panniers, delicately picked its way down the stony, slippery path. The two guards walked behind, similarly cloaked and hooded. Beneath their cloaks, they all carried bayonets honed to razor sharpness.

They entered from the far side of the camp, distant from the tents and campfires of the centre, an area of baggage trains and storage. They made their way past piles of sacks and barrels. There were few about, the men too intent on finding a fire, hot food, rum, a place to shelter from the penetrating rain. They plodded on past the tethered mules and horses, Webster cutting the lines as they went. They followed the mud-churned roadway, making for the heart of the camp, ignoring the growing muddle that followed them as horses and mules began to break free. Just as quickly, just as efficiently, Webster and Roberts slashed the guys that held the tents, causing the heavy canvas to collapse, trapping the men inside with outbursts of swearing and startled, muffled cries.

The bayonets disappeared back inside their cloaks as they neared the command tent. Here they split up. Tom signalled to Roberts to go left, Webster to go right, tipping braziers over as they passed. The glowing hot coals tumbled on to the oiled-silk panels, burning through to the dry canvas beneath. Flames shot up the sides of the tent; smoke began to billow. Tom held his mule steady as a big man came out, looking bewildered. He was very stout with a little pointy head. He moved stiffly, as if he was wearing some kind of corset; Tom could almost hear the creak. He was in his shirtsleeves, braces down—he must have been caught at his toilette. Equerries followed, throwing his shaving water over the fire.

While all this was happening, Tom was steadily backing his mule into the flagpoles. First one then the other toppled over into the mud. Tom took out his bayonet and severed both flags. He flung them over the back of the mule and then threw his cloak over them to disguise the red and gold. He plodded off through the shouting and spreading confusion, Roberts and Webster falling in beside him as they took the track to the other side of the camp. From there, they would work their way back to the ridge.

"Here." Tom spread the flags before her like a carpet, like a challenge.

"That's the easy part," Augusta said. Nevertheless, she was impressed. She smiled, remembering the Duke running out, braces dangling. "Lions rampant, gules with cross argent and five roundels; cross argent on sable, quartered with scallops." She walked over the flags. "The arms of my enemies, the ancient family of Wellesley. Now we have to defeat them in battle."

She was looking at him now like she was pleased he'd passed her test. More than that—as if she was expecting something from him.

He stepped back from the standards with their lions, spots and shells embroidered in silver and gold, and knew that he would help her. She needed him, and that gave him a sense of purpose. He felt the strange, lost feeling receding. Maybe it was what he was here to do.

"Let's have a look at the map," he said.

She was right. Getting those flags was the easy bit. He frowned down at the blocks of colour. Red marked the enemy on the plain; her troops, along the ridge, were shown in blue. That told him very little, except how small her force was compared with theirs. He picked up the telescope and went out.

Tom inspected the lines and found a few cannon, infantry armed with muskets, plus the men he'd brought with him, but no cavalry that he could see. Then he went to the ridge to look at the army below. The weaponry, the uniforms, looked Napoleonic. From somewhere in his scrambled-up memory, a game came back to him: a multiplayer, turn-based strategy game set in those times, so he knew a little bit about munitions capabilities and battlefield tactics.

"What do you think?" she asked when he returned to the tent.

He snapped the telescope shut and handed it back to her.

The dog growled softly as if it still didn't trust him.

You've got no chance, he wanted to say. *What we need is some decent field artillery and some heavy machine guns. A tank or two would be nice—why not? And maybe some attack helicopters. Let's chuck in the lot.* For a minute, he could see it. That would throw a scare into the opposition. But that wasn't going to happen. He looked down at the map instead.

"We deploy the artillery, here, here and here." He pointed to spots along the ridge. "Muskets here, rifles there. We have the advantage of higher ground but they have the numbers. We re-enforce our flanks, set men to dig ditches, cut and sharpen stakes to foil their cavalry and we hit them when they least expect it, so we attack at first light. Meanwhile, Webster and Roberts can go down in advance with a couple of other men, use darkness as cover, do their best to sabotage things a little bit."

She seemed impressed by his decisiveness. He was a little impressed himself.

"Sabotage?" she asked, shaking her head as though the word was unfamiliar.

"You know, mess things up. Set the horses free, make sure their gunpowder's wet, that kind of thing, and nick—steal—whatever they can. Webster, Roberts—with me."

These two would be his own special forces. On their little trip to steal the standards, he'd kind of bonded with them. They were big guys, strong and capable; they moved quietly and thought quickly.

"We know what to do, Cap'n." Webster grinned. "Me and Robbo'll tak a couple of donkeys down there, crack on. We've been told to move gear up the lines and help ourselves to what we can carry. We'll open the black powder barrels." He turned his face up to the fine rain. "Should be good and wet by morning. We'll cut the horse lines while we're at it."

Tom wandered the ridge, thinking about tactics. It was boggy down there, marshy, and this constant rain had made it more so. There was standing water between the reeds and rushes at the base of the scarp. Tricky going for men and horses alike. He'd seen it in some war game, the name of which he couldn't recall. Not set in this era—there had been knights on horseback and archers—but, just like here, a small force had faced a larger, and the terrain had meant the difference between victory and defeat. Funny how things like that came back to him, when he'd temporarily misplaced his own name. Augusta must have thought he was really stupid.

Tom's memory was coming and going like a dodgy signal. He shook his head, as if that would rattle everything back into place. *What am I even doing here, thinking about tactics and stuff? If this is a game, whose is it?* Whatever the game, he was in it now. He had to play it. He didn't appear to have any choice.

He prowled, restless. The camp was quiet. Some men tried to sleep, but sleep comes hard before a battle. Someone played softly on a penny whistle; others spoke in quiet whispers or kept their own counsel, thinking on what the next day would bring, as they busied themselves at little tasks: repairing kit by the light of the campfires, cleaning their weapons, honing blades with the patient sweep of a whetstone. Tom wasn't above a few butterflies himself.

The light was creeping up into the eastern sky, too soon for some; for others it was a relief, as though they had thought morning would never come.

He made his way up on the ridge.

Augusta hadn't been able to sleep, either. She joined him under the pine trees.

The rain had stopped; a thin mist was rising. The camp below them was still in darkness, little stirring.

There had been no retaliatory raid to repossess the colours, or punish their taking, although she knew that they would feel it as cruel insult and humiliation. That did not fill her with confidence. *Why would they bother?* They would take them back soon enough and pay any insult with interest.

Tom and Augusta gazed down, taken up with their own thoughts, both of them wondering what the day would bring and who the other might be.

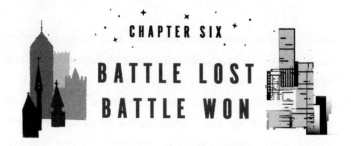

CHAPTER SIX
BATTLE LOST
BATTLE WON

THE GUNS WERE LOUD. They filled the air and shook the ground, the thudding carriage recoil sending shock waves up through Tom's body. Smoke billowed in drifting clouds of white and grey, catching in the throat and bringing stinging tears. The gunners' faces were already black with it, just their eyes showing white. The air reeked of gunpowder; he could taste it, along with the metal tang of adrenaline. No game had ever been as exciting as this.

Cannonballs flew, hitting the camp below, smashing tents, catching men as they ran out into the open. Screams and yells, thinned by distance, came on the wind. The sudden bombardment was causing just the kind of chaos that they wanted. His riflemen and musketeers were ranged across the hillside, one line behind the other. Their guns were cumbersome, loading slow, neither rifle nor musket accurate over any distance, but with one line loading while the other fired, they were keeping up a steady rate of fire. His orders were to make every shot count. Men below them were falling under the fusillade. He had the best shots next to him, aiming at the officers as they tried to organize and rally the men. The object was to harry and confuse, not to allow their enemy to form up and mount any kind of attack.

Augusta had told him to keep his sights on the big tent and wait for the commanders to emerge. There was no mistaking them. The first to come out was the fat guy with a pointy head, bursting out of his buckskin breeches, his blue jacket stiff with gold facings, with epaulettes the size of dinner plates, boots polished to mirror brightness and wearing the biggest bicorne hat that Tom had ever seen. He was joined by another, younger, in the red of a foot regiment, the white plumes in his tall hat waving in the wind. They were both making for horses that were being brought up for them. Tom had them in his sights, but with this weapon from this distance...

Before he could take his shot, the hat went flying. Augusta was standing above him, reloading, oblivious of the musket balls flying around her, cursing that she'd hit the hat not the head inside it. His own shot went wide and, by the time they were ready to fire again, both generals were spurring away—never mind the soldiers being blown to pieces around them—thundering through their own troops, the confused mess of the camp, riding over the dead and the wounded, making for the rear as fast as their horses could carry them.

The Duke and his son, Douro. She was not surprised at their pell-mell retreat. It was only to be expected.

Their army was mostly for show, to parade and intimidate by sheer numbers. The officers were more interested in strutting round Glass Town, showing off their elaborate and expensive uniforms, than actually fighting. Her smaller force was made up of men from the North, loyal and unwavering, fighting for their land, their homes and villages, their way of life.

The strange young man who had appeared from nowhere seemed to know what he was about, but it wasn't won yet.

She put the glass to her eye to scan the ground below her. The generals turning tail, with most of the officers behind them, seemed to have taken the heart out of the troops.

Augusta looked to her own lines. Their bombardment was constant but the piles of shot were diminishing. They couldn't keep this rate of fire up for long.

She swung the eyeglass back, attracted by a movement below her. A line of battle was forming, organized by an officer on horseback, hatless and helmet-less, his long, curling chestnut hair streaming behind him as he galloped back and forth, shouting orders and waving his sabre. He was keeping on the move, riding up and down the line, turning and wheeling, deliberately making himself a difficult target. He was getting the men in place, getting them organized. They seemed to take on some of his reckless defiance; as soon as one man fell, another stepped up to take his place.

"Rogue" Percy. Whatever the odds, he would not turn and run. Neither would Captain Dorn. She could see his short, powerful figure marshalling the infantry, directing the men forward, bayonets at the ready. The line came on steadily through their own thinning cannon fire.

Rogue wheeled away, leaving the command of the infantry to Dorn. His return was just as sudden, at a thunderous gallop, sabre pointing forward, at the head of a column of heavy cavalry. Carabineers, armed with short muskets and horse pistols. Big men in plumed brass helmets, armoured front and back, bandoliers crossing their shining breastplates. He must have been keeping them in reserve. The mix of flamboyance and cunning was typical of him.

At his command, their sabres flashed red in the rising sun. At Dorn's shout, the line of infantry broke apart, the cavalry streaming through the gap, preparing to fan out and charge up the slope, sabres drawn to cut to left and right, their big horses ready to trample the men on the ground.

Well, let them come…

"Back! Fall back!" Tom ordered, directing his men to higher ground. "Hold position!"

Their apparent retreat accelerated the charge, which was just what he wanted. The heavy horses, weighed down by the big men in their armour, were caught in the marshy ground at the base of the slope. The charge halted as the carabineers tried to free their horses from the sucking mud. Ball and bullet pinged off metal as the horses struggled. The air was filled with the frantic neigh and snort of frightened horses and the shouts and screams of the men as the musket balls found their mark. Horses and riders went down, adding to the melee and confusion. The carabineers returned fire from horseback, but they couldn't gain the slope and their horses were sinking deeper into the quagmire. The helmetless officer wheeled his sabre three times as the sign to withdraw.

A ragged cheer went up along the line of riflemen and musketeers lying prone on the hillside. They had won the day.

Tom stood up, slightly unsteady, light-headed with elation. He'd never felt such a rush, such a buzz. He waved his hat, grinning and laughing, accepting the salutations of his men.

Below him, the young officer turned back, steadied his carbine over one arm and took aim. A punching blow to the shoulder threw Tom backwards. He looked down in wonder at the hole smouldering in his jacket, at the bright blood welling from it. For a long moment, he felt no pain, and then it hurt like hell.

Augusta didn't see him go down, her attention taken by the enemy forces disappearing into the smoke and dust. The retreat was as unexpected as it was sudden, and not altogether to be trusted...

The enemy camp was strangely empty except for ragged women and children picking their way through the wreckage. Where they came from was a mystery but every battlefield knew them; they descended like the carrion birds—crow, raven and kite—wheeling in the sky above, ready to descend to feed on the dead and dying.

The boy. What had happened to the boy? Without him, the day would have been lost. This victory was his.

"Come, Keeper."

The dog followed as she strode down the hillside. He had stayed by her side, steadfast through the fighting, undaunted by the din of battle and the cannons' roar.

They found the boy being helped to his feet, supported by Webster and Roberts.

"He's hurt, my lady. Hit in the shoulder."

The boy was deadly pale and near to fainting.

"Take him to my tent. Have him tended to and look to the other wounded."

The two men carried him between them, trying to be gentle, trying not to hurt him, but every jolt sent pain shooting through him and fresh blood leaking. He could feel it running down his arm, dripping from his dangling wrist. His sleeve and the front of his jacket were soaked, the stain black on the bottle-green cloth. *What kind of game is this, where you feel real pain and bleed real blood?*

He was lying on a small camp bed, Webster cutting his coat away for Roberts to inspect the wound. Roberts frowned and rolled up his sleeves. He washed his hands in the basin on a stand by the bed and dipped a cloth in the ewer to swab round the wound. He wrung the reddened water into the basin before soaking the cloth again.

"Here, lad, drink some of this." Webster helped Tom to sit up and brought a bottle to his lips.

Tom coughed and gasped as the fiery liquid hit his throat.

"Steady, steady. Bit more. That's it. You're in good hands, lad. Roberts were 'prentice to a barber. He has medical interests, you might say. Heard tell he were a resurrectionist for a doctor who weren't too fussy where the bodies come from, ain't that right?"

The other man laughed. "Aye, right enough. Dr Bady. Used to stay and watch him working. Learnt a thing or two that way."

He unfurled a roll of fearsome-looking instruments, selected a probe and a pair of long, pointed tweezers and thrust them into the glowing coals of a brazier. He took a swig from the bottle Webster was holding and handed it back to him.

"Pour some of that into the wound and the rest of it down his throat. Hold him!"

The pain from the spirit was searing. Tom bucked, gagging and choking as rum spilt from his mouth. He struggled even more as Roberts loomed over him, probe in one thin, long-fingered hand, tweezers in the other, but Webster was too strong for him. Roberts's movements were quick and decisive.

The probe entering the wound brought a white-hot bolt of agony. Blackness gathered all around him and he seemed to be falling, falling…

"It's for the best," he heard a voice say. "It'll be for the best."

And then there was nothing.

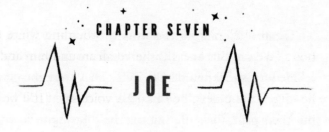

CHAPTER SEVEN

JOE

"YOU DON'T HAVE TO DECIDE YET. There will be other tests..."

He was aware of people standing round his bed. A doctor, his parents. His mother, tearful, being comforted by his sister. They were talking about him, he realized. Trauma to the brain. Oxygen deprivation. What had happened to him? And what were they going to do to him, or with him now?

He tried to move, to speak—but nothing. Not even an eyelid flicker, no matter how hard he bent his will to it.

How long had he been away? He thought about it like that. *Being away.* He had no sense of time, no way to measure its passing, apart from whether it was day or night. It was daytime right now, with the sun coming through the window, but was it the same day, or another, or another? It had been winter when he came in here. Days short. Decorations going up and being taken down again. It was different now. The days were longer but was it spring or summer? He couldn't tell. No way of knowing. For some reason that bothered him. People came to talk to him but they never told him anything that he wanted to know.

"Shall we?" The doctor was shepherding them out now. "We can carry on the conversation in the office."

He was glad when they'd gone. They were the people he loved, the people he cared about most in the world, but their pain, the suffering that he'd brought down on them, made it worse somehow.

#heroinacoma Milo had called him. He remembered the match heading for a one-all draw, then the player running to the corner, shouting, arms raised, team mates around him, the roar of the crowd erupting. After that—blank.

"Hi there. How are you doing?"

It was the male nurse he liked. The other nurses called him Joe. He spoke with a slight lilt that marked him as coming from somewhere Tom couldn't quite place. Tom liked his voice. It was quiet and soothing, with a spark of humour and just a little mischief. You could hear the smile in it. He spoke as though Tom could hear him, as if they were having a conversation—one-sided but still a conversation. He was wearing fresh scrubs. Tom could smell crisp laundering. Tom sensed that he was not tall, but broad and strong. His touch was gentle, subtle, but Tom could sense the strength in his hands.

"Let's get you sorted out, shall we?"

Joe bathed him, gently, a bit at a time, turning him this way and that way. Sometimes he gave Tom a massage. Other times, he just moved his hands over Tom's body in a kind of hovering way, not even touching, but Tom felt a tingling—the nearest thing he'd had to any kind of sensation. Afterwards, Tom felt better—quieter in his body, calmer in his mind.

Every day, Joe moved Tom's limbs for him, working round his inert body with infinite patience, keeping the muscles and joints in working order ready for when he could move by himself. Tom sensed that this was what Joe was doing—that while he was working, he was thinking not *if* but *when*. Tom liked that. He saw it as an act of faith. Tom sensed the power in Joe's touch, like heat coming through his palms and fingers, as if he was giving some of his strength to Tom.

"Where you been, eh?" Joe whispered as he worked on flaccid muscles. "Where do you go when you travel away from us?" He straightened up. "There. That's better, huh?"

Joe checked the instruments, the drips and tubes snaking in and out of him.

He was washed, powdered, dressed in clean pyjamas. Bedclothes tucked in around him. It made him feel better, fresher, like a very clean baby.

"He's all yours."

The girl came in. The one who had been reading. She settled in the corner and opened the book.

The sound of her voice soothed and he thought maybe he'd sleep now.

He drifted, Joe's question echoing. *Where* do *I go?* What was this place he was visiting? Would he go back there if he went to sleep? Was it like dreaming? Lucid dreaming, maybe? Although it wasn't like any dream he'd ever had, lucid or otherwise. You were supposed to be able to control lucid dreams, right? He'd had as much control in that place as he did here. What *was* that fish thing that Milo had planted in his ear? Kind of like a game was how he'd described it but it wasn't like anything Tom had ever played. In games you could kill, see people die, but it was never real, not like that battle. If you were hit, even killed, you just lost the game, lost points, went down a level, whatever. You didn't hurt and you didn't bleed. He'd moved from a world where he felt nothing to one where pain was all too real. If he'd been able to, he'd have laughed at the irony of it.

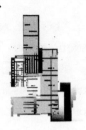

CHAPTER EIGHT

THE JINN

"WILL HE BE ALL RIGHT?"

Augusta frowned down at the young man stretched out on her camp bed. His wound had been cleaned, his shoulder bandaged.

"'Appen he will." Roberts shrugged. "'Appen not. I've took out the ball." He rolled it between finger and thumb before handing it to her. "He might like to keep it. Some do. I've cleaned the wound. Best he sleeps now. He's a reet brave lad."

Augusta nodded in thanks and agreement. Roberts was the nearest thing to a doctor that they had. Better than a doctor. She didn't like doctors. Didn't trust them. Full of pompous bluster and liable to make patients worse, not better. As likely to kill as cure. Roberts had medical knowledge; where he'd acquired it, she didn't care to enquire. His mother and grandmother had been Herb Wives, she did know; Hedge Witches some called them. Perhaps there was truth in the latter name. Ordinary folk had certainly revered them, even feared them. They were said to keep to the old ways, but they knew about cures and they knew about healing. Roberts's skills came mostly from them.

"Let him rest here," she said. "We'll be on the move soon enough."

Roberts left her looking down at this stranger, his unconscious state giving her leave to study him. Not very old—sixteen or seventeen? Well built, but the skin over the long muscles was fine, delicate, as milk white as a maid's. His face was well favoured: a wide forehead under coal-black curls, dark straight brows over slightly slanting eyes, long eyelashes above high cheekbones, a straight nose and a firm mouth, the lips full and curving up slightly at the corners. Lying there, he looked sculpted from marble, like the beautiful youth Endymion, lover of the moon goddess, lying in his cave on Mount Latmus, choosing the sleep perpetual so he could stay young for ever.

She turned away from the sleeping boy, a little embarrassed by the intensity of her scrutiny, and turned her mind to other matters.

This was by no means the end of it. A lull, merely. She distrusted that sudden withdrawal. They were bloodied but by no means defeated. "*If you can't win one way, find another.*" Rogue's words. He was no coward, not like the others, but he was devious and he'd left so abruptly, galloping off with his cavalry. It didn't make sense. He had to be up to something…

She went to the campaign table to study the map. Her lands lay to the north and west of this ridge where she had made her stand. The little clusters of buildings that marked the hamlets and villages were scattered, isolated…

"My lady, a messenger…"

Young Wainwright. A sheep farmer from Windhover Crags, a high point at the end of the ridge. He'd been riding hard. His face was wet; although with rain, sweat or tears, it was hard to tell. He stood, chest heaving, gasping out his news.

"Marauders, milady. Flying black banners, reiving through the country burning and pillaging. I thought to warn you. Wit' main force here, tha' country is reet easy pickings."

"Show me."

"They come across here not an hour ago, spreading out across the land." Wainwright pointed to the map. "I seen 'em from the Crags. Layin' to waste. I seen smoke rising from farms and farmsteads, village and hamlet."

"What about the people?"

"Killed, I reckon. Or took off."

She turned from the man, dashing away her own tears. Her people taken to build the city, or slave in the mills and factories, or on the docks. The work in Glass Town never stopped.

"Thank you for taking the risk to come here and tell me." She turned back to him. "But go, now. Save yourself."

Black banners meant Rogue's men. So *that* was what he was up to, why he'd left the field of battle. Allowed her to think that she had won, so he could attack the land she'd left defenceless. Damn him! Rogue was as handsome as the devil and just as vicious. They had known each other since childhood and she knew him as only one child could know another. She'd learnt to her cost that he could never be trusted. She had seen his cruelties. As a boy, he'd delighted in torturing birds and small creatures. Now he went after bigger prey. He would take a great satisfaction in ruining her land, taking her people into slavery or putting them to the sword. She had once been promised to him and had broken that promise. This was his revenge for that insult. Women swooned over him but he tortured them with the same exquisite precision he'd lavished on his captive birds and hapless frogs. She'd rather be married to a Barbary ape, but Rogue would always want what he couldn't get.

"There—there's more, milady." Wainwright stepped towards her. "And worse…"

Augusta frowned. What could be worse?

"Jinn." The man spoke low, as though someone, or something, might hear. "I saw them. Rising up in the North like a gurt swarm o' hornets…"

"Show me!"

Far on the northern horizon, two pillars were forming above the distant peaks of the Jibbel Kumri, the Mountains of the Moon; one was dark, as if made of dust and smoke, the other of flame and fire. They were growing at frightening speed, spiralling up, expanding and contracting like a murmuration of starlings as they took on more and more power. Within the clouds, threads of silver lightning flickered, but they were too distant to hear the roar of thunder. As they watched, the columns began to bend and twist and spin across the land.

"We must not be caught out in the open!" Augusta shouted.

As she spoke, the columns leant out, fingers of flame, fingers of darkness growing and stretching, groping, searching, reaching like grasping hands. Fear was spreading through the camp like a contagion. Everywhere, men were running. The air was filled with their shouting and the whinny of panicked horses. They all knew what the Jinn could do.

"Every man for himself! Get as far away as possible," Augusta ordered. "And seek cover! You, too," she said to Webster and Roberts. "You must get far away from me. I'm the one the Jinn are seeking."

"We'll not leave yer, milady." Webster stood square, arms folded.

"That we will not," Roberts agreed.

"What about the boy?" Webster looked to the command tent. "We can't leave him."

Augusta felt tears prick, at their loyalty and the sudden relief that she would not have to face this alone.

"We'll have to take him with us. Webster, go and find a cart. We'll make for Shucksgill Gape. Head into the Deeps."

Augusta helped Roberts to dress the boy, binding his arm tightly to his chest and draping his coat over him. They carried him out between them and loaded him on to the back of a cart piled up with canvas and bedding to try to make him comfortable.

They left the camp, Webster driving the wagon. The moorland ponies instinctively turned to the old track across the moors.

Taking the boy would slow their progress but Augusta could not leave him. She rode with the cart, Keeper loping along beside her. The boy was still unconscious, pale as death, pale as milk, but still breathing. He must have been sent for some purpose; the part he had to play still unknown. He was a mystery, and mysteries added the unexpected—the unexpected could give her an advantage in the intricate point-counterpoint of the Glass Town Game.

And she needed something. Her enemies had evoked the Jinn, the Genii, and were using their terrifying physical manifestation to hunt her down. She could feel the power and malice, scorching the back of her neck, pitiless as the desert sun. She risked a look behind. The columns were growing steadily, gaining more substance, becoming more *solid*, moving ever nearer. When they were close enough, the columns would dip and swoop, fingers spreading out to trap anything underneath in giant fists of darkness and fire.

The old track was paved with great slabs placed there by those who had built it a thousand years ago and more. It was wide enough to take a cart easily and it cut through heather and bracken straight as an arrow shot. The top of the ridge was marked by a line of stunted thorns, their branches bent and twisted away from the direction of the prevailing wind. They were black and ancient with no sign of greening, but here and there white flowers showed. Augusta picked a clump of tiny blossoms as she went, avoiding the long, vicious thorns that grabbed at her fingers. These trees were planted by the Fairish and still offered protection.

Augusta felt easier once they had crossed the invisible border into their lands.

At the base of the hillside, the track ran beside a fast-running stream joined by tributaries from smaller valleys to left and right. Shucksgill Gape lay up one of these valleys, but which? They must gain it, and soon. The Jinn were getting ever closer.

The Gape was named for a mouth wide enough to take a horse and cart—and deep enough to save them from the Jinn. It led to the Deeps and was one of the ways into the Fairish realm under the hills. It promised a place of safety, but Augusta had never come to them by way of Shucksgill Gape. She'd always stumbled into their realm without knowing quite how she'd got there. She'd been a child then. There was no knowing if the Fairish would welcome her now. The Fairish were notoriously fickle. The way might be closed against them, or worse, but that was a worry for later.

Roberts had visited the Deeps with his grandmother. He rode forward, looking for signs. He thought that the

Gape was off to the right but the ways to the Fairish were never easy to find and he hadn't been there since he was a lad. They had to make the right choice. If they took the wrong valley they would be trapped, with no way out, at the mercy of the Jinn. Behind them, the sky was dividing, one side the deep red of a summer sunset, the other as dark as a winter storm.

"Up 'ere!" Roberts beckoned.

Webster whipped the horses on, using the wide, shallow stream as a roadway. The boy was still sleeping, which was probably a blessing. The jolting and jauncing would hurt him cruelly.

The wind was getting up; a hot wind, carrying twigs and leaves, grit and dust. They pulled their cloaks up over nose and mouth as they rode on, eyes narrowed. The deep, narrow-sided valley might save them but there was no surety. They hurried now, the fierce wind pushing them on.

"Round the next bend!" Roberts shouted.

Augusta hoped he was right. The Spirit Wind was increasing in strength, howling in their ears; branches and heather bowled past them, catching on rocks and wrapping round their horses' legs. The Swooping was near.

"It's up ahead!" Roberts yelled above the shrieking voice of the hot wind.

The valley was a dead end. A cliff face frowned down at them, the cave at the base like an open mouth. A stream issued from it, the fast flow chattering and clacking over the rocky bed. The rock above the entrance was worn smooth by running water that dropped down like a beaded curtain. Effigies and offerings hung on strings in the dripping fall: gloves, boots, dolls, hats; all had petrified into shapes strange and sinister: a head, a hand, a foot, a human child. Some were shapeless lumps, unrecognizable as anything. Folk had been leaving things here since time out of mind as gifts and offerings left in thanks, to ask for attention or turn it aside, for this cave was known to be home to the Fairish, an entrance to their land.

Webster drove the horses on and they gained the opening just in time.

Behind them, the strings of objects clanged together, creating a weird, discordant music as the fierce wind passed through them, howling like a thing denied.

The sound funnelled down the cave and echoed back, amplified.

Webster crossed himself. The noise might penetrate deep into the cave, reaching the Fairish, and they didn't like to be disturbed. The wind was screaming, searching; the strings swung wildly, as if pushed apart by a giant hand reaching in for them.

"Never mind the Fairish, Webster! They're the least of our worries," Augusta shouted. "Get further in!"

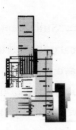

CHAPTER NINE

THE GAPE

Augusta dismounted. Roberts and Webster uncoupled the horses from the wagon. They would have to leave them here. There were torches by the entrance for those who visited and wished to venture inside. The two men fashioned a makeshift stretcher to carry the boy between them while Augusta lit a torch to guide them deeper.

The roaring diminished. The Jinn wouldn't be able to reach in here, but the phantom wind moaned around them and bent the torch flame. Augusta wouldn't feel entirely safe until they'd gained the innermost cavern. The roof disappeared into darkness. Stumps and pinnacles dotted the floor like melted candles. The torch illuminated walls ruffled and fluted like petrified curtains, slender columns of pearly deposits that had been laid down since the world was young. Local folk called this the Gallery, for the shapes that the rocks made and because, here and there, the walls were scratched and etched with the shapes of animals swept away in Noah's flood, put there by a people older even than the Fairish.

"We'll stop here. Put the boy down." Augusta knelt next to the stretcher. "How is he?"

"Still sleeping." Roberts scratched his head. "He lost a deal of blood but his pulse is strong. I'd have thought he'd have woke by now, what with all the bouncing about."

"'Appen he'll come round in his own fair time," Webster said as he looked down.

"'Appen he will." Augusta frowned. His condition was strange. She'd never known a swoon last much of a day. It was as if he'd taken laudanum, or some drug that had rendered him insensible. "Make sure he's comfortable and build a fire." She clutched her cloak to her. "It's cold in here."

The fireplace was marked by a heap of grey-white cold ash surrounded by baked and blackened stones. A supply of wood and torches had been left by outlaws and others, who used the cave as a hiding place or refuge. Augusta wondered how her own folk were faring. She should have been out there defending them, not skulking here, as much a fugitive as they.

"You did what you could, lady," Webster said, as though he could read her thought. "We saw 'em off, a right bigger force. Who'd know that they'd summon the Jinn, or that Rogue lot would go skirmishing behind the lines?"

His words were kind but he'd left the greater truth unsaid: hers would always be the smaller force; they would always be at a disadvantage. Beneath that, a small voice whispered, *You should have known that is* precisely *what he would do.* Letting her think that she'd won would make her consequent defeat more bitter and sweeten his triumph.

They set up camp, not knowing how long they would be here. There was precious little to eat but what they had they put together. Webster collected water from the pools on the floor of the cave and put a pot over the fire. In it went dried beef and beans, barley, a few withered roots, a handful of salt and a good pinch of red pepper—one of Parry's gifts. The result was palatable enough. They sat together to eat from rough bowls with wooden spoons.

The boy stirred. Perhaps the smell of food had woken him.

He looked round, bewildered, and struggled to rise. "What's wrong with my arm?"

"You were shot." Roberts went over to him. "A ball in the shoulder. A right big 'un. I've taken it out, lad, and treated the wound wi' a poultice of comfrey, but you'd best not move around too much or you'll set t' wound a-bleeding again. Here, have a bowl o' this. Put some strength in you."

"Thank you." Tom sat up with Roberts's help, the bowl balanced on his knee. He was surprised at how good the soup tasted, at how hungry he was. "What's happening? Where are we?"

"We took refuge here," Augusta said. "Fleeing from enemies."

She didn't say what sort. Best not mention the Jinn. He was a stranger and unlikely to comprehend the danger they posed.

"Fleeing?" He frowned. "I don't understand. I thought we won."

"We did, too! You fought bravely, but there were other enemies, other *threats*, that took us unawares. We are safe here."

"For the time being."

"As you say, Webster." The Jinn must have passed by now. "Go to see what's happening outside. Take Roberts with you."

As the men set off towards the entrance to the cave, Augusta took out a small black bottle. Another gift from her man Parry.

"Have some of this. It will help with the pain. Not too much! That's enough."

"That's good stuff." Tom passed the bottle back. The pain in his shoulder was easing, the stiffness going.

"How are you feeling?"

"Better. Stronger. It's cold in here."

He tried to pull his coat around him. She reached to help him. There was something about her touch, her closeness as she leant across him, like a current passing between them. Her sudden shiver showed that she felt it, too.

"I hope I didn't hurt you." She stepped back, for once uncertain. Her smile almost shy.

"No, ah…" He smiled back. "Thank you, Augusta. Or should I call you my lady?"

She coloured slightly. "Augusta will do."

"Can you help me?"

She offered her hand to pull him up and their eyes met. Hers changed all the time, like clouds on a windy day.

"You're right." She turned away, wrapping her arms around her. "It's cold in here."

The dog at her side gave a gruff, growling bark.

"Quiet, Keeper!"

"I'm a friend." Tom reached to scratch the dog's broad head. "No need to be jealous."

"I don't think he's growling at you…" The dog's short ears flicked up and he gave a yelping whine, stationing himself at the entrance to the cave. "He must have heard something."

"Webster and Roberts coming back?"

"Perhaps…"

The dog let out a sharp, deep-throated bark.

"Hush, Keeper. I'm trying to hear…"

She stepped away as Webster and Roberts ran back into the cave.

"Jinn's gone," Roberts panted, hands on his knees. "Webbo climbed up t' bank. Tell 'm what you saw."

"McMahon and his dogs." Webster shook the rain from his hair, his eyes. "They must've picked up our scent by the river. They're coming this way."

The belling of hounds reached them, faint but distinct, carried by the cave's peculiar acoustics.

"They've gained the entrance. They'll be here any minute!"

"McMahon will be tracking for Rogue," Augusta said.

"Aye," Roberts agreed. "His forces won't be far away."

"We'll have to go further," Augusta directed. "Into the Deeps."

It was the way to Fairishland.

Webster frowned, his big face full of worry. "But we could get lost down there!" he protested. "The only folks knows them tunnels is the Fairish. Men going down there are never seen again. Lost their way or led astray deliberate."

"I used to visit here wi' me nan," Roberts said. "And I'm here, ain't I?"

"We have no choice, do we? We have to take our chances." Augusta picked up a torch. "It will be as dangerous for them as us—perhaps more so. The Fairish have no liking for McMahon and his dogs. Roberts, you show the way."

They lit more torches and took extra, as many as they could carry.

One by one, they followed Roberts through a smaller entrance in the opposite wall. The tunnel was lower, narrower, the walls rougher, leading sharply down and deeper. The caves ran for miles under the hillside, branching and branching, with no indication as to which might taper to a dead end and which lead out into the world again—or which world that might be. There were other dangers, too. In some places, the torches burned blue and started to gutter, showing that the air was foul, or scarce there at all. Heavy rain could turn the little freshets that ran everywhere into raging torrents, filling up the whole system of tunnels, drowning anyone caught there, leaving them to float lifeless in the water-filled space.

It was raining outside. Webster had come back wet with it but it was best not to think about that as they moved from one tunnel to another, with Roberts as their guide. He seemed fairly certain that he was leading them in the right direction, but where that direction might be was less than clear and he had no control over the weather.

The rain must have been getting heavier. The water was rising, flowing faster, up to their ankles with more pouring down the walls. They would be wading soon.

They could hear splashing behind them. Keeper's coat bristled; the growl in his throat erupted in a deep bark at red points sparking in the darkness. Augusta could hardly hold him. Whoever—whatever—was following was gaining steadily.

Roberts was examining the right-hand wall of the cave, his torch shaking as he held it close to the rock.

"The way to the Fairish is here, I could have sworn. Me nan showed me. Here, Webbo. Hold the torch."

Panic glittered in Roberts's blue eyes as his hands fluttered like an old man's over the rough surface. They were all drawn to what he was doing, staring at the rock face looking for clues, despite the splashing and the little red lights coming closer and the rising water and the prospect of them all becoming floating corpses.

The dull ache in Tom's arm was a reminder that this was no *Tomb Raider*. This world was for real; you could get hurt here. His shoulder was throbbing now. Despite the cold down here, he was burning up, the sweat trickling down his back and stinging into his eyes. He remembered reading somewhere about gunshot wounds, fragments of cloth and God knows what driven deep into the flesh, setting up infection. He felt faint and a little sick at the thought of it, but maybe he was feeling sick anyway. A handful of leaves wasn't the same as a dose of antibiotics. *If you hurt here, can you also die here? How far do the rules of this game extend? Are there no limits, or is the limit death?*

To stop from passing out, he focused on Roberts exploring the rock wall like a blind climber searching for holds. It had got to be one of those puzzle things, like you get in some games, but they didn't exactly have time to collect clues and figure it out. Either that, or…

"Open for me."

There was a grinding of stone on stone and a whole section of wall began to move and pull apart, slowly at first, then like a lift door opening. As soon as the last of them was through, the wall snapped back, smooth and grey and blank with no sign of a crack. Wherever they were now, there was no going back.

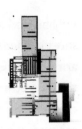

CHAPTER TEN

FAIRISHLAND

THE SMOOTH WALLS of the tunnel glistened with pearly opalescence streaked with shimmering colours, as if a rainbow had melted and seeped underground. A faint glow lit the way, making the torches unnecessary. The floor was completely dry. The dog's claws skittered and clicked on the soft sheen of worn marble.

Tom was wondering just who the Fairish might be. *Are they fairies, as their name suggests?* Would they be tiny with wings, their queen no larger than an agate on an alderman's ring, or would they be big and scary?

The passage opened out into a large cavern, the roof supported by slender pillars and columns sculpted from the stalactites and stalagmites that had joined together. The pillars branched and arched into walkways and bridges that crossed and recrossed, spanning the heights. Soft lights, silver and golden, gave the space a feeling of lightness and airiness, although they were deep underground.

They were stopped by an invisible barrier, some kind of force field.

"These Fairish, are they—?" Tom whispered.

Before Augusta could answer, two of them stepped out. They looked like a cross between kick-boxers and ninja warriors. Tall, with narrow hips and broad shoulders, short leather jerkins sculpted to their muscular torsos, long arms and legs clad in wool and soft leather. They wore their silver hair braided, twined with threads of different colours and bells that chimed softly as they crossed long spears tipped with flint as thin and delicate as a leaf, the edges translucent and sharper than any sword.

"Who goes here?"

Augusta stepped forward. "We seek sanctuary. We would speak to the Summer Lord."

The guards exchanged looks. No words passed between them.

"Very well, but leave your weapons. Anything made of iron must be left here."

Swords, guns, knives were left in a pile along with belts, buckles, even steel buttons. The men clutched their trousers as they followed the two guards along a narrow raised walkway leading them deeper. The walkway branched left and right into further caverns, lit with the same golden light. Caverns within caverns; it was like being inside a honeycomb.

At last, they came to a great hall so wide that they couldn't see the walls, so high that the slender columns disappeared into the darkness above them. At the centre stood a tall throne made from gleaming white travertine, laid down and formed to the shape by millennia of dripping water. A halo of silver lights seemed to float around it. Fairish soldiers stood to either side bearing long, bronze, leaf-shaped blades. Their own guards prodded them forward.

"Bow before the Summer Lord!" they commanded and stepped back.

"Who do you bring me? Who enters by the Deep Way?"

The Summer Lord spoke from his stone throne. He seemed young, lounging as though in an armchair. He was wearing a suit of soft leather, dyed the deep green of mid-summer. His handsome face was compelling: light hazel eyes under straight black brows; his skin a flawless golden brown; his beard, close cropped, as soft as otter fur. His hair was a deep bronze gold. Three pronged horns jutted forward through the curls. At first, Tom thought he was wearing some kind of crown or headdress, but when he looked closer, he saw that the horns were a growing part of him.

Augusta stood before him, spokeswoman by unspoken consent.

"We ask for sanctuary."

"Lady Augusta." He stood in one lithe movement. "It is a long time since you thought to visit us." He came down the steps in a sideways dancing movement. "Why should I grant you sanctuary? Your people have not been friends to me and mine this very long time." He paced up and down before her. "They have made our lives impossible with the din of their machines, their great wheels churning and turning in the waters of our streams, and everywhere the ring of iron upon iron. Few of their folk respect the old ways or are friends to us. They block our trooping paths; fill the air with choking smoke so we can no longer breathe it. Even Robin can no longer go among them. Our places grow fewer; we are cut off from our fellows." He paused. "We have many grievances against you and your kind."

He looked at her, his eyes the light peaty brown of pools in a moorland stream: to gaze too long into their clear depths was to drown. Augusta paled under his scrutiny but she held his gaze steadily.

"Not I, my lord," she said in a quiet voice. "I would do nothing to hurt you and your people. Robin Goodfellow is always welcomed among us."

"Who speaks my name?"

A boy appeared beside the Summer Lord—or Tom took him for a boy. He was half sized anyway, dressed all in skins, his thick hair in roped dreads, braided and stuck with wisps of wool, beads, acorns, shells and the bones of small animals. He had the face of a child, rounded with wide brows, a short nose and a pointed chin, his skin as brown and smooth as a hazelnut, but his eyes were as old as time: cloudy, yellowish, semi-translucent, like flakes of flint. He had a quiver on his back and held a short bow, half drawn, an arrow already nocked and ready to fly.

"What think you, Robin?" The Summer Lord put a hand on his small companion's shoulder.

"Let me kill them," Robin said, his voice disconcertingly gruff and deep. "They have no place here." He drew his bowstring taut, aiming at Augusta.

She didn't turn or flinch but stepped backwards and held up her hand to ward him off.

"There are no good folks any more. No merriment to be had."

"Now, Robin." A woman's voice sounded, soft and silvery. "You know that's not true and that this is not the way we treat our guests."

She stepped out to stand on the other side of the Summer Lord. They could only be brother and sister: the same height, the same hair, the same eyes, although hers were paler, a strange tawny gold. She wore no antlers but they were not the eyes of humankind. She wore a hat banded with feathers: long, barred pheasant tails; tawny owl wing, short and speckled; the blue-black iridescence of crow and raven; the russet spray of a grebe's crest.

"Augusta!" She stepped over and embraced her. "I haven't seen you since you were quite a child and you would get lost on purpose to find the glen. You visited us often then."

"I remember." Augusta returned her embrace. She smelt of flowers and sweet summer grass. "I thought you might have forgotten."

She held Augusta at arm's length. "We do not forget. Forgive Robin and my brother. Much has happened to darken our feelings against your kind. But *you* have done nothing against us. You have always been our friend." Her fine nostrils flared and she walked along, looking from one to the next. "One of your party is hurt. I can smell the sweat on him, the wound."

Tom felt her touch on his shoulder, as light as one of the feathers she wore. His knees went from under him.

Roberts and Webster jumped forward to support him.

"Bring him this way," the woman ordered. "I will see to his wound. Meanwhile…" she smiled at her brother, "treat our guests kindly."

"His fever has gone." The Lady touched the boy's forehead. "He'll sleep now."

The Fairish were great healers; the Lady the most skilled of all. Tom already looked better, lying on a low wooden bed in a clean shirt with his wound bound, the colour returning to his face.

Augusta felt relief fill her like the healing fragrance of the herbs that hung from the ceiling of the cool room: camomile, lavender, thyme, sage and others she couldn't name. The walls were pale grey stone, carved from the living rock. A spring, pure and silver, bubbled in one corner and fell into a clear stream that flowed round a great tree growing up through the roof. Light filtered, pale and diffuse, from tiny windows set at angles to catch the light from sun rising to sunset.

"He will sleep now. It's the best healer of all." The Lady paused, her hand resting lightly on Tom's brow. "There's something strange about him." She looked up at Augusta. "Where did he come from?"

"I don't know," Augusta replied. "He just appeared at the head of a troop of soldiers. I thought he'd come from Parry, or Ross, but they are far away so that's impossible."

"Have you asked him?"

Augusta nodded. "He doesn't seem to know or—"

"Or he chooses to be silent on the subject?"

Augusta shrugged. "Do you know?"

"Not from this place, or this time. I sense something else. A great hurt. Not this." She touched his shoulder. "Something deeper, more… profound."

"Perhaps he's come here so it can be cured."

"Maybe. But it is beyond my healing. He is out of time, out of place. He may become lost here, unable to return." She shook her head. "I can get no sense of him but what I do know is that his very presence here holds danger."

"For whom?"

"For himself." She looked at Augusta, her golden eyes distant and sad. "For you."

"Can you not see?" Augusta asked. "Can you not look now?"

The Fairish were famous for having the Sight. In the centre of the room was a basalt basin, fed from the spring but never filled, the water always dark and still. It was called the Black Water and it was said that the Fairish used it to overlook the present, to view anyone, at any distance, and see into the past and into the future. Augusta could see nothing in the surface, only her own reflection, but for the Fairish woman, the waters would clear and she would see as through a window.

"I'm reluctant to try the Black Water. The Sight is not for humankind. Very few of you have it, and for those that do it is an affliction. To see all is to see too much for most to bear. I will have to think on it. Sometimes, it shows us what we don't want to see." She brushed back a lock of Tom's dark hair. "He's here for a purpose, but for good or ill, I cannot tell."

"He's here now, so there's no escaping whatever he brings with him." Augusta looked down at the sleeping boy, surprised, shaken by the emotions he stirred.

"Have a care." The Fairish Lady looked at her. "Remember he doesn't belong here. Don't get too close to him."

Augusta met her eyes. "Maybe there's no escaping that, either."

When Tom came round, he was lying on a low bed. The pillow smelt of lavender; the mattress beneath him was soft with down and feathers. The uniform he'd been wearing had been removed. He was wearing a finely woven woollen shirt and soft leather breeches. He flexed his shoulder. It didn't hurt at all. When he pulled his shirt aside to see the wound, there was nothing there, just a slight discoloration, a small indentation the size of a penny where the wound had been.

"The Fairish are skilled at healing." Augusta stood up from the chair where she had been sitting.

Tom struggled to sit. He looked down at his clothes.

She laughed. "Don't worry. Roberts and Webster did the honours. Nothing to do wi' me!" She was dressed similarly in wool and leather, dyed in different shades of grey. Her hair was wet, tied back in a knot. She looked younger, prettier. "It was good to bathe and to get out of that uniform, even if I'm wearing borrowed clothes. These things are much more comfortable. How are you feeling?"

Tom swung his legs off the bed. "I feel fine. Never better."

"You must be ready for something to eat. Come. They are waiting for us."

Tom followed her down a long corridor to a great hall. They were shown to their places at the high table, the host ranked below them like at a medieval banquet. Tom tried not to stare. Apart from the guards, who Tom had privately named Thranduil and Legolas, most of them were small of stature, more like Robin than the man with the horns and his sister. The Summer Lord and the Lady were the most normal-looking, even with those weird horns. Some of the others were *very* strange. The further away from the top table, the stranger they got: big heads and small bodies, small heads and big bodies, pointed ears and long noses, slanted eyes and wide mouths, teeth sharp and pointed and, yes, some of them *did* have wings. None of them looked anything like the pretty little fairies in books or films. He guessed that was just an idea of them. No one had actually ever *seen* one, so people were free to make up what they wanted. Yet here he was with them. Wherever *here* was and whoever *they* were…

"What *are* they?"

Augusta put a finger to her lips. "They don't like to be talked about," she said, although he hadn't been aware that he was speaking out loud. *Is she reading my mind now?* "Or stared at."

He took his eyes off the host and stared at the wooden platter in front of him. *Is this real?* He touched the polished grain of the wood, inhaled the steam coming off the dishes being placed before him: the venison smelt really good, as did the mushrooms, and the greens and roots. He was reaching for a slice of bread—crusty, yeasty, warm from the oven—and yellow butter to spread on it, when a memory came back from somewhere. Didn't something happen if you ate the food in Fairyland? Like you'd never get out again?

"Stop sniffing everything," Augusta whispered. "They'll be even more offended. Whatever you've heard, their food is fine."

He shrugged and picked up his goblet. Real or not, he could pinch himself all he liked but he wouldn't wake up. The wine tasted like wine. The food looked like any other food, and he was hungry.

Everyone was eating heartily. Except Webster—it seemed like he'd bought into the same stories Tom had about eating the food. He could hear Webster's guts rumbling but he wasn't touching a thing.

"What is wrong, my friend?" The Fairish King smiled. "You will not be poisoned and no harm will come to you. We take what the land gives us and trade for the rest. Some of the countryfolk are glad to give us salt for our meat, flour for our bread, hops and barley for our beer, milk and butter for our table in return for our favour. Thomas—"

"What? I'm sorry." Tom realized that he was being addressed.

"We had a Thomas as a guest at my mother's house in the Northlands. True Thomas they called him. I remember him. He was a poet."

"When was this?" Tom asked.

The Summer Lord frowned, thinking. "Our time runs differently, like a slow stream compared to your fast-rushing river. I remember him telling me that he was born in your year twelve hundred and twenty."

Tom made a quick calculation. "That would be eight hundred years ago."

Augusta looked at him strangely. "*Six* hundred years, surely?"

The Summer Lord laughed. "I told you time runs differently. In your world, too, it seems. Come, my friends, eat and drink. Afterwards, rest. You are free to stay with us as long as you wish."

"A word." After the meal, the Lady drew Augusta aside. "I have done as you asked. I looked into the Black Water."

"What did you see?"

"Many things."

"Did you see me?"

"Yes. I speak to you as you really are. Not as you pretend to be. Be warned: this game you play with your brother and sisters, that you've played for these many years—it is no longer a game and you are no longer a child."

"What else?"

The Lady shook her head. "I saw greatness about you—fame, acclaim, honours. A life beyond a life. The reverence of people you don't know, will never know…"

"In this world, you mean, as Lady Augusta?"

"No."

"In my real life? That can't be right!" Augusta laughed at the very idea, although suddenly she felt cold, and goose pimples stippled her arms.

"The Waters never lie. It's perhaps a blessing that what we see is rarely believed."

"What else? What else did you see? Did you see Tom? Do you know where he is from?"

"Yes, and no. What he said as we dined was no mistake. He is from the future, from a further two hundred years of the world's turning. The Waters became as cloudy as a stormy sky shot through with lightning. I was in a world I hardly recognized. I fear that it is as my brother has foreseen: there is no longer room for us there. There are more and more of your kind, destroying the wild places, poisoning the air and the waters. We are of the Air and to the Air we will return."

"What does that mean?" Augusta frowned. Why did the Fairish always retreat into oracular obscurity when they had something important to say?

"I don't know." The Lady sighed. "I saw much I didn't understand, and I can't explain what I don't know. When I returned to myself, I was wearing this."

She was wearing two bracelets, silver bands, with oblong, dullish black stones set into them. She took one off and fixed it round Augusta's wrist.

"What is its purpose?" Augusta held up her arm. The bracelet was a very fine mesh, made of some light metal, and sat close to her skin.

"I don't know. But I feel it will give you protection and that, if you are in danger," she said, holding up her own arm, "you will be able to summon me. Now it is time to rest. An attendant will show you to your quarters. Tom and his companions have already retired."

At least I won't lose it, Augusta thought, as she got ready for bed. For turn and turn the bracelet as she would, she could find no break in the mesh for a hinge or clasp. She could see no way that she would ever be able to remove it from her wrist.

CHAPTER ELEVEN

MCMAHON'S DANDY DOGS

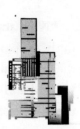

THE NEXT MORNING, they breakfasted alone on oat-cakes and honeycomb. The Summer Lord was out hunting with his host and the Lady was collecting herbs while the dew was still fresh on the ground, Augusta explained, and Roberts and Webster had gone with Robin to collect their weapons and to scout the countryside around.

"What's that on your wrist?" Tom frowned. "I haven't seen that before."

"The Lady gave it to me."

"Let's have a look." Tom peered closely. "That's odd."

"What's odd?"

"It looks like—" Tom started, then he stopped.

"Looks like what?"

"Oh, nothing."

The thing on her wrist looked like a Fitbit or a smart-watch, which, given the circumstances, was extremely odd, but how could he even begin to explain it?

"Have you finished?" Augusta stood up from the table. "Come on then. Let's go."

Tom followed her out into sunlight dappling through new green leaves.

"No matter the weather or season, it is always summer in the Vale of the Summer Lord," Augusta said.

They walked down to a clear, fast-flowing stream, braided and starred with water crowfoot, that ran along the bottom of this hidden valley. The meadows on either side were full of flowers: primrose, cowslip, forget-me-not; the air filled with the scent of violets and lily of the valley.

"It's so beautiful," he said. "I'd like to stay here for ever."

What he really wanted to do was take her hand and wander to the willow tree that hung over the water, pick flowers for her, make daisy chains, just lie in the warm sun gazing at the river until evening came. He didn't say any of this. She might be upset if he took her hand, offended. He didn't even know where any of that had come from…

She smiled, as if she felt the same, and took his hand anyway. It was as if all that had happened, the battle and their flight, his wounding and his healing, had made a connection between them. Either that, or it was part of the enchantment of the place…

"It takes some people that way," she said as they walked along together. "It would be easy to stay but therein lies the danger. It is true what the Summer Lord said: time does run differently here. More slowly. Meanwhile, our years would be fleeting by like days, speeding as swiftly as leaves on the water, so we would not be able to go back. All we knew would be gone. And if we remained here? Eventually we would grow old, while the Fairish would remain as they are now, neither old nor young. So we must go. They know it, too. I've already taken our leave."

Two horses had been readied for them, a chestnut and a grey, smaller than the hill ponies, more delicate and dainty. They weren't shoed and had no saddles; their reins and headgear were woven from withies. The Fairish rode only through grass and woodland, and they rode bareback. Tom's feet almost touched the ground. He wasn't used to bareback riding. His mount seemed to know and behaved accordingly. When Augusta had finished laughing, she showed him the trick of staying on and how to control the horse.

They rode along the valley with Keeper loping beside them. The sun shone bright on the stones in the shallow water; flag iris and water marigold splashed the margins with yellow; purple-headed flowers drooped over the clear, fast-flowing water. It was a fairy glen, an enchanted glen, a hidden crease in the land, a crease in time. Water fell and streaked silver through stands of tall beeches rooted into the steep sides of the valley, their smooth grey trunks straight and slender, their drifts of young leaves impossibly green. It was like riding through Rivendell, actually *being* in *The Lord of the Rings*. Secretly, Tom had always wanted to be an elf...

The river disappeared into a cave under the hill. Augusta urged her pony up the steep track that ran by the side of the entrance, through the hanging beeches and into the trees that surrounded and protected the hidden glen.

Here, the track widened into a broad path. The trees spread out on either side, huge thick trunks, twisted and gnarled; Tom thought he even saw faces, or what looked like faces, on some of them.

Augusta noticed that the trees were changing from summer to autumn, leaves drifting down. Maybe the Fairish Lady was right: their time here was ending.

She kicked her horse on. A thick carpet of leaves deadened their canter. Around them, the woods were quiet—just the odd bird call, the staccato drill of a woodpecker.

"I feel like we're being watched," Tom said, to break the silence between them.

Augusta laughed. "Of course we are, but we won't see them. These are their woods, their country. They've given us sanctuary, but we're human. Robin and his like will be keeping an eye on us."

Tom looked across at her. When she laughed, she looked about his age, even younger. When they'd first met, she'd seemed older, distant, cold even, but with her hair down, falling over her shoulders, and wearing a hat stuck with feathers, she looked a little wild, raffish. Different, anyway. She was dressed like the Fairish, in trousers and jerkin of soft, supple leather. He was wearing something similar but the clothes looked better on her. Her shirt was open at the neck and her tight-fitting jerkin moulded itself to her figure. Her long legs nearly reached the ground. She wasn't pretty—never could be—but she was more than that. Good-looking? Handsome? He searched for a word to describe her. With an uncomfortable jolt in the region of his heart, he found the word he needed. She was beautiful. He glanced away quickly, not wanting her to see him looking at her that way.

"What are you staring at?" she asked.

"You," he said. *Might as well be honest.* "I was thinking I like you better how you are now."

"I could say the same about you." She looked over at him, her grey eyes frank and appraising. "Race you."

She set off, Keeper bounding along beside her. She beat him easily. She had a good start and was much better on a horse, especially without a saddle. It was all he could do to stop himself from falling off.

They rode on while Keeper ranged away from them into the woods, following wherever his nose took him. The sunlight fell in shafts through the canopy above, dappling gold across the ride they were taking. Trunks and stumps, mossed a deep green, stood out against the haze of bluebells that carpeted the woodland floor and added their heavy, musky scent to the smell of sap and growing things.

At last they came to the end of the trees. The margins of the wood marked the limits of the Fairish realm. The wide green road winding away across the moor led out of their kingdom and into her lands. This was the way that Augusta had taken when she first came to the Fairish, straying from the moors and into the wood and enchanted glen.

Augusta kicked her horse to a gallop. Tom followed, chasing her through the gorse and heather, the sky huge above them. She stopped at a path that led from the main track and up a steep slope to a craggy outcrop of yellowish brown stone. It was topped by a tumble of huge rocks, jutting this way and that, as if piled by a giant.

"We'll leave the horses here," she said. "Walk to the top. They call these the Hangingstones. Local folk say an ogre is buried here. This is my favourite place to be."

Augusta leant against a tall, weathered slab, the rough rock marked with a faint pattern of grooves and cups. The wind was everywhere, tugging at their hair, at the tough tufts of heather, rippling through grass and sedge, ruffling the white nodding heads of trembling bog cotton. Cloud shadows chased across the land in restless, changing patterns of light and shade. She led him to a cleft in the rocks wide enough to shelter them.

"Close your eyes," she told him.

Tom did as he was instructed. Out of the wind, the sun was warm on his skin.

"Listen," she said. "Can you hear the high, mewing cry? That's a hawk. That chirring is a red grouse and that peeping? A golden plover. There, that is the curlew. Some say they are birds of ill omen, especially if you hear them at night. The Seven Whistlers, they call them. Miners especially think they herald disaster, but that's just superstition. Besides, I've only ever seen them in ones or twos. My brother used to collect birds' eggs until I stopped him. I like to come up here whenever I can. It's the only place where I'm really happy." She shook him. "You can open your eyes now."

She was turned towards him, her eyes as grey and wide as the sky. She was different again. The sun had brought out a scattering of freckles and she looked like a girl, an ordinary girl, but still beautiful. She was sitting near, their shoulders touching, her face close to his, her breath warm on his cheek. If he turned right now, he'd encounter her mouth, the curve of her lips, that slight gap between her teeth… In his own time, he knew exactly what he'd do, but in *this* time—whatever time this was—he didn't know if such a thing was acceptable, if such a thing might upset her. He turned to find her face was even closer than he thought, and the look in her eyes said she wouldn't mind at all…

By her side, Keeper stirred, his ears pricked, ruff bristling and a growl deep in his throat.

Tom sprang away from her, thinking the dog might be growling at him again, and the moment was gone.

Suddenly, a hare broke cover right in front of them in an explosion of long ears and brown fur. Tom expected it to veer away when it saw them, but it came on.

Keeper leapt to meet it but Augusta held him back.

"No, Keeper. Leave the puss be."

The dog obeyed, staying beside her as the hare dodged and jinked round to the far side of the rocks. Keeper quested, scenting towards where it had gone, whining his protest at the strong hand that held him, then his ears pricked, his broad nostrils widening as if he'd caught another scent. He turned his head, fixing on a different direction. His fur bristled into a ridge down his back; his whine turned into a growl, then a deep-throated bark.

Augusta stood up. Tom joined her, curious to see what had alerted him.

Thin on the wind came the sound of a horn, and behind that the baying of dogs.

"McMahon and his dogs. Come on," she said to Tom. "Keeper, with me."

Augusta set off round the rock. She was searching for the hare's hiding place. Keeper followed, reluctant, turning every so often. She shouted for him to stay with her and held him by the collar for good measure. He was brave and strong. He might take down one or two, even three or four, but the whole pack would tear him to pieces. She hated McMahon, and she hated his dogs as much as she loved the hares they hunted for. She would not see them brought down, tossed and tumbled—their speed and agility, their cunning and bravery, their grace and beauty torn into tattered rags of fur. She had forbidden McMahon from hunting over her land but still he defied her.

The hare lay flat, huddled in a crevice. She could feel its fear in its quick, panting breath. Augusta stood in front of its hiding place, legs apart. Below her, she could see McMahon on his horse, the long curving horn to his mouth. His dogs, black and white, red, brown and yellow, had caught the scent now and were leaping up through the heather. It was all she could do to hold Keeper as they streamed up the hill towards her.

It was rumoured that McMahon lived under a curse, that his dogs were not quite of this world. They were certainly big and fierce. The first to arrive was a rough-haired red and white bitch, easily the size of Keeper, long legged, deep chested, with great white, curving teeth; her red tongue lolled from the side of a mouth foaming saliva.

Augusta fixed her with a steady stare. She backed off, her growl turning into a yelp, and lay down, wary, head on her paws. Augusta stood her ground as the other dogs came crowding up. They milled in confusion before lying down around their leader.

McMahon pulled up. He'd been riding his horse hard; its nostrils were flared wide, its flanks sweating and bloody. A thickset man with a face like a ham, he glared down at them with small ferocious eyes. Fierce black side whiskers grew past his ears and turned up to meet in a thick moustache. He wore a battered top hat, his curving horn dangling from a baldric over his shoulder. He swept his long huntsman's coat aside to show a curled black whip hanging from his saddle. He shortened his reins and drove his spurs in hard, making his horse rear.

"Get out of my way!" he shouted. "Let the dogs at it!"

Augusta ignored the raking hooves and stepped forward to face him. "Whip in your dogs, McMahon. You know you're forbidden to hunt over my land."

"Your land, is it?" He laughed. "Are you sure? You no longer hold sway here." He unhooked the thick whip. "Step aside, I say, or I'll take this to you!"

The tapering length of plaited leather leapt like a live thing. The metal tip snapped an inch from Augusta's eyes but she didn't flinch, or even blink. As McMahon made to draw his arm back, she grabbed the whip.

"Do as I say, or I'll have you off your horse." She gave the whip a tug. "I don't know how long you'd last on the ground with these half-starved dogs of yours."

The dogs were suddenly up, baying and barking, circling horse and rider. McMahon's mount shied, rearing away from them, threatening to unseat him. McMahon had to let go of the whip to free both hands to regain control.

"Call *Going Home*." Augusta had the whip now. "There will be no more hunting today."

"On the contrary, madam, I'll be calling the hounds on. We'll be hunting for as long as there is light to see, and it won't just be four-legged quarry that we will be chasing down."

McMahon put the hunting horn to his lips and with a succession of quick, piping blasts, he wheeled his horse and galloped away, his hounds streaming along behind him.

Augusta cast the foul whip aside and climbed up to the topmost rock, the better to see if he had really gone, before she went down to the crevice where the hare was hiding.

"You can go now, puss. Go. Go on!"

The hare looked up at her from its stone covert, ears flat, its large amber eyes almost human. Then it rose in a leaping bound and zigzagged away to live another day.

Augusta watched it disappear into the heather.

"I've been too long away. I've left my people as vulnerable as old puss there, to be harried and hunted by McMahon—and worse than him."

She led the way to the bottom of the hill and let out a piercing whistle. Their ponies came as if by magic—which it very probably was. Tom didn't know what the rules were here. There didn't seem to be any…

"I'm going to my home. You can come with me if you want." She swung herself up on to her horse. "Or you can go back. The horse will take you to the Fairish."

"What will I do there?"

It was a genuine question. Tom had no idea. It seemed he had no choice but to go with the girl—everything seemed to be tending in that direction—and besides, if he left, he might never see her again and, suddenly, that mattered. It mattered very much.

CHAPTER TWELVE

PARRYSLAND

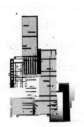

SHE WAS GLAD he'd chosen to come with her. She'd grown to like his company and she didn't want to go on alone. There was no knowing what she might find when she got to her home and he'd proved himself brave and loyal. The strangeness about him only made him more intriguing...

Their narrow path joined a wider track that ran alongside another shallow, swift-running river, the water darkened by peat to a deep brown; trout darted under the surface like swift black shadows. The landscape was changing from the high moors to greener, lusher lands, the hills more rounded, gentler altogether. Augusta would have expected to see sheep dotted about in the small stone-walled fields that divided the steep valley sides, lambs with their dams, but there was none to be seen. The fields were empty, gates torn from their hinges. A shepherd's hut stood charred by fire, the roof gone.

Augusta reined in her horse.

A sign by the side of the road that announced this to be *Parrysland* had been knocked down.

"I don't understand," Tom said. "I thought this was your land. How come it says *Parrysland*?"

"Because Parry is my man, so his land is my land. To understand it you'd have to understand the Glass Town Federation and how it was founded. It's complicated and we don't have time for long explanations. I'll tell you as much as I know, but not now. I don't like the look of what's been happening here. Come on!" She kicked on her horse.

At the end of the valley, their track joined a wider road. The surface was churned and rutted, the verges trampled and muddy; wagons, horsemen and many marching feet had passed this way.

They followed the road to a village. A mill stood by the side of the river; next to it an inn. The road was bordered by grey stone walls with houses of the same stone ranging up from the road, tucked into the hillside, each with a little garden in front of it. At a distance, all looked ordered and peaceful—perhaps too ordered and peaceful, for there were no people about.

As Augusta turned to take the steep main street, her worst fears were confirmed. Doors hung off hinges, glass glittered on the cobbles, broken chairs and furniture lay upended, along with chests broken open, their contents strewn in the mud. The wind had dropped. The air hardly stirred. The deadly quiet was only interrupted by the caw of crows and carrion birds gathering on the roofs and in the branches of the trees.

They dismounted. Augusta called Keeper to her. He followed close at her heels, his ears back, as if he didn't like what had happened any more than she did. They went from house to house. All seemed deserted, until they reached the green space that marked the centre of the village. Cows cropped the grass, ducks swam on the pond and a row of bodies, hands tied, lay crumpled against a wall pocked with bullet holes and stained with blood.

Augusta walked over to them, unable to hide her tears.

"These were my friends," she said. "My neighbours."

She knelt down and whispered to Keeper. Whatever happened, she would not put him in danger. She had a good idea who had done this to her people and he was probably up at the house—*her* house. He'd enjoy using it as a command post for him and his officers, eating her food, drinking her wine. He would like as not kill the dog for spite. Keeper looked at her, whining his reluctance.

"Go on. Go on!"

The dog loped away. He would not go far but he knew to stay out of sight. When she was sure he'd gone, she strode off.

Tom followed her towards a pair of tall grit-stone pillars, the gateway to a handsome house that stood above the village. Solid and stone built, it nestled into the side of the hill as though it was part of the landscape.

"What have we here?" A soldier stepped out. He wore sergeant's stripes but he was bareheaded, his uniform unbuttoned and dirty, and he was more than a little drunk. "A pretty girl and a pretty boy. Dressed in strange fashion. What are we to do with you?"

He looked to a group of soldiers who were lounging nearby, passing a bottle between them. They grinned in anticipation of sport to come.

"Take me to whoever is in command here." Augusta stared back at him, arms folded. She would not be intimidated.

"Ooh." The sergeant looked to his comrades. "She likes to boss, eh? Likes to give orders? We'll see about that."

He reached a hand towards her but Tom stepped between them.

"Don't you touch her."

"Yours, is she?" The sergeant shoved Tom out of the way. "Well, she's mine now."

"Save some for us!" One of the soldiers pushed himself off the wall and came towards them.

"There'll be plenty." The sergeant's hand went to his belt buckle. "Keep an eye on t'other 'un while I'm about my business."

A man stuck a pistol in Tom's back. "What you going to do with 'em after?"

"Put 'em in the barn with the rest of 'em. Set fire to it before we open the doors, then when they come running out—shoot 'em like rats. We'll have some fun first, though. You see if we don't!"

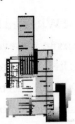

CHAPTER THIRTEEN

ROGUE

THE SERGEANT HAD HIS ARM across Augusta's throat and was pushing her back against the wall.

There was a roar as Keeper leapt for him, but the man was already going down gargling and choking on his own blood. He plucked feebly at the feathered flight of the arrow, no bigger than a dart, buried in his neck as he fell forward into the mud.

His men were dead before they could help him. Stuck with arrows in eye and throat, and one with a pike in his back.

Roberts went to retrieve his pike from the dead man, while Webster plucked the Fairish arrow from the neck of the sergeant. He looked up at Augusta and grinned.

"Canny little fellas, them Fairish. Can hit a sparra's eye." He stood up and dusted his hands. "The Summer Lord sent Robin and his men to see you safe. We came with 'em." He looked round. "Like as not they've gone now."

Augusta called her thanks anyway, to Robin and to the Summer Lord and his sister for their protection. The Fairish were touchy about such things, and who knew when she might need their help again.

"Webster, Roberts—" Augusta looked at them with tears in her eyes.

"No need to say more, my lady. We come past Tranter's Field," Roberts said. "Seen what they done. The bodies…"

Webster bowed his head. "A sorry sight."

He looked away with a shake of his head; those lying there had been friends, neighbours, kin.

"They are holding the rest of the people captive in the tithe barn," Augusta said. "I don't know if it's guarded…"

Webster drew his sword and Roberts brandished his bloody pike.

"Don't matter if it is."

"Once they're out, get them away, as far and as fast as you can. Go back to the Fairish, up on to the moors, join the Dark Lantern Men and the rebels who have fled from Sneachiesland and Rogue."

Webster and Roberts nodded. Sneachiesland lay to the north of them. Its lairds ruled in Rogue's name and they were as cruel as their master. They knew why folk had fled.

"When you are ready, get a force together and come back and fight to free our land. I put you in charge until my return."

"We won't let you down, my lady," Webster said.

"That we won't." Roberts grinned. "We'll make you proud. We'll get some good lads together." He nodded to the house. "Knock seven bells out of yon."

Augusta held out her hands to both of them. "God speed and good luck!"

"And to you, my lady." Webster looked to Tom. "You look after her."

They made their way to the barn, moving quietly and stealthily. The guards had fled or lay dead with a flint arrow protruding from eye or neck. Webster lifted the length of wood that barred the double doors. Roberts beckoned those inside to come out quickly.

Rogue was behind this, Augusta thought as she watched her men shepherd the people out of the village and towards the moors. Even though she hadn't seen him yet, she could sense his presence, feel his malice. Like brimstone in the air. He would make her people suffer, and delight in it, just to hurt her. Those he hadn't killed he would enslave.

Augusta sighed her relief as the last of the villagers disappeared into the trees, then she turned at the clatter of hooves on stone and pulled Tom back into the shadows as a man came riding out of the gateway to the house.

He was mounted on a black stallion and rode with one hand on the reins, the other on the sabre that swung by his side. Dark chestnut hair curled to the wide silver epaulettes of his midnight-blue jacket. His high boots and white breeches were splashed with mud. He was followed closely by other horsemen, some in uniform, others not.

"What's this to-do?" he said as he rode towards the village. He looked round at the officers accompanying him. "Where are your men? Why is the barn door open? Go and see what's happened!"

One of his men rode over to the barn and back again.

"It appears to be empty, my lord. There's been some sort of attack. Someone has freed them."

"And the men who were supposed to be guarding them?"

"Dead."

"Let me see." He dismounted next to the first body, knelt to touch the feathered arrow flight protruding from the man's eye. He stood up with a look of distaste, brushed his hands together and dusted specks of dirt from his breeches. "Fairish arrows. It's about time we cleared out that nest of adders."

His men looked around, apprehensive. Guns to the ready. Hands on swords.

"They'll be gone now, you fools. They won't stand and fight. Their way is to shoot from the shadows like cowards."

"Flint against flintlock?" Augusta stepped out. "Who can blame them?"

"Augusta. My lady." He swept off his hat and gave an elaborate mock bow. "I might have known. You were ever their friend, as I recall. Who else could it be?" He looked her up and down. "Even dressing like them now." At her side, Keeper growled. "Get that beast under control or I'll have him shot."

He pushed back his chestnut curls and smiled. He was undoubtedly handsome. He was known for his fine eyes: large, dark blue, almost black, under arching brows and the exact same colour as the sapphire pin, as big as a pigeon egg, that fixed his snowy-white neckcloth. Vain, too. His side whiskers sculpted to show off his high cheekbones. His nose was long and narrow with a patrician hook to it. The cruel twist to his mouth made him even more attractive in some eyes, less so in others. Augusta was of the latter mind.

"Rogue. I could say the same thing." She looked about her. "A trail of destruction and senseless killing. I might have known it was you." She echoed his words. "Who else could it be?"

"Any one of a number these days, I'd have thought. We live in murderous times and you have many enemies. And it's 'my lord' to you. You have the honour of addressing the new Duke of Northangerland."

"Since when?"

"Since I was given the title."

"Gave it to yourself, more like."

"I'll ignore that. And who is your esquire?" Rogue's scrutiny intensified. "Who, or what, do we have here? Dressed like one of the Fair Folk but without their... peculiarities."

"He's with me."

"Is he? We'll see about that. He looks a wrong 'un to me." Rogue turned to the officer at his elbow. "Take him away and have him questioned."

"No." Augusta put a hand on Tom's shoulder. "He stays."

Rogue's blue eyes stayed on Tom. "For now, perhaps," he said after a long moment, "I'll indulge you." He nodded towards the house. "Shall we? I marvel that you can live like this, Augusta. You could have palaces and yet you choose to live in a hovel, this perfectly dreadful place, surrounded by all these boring little people. You *are* letting the side down."

"You wouldn't understand," Augusta said. "So why try? All I ask is to be left in peace."

"That will not be possible. Let's continue our discussions up at the shed that you like to call home."

Tom followed them up to the house. The afternoon sun winked on rows of small leaded windows under pointed gables. It wasn't a mansion but it was pretty big. It looked all right to him.

There was a date above the portal, so eroded that Tom couldn't make it out. The front door was weathered oak, studded and banded with iron. It was opened by a young-ish woman dressed in a white cap, with a white apron over her plain blue dress.

"My lady! We've been that worried! What with *these* coming…" She flashed a look at Rogue, anger and defiance in her brown eyes.

"Don't fret, Annie. I'm perfectly safe and well."

"Bring us some refreshment," Rogue ordered. "Wine if you have it."

"You drank all that," Annie answered back. "We've good ale and cider."

"Less of your lip, woman," Rogue rapped out. "Bring us what you've got and be quick about it."

He led the way into a large room, oak panelled, with logs burning in a fireplace big enough for a man to stand in.

"Not you," he said to Tom. "This is to be a private conversation. Nor that dog."

Keeper was still growling. Tom took him by the collar. He hesitated, reluctant to leave Augusta.

"It's all right." She smiled and touched his arm. "I can look after myself. Take Keeper outside."

Tom left reluctantly, dragging the dog with him.

The hand on the arm, the easy closeness that there seemed to be between them, was not lost on Rogue.

He went over to a long, polished table littered with maps.

"My orders were to subdue your lands, which, you have to agree, I've done most effectively, and to bring you to Glass Town. When that woman comes back, tell her to find suitable attire. For him, too. I'm sure one of your menservants will have something for him to wear. You're not going to Glass Town dressed like that." He studied his fingernails then looked back at Augusta. "You may want your maid with you, and whoever else you require. You will need your women, I suppose."

Augusta studied his face. There was something suspicious about the way he was looking at her, gleeful and mocking at the same time.

"Why would I need them particularly?" she asked.

"You are to prepare for your wedding, madam, so you will need women about you."

"Wedding?" Augusta couldn't disguise her shock.

"Yes. You are to marry."

"Who says so?"

"The Duke, of course. If you hadn't run off to start this futile rebellion, you'd know all about it."

"To whom, may I ask? Not Douro!" Augusta held on to the edge of the table as the dawning horror of it threatened to overwhelm her. "He loathes me and the feeling is mutual. It would be worse than—"

"Marrying me?" Rogue grinned. "Infinitely."

"Besides," Augusta said, frowning, "I thought he already had a wife."

"Passed away, sadly." Rogue examined his fingernails again. "He doesn't have much luck in that respect." He looked up. "So, you see, both of us are free." He came towards her. "Which is it to be? The Duke has yet to decide between me and Douro. You know how capricious he can be—changes his mind as often as he changes his uniform. But on one thing we are all agreed. It was decided in Council. *You* are in need of a master." He took her chin in a hard grip. "And I'm to bring you back to Glass Town, willing or no."

Annie came in and banged the tray of cider down on the table. Augusta used the interruption to pull away from him.

"You both have mistresses aplenty," Augusta said. "Women are queuing up. And I don't want either of you, so why me?"

"For myself?" Rogue laughed. "That would be a good enough reason. But the real answer is simple." He spread his fingers like bat's wings across the map on the table. He looked up at her. "Whoever marries you gets all your land, all your property. All your wealth."

Augusta turned away from the greed she heard in his voice, saw in his eyes. Rogue or Douro. The devil or deep water… *He wants to win this contest,* she thought, *and what he wants, he generally gets.*

"What if I refuse? The Duke and the Council can't make me."

"Oh, I think you will find that they can." Rogue's smile widened, showing sharp, white teeth. "If you refuse, or make any kind of fuss, your lands will be forfeit and *this* will happen. The choice is yours."

Where his fingers touched the map, the paper began to smoulder, tiny flames eating outwards from the lettering of Parrysland, until there was just a scorched hole, fringed with black.

"Here, lad." Annie came out to Tom sitting on the steps outside. "I brought you a bit o' summat. You must be hungry. Thirsty, too."

She set a plate of crusted bread and crumbly white cheese on the step beside him and passed him a mug of ale.

Tom took a long drink and put the tankard down. He was struggling to keep his temper. He didn't like Rogue and he didn't like being sent out like that, as if he was no different from Keeper. The dog seemed to know how he felt. He whined and licked his hand.

"Don't mind Rogue," Annie said. "And don't worry about milady—she'll give as good as she gets."

"What are they talking about in there?"

Annie sat on the step beside him. "Marriage."

"Marriage? Augusta is to be married?"

Annie nodded.

Tom was shocked. Augusta seemed so young—too young; his age or younger. Marriage was a thing older people did.

"She's too young, surely?"

"That's the way wit' gentry. Some of 'em married off by fifteen, fourteen even. Promised even younger."

"Is she to marry Rogue? She loathes him."

"Rogue or Douro—they ain't quite decided. She ain't too keen on t'other one, either, but feelings don't come into it. It's all about land and property. Whoever marries her gets everything." Annie paused, looking around. "They might have all this, lands and houses, but I don't envy 'em. Not one bit."

"It seems wrong. Barbaric."

"'Appen." Annie stood up. "But that's the way of it. Now eat yer bit o' bait, young fella, keep yer strength up."

Tom didn't feel hungry any more. He drained the tankard and gave the food to the dog. He stood up and walked along the gravel path below the big bay window, treading softly so as not to draw attention, and watched them through the distorting glass in the little diamond panes. He saw Augusta turn away; saw how Rogue looked at her as he spread his big hands over the map of her lands. All the time wondering: *What am I doing here?*

Why should he even care who she married, or if she married? But he did.

CHAPTER FOURTEEN
THE WHITE ROAD

THEY TRAVELLED in a long column, Rogue at the front, his escort behind him and then a line of carts and wagons carrying what he had plundered. Augusta and Tom followed, under guard. They rode along with two soldiers, one in front and one behind, with Keeper loping alongside.

Augusta's servants walked beside the cart that held her luggage; her maid, Annie, riding on the trunks and cases, guarding her things.

"I don't trust them soldiers, milady. Thieves to a man."

Tom liked Annie. Fierce in defence of Augusta, she bowed to no one. Even Rogue felt the rough edge of her tongue. She had particular contempt for the men he had around him, calling them murdering scum to their faces, telling Rogue he should be ashamed to be associated with such as them. Only Augusta's intervention prevented her from making the journey over the back of a mule, gagged and bound.

As they began to descend into a wide, undulating plain, they were joined by another column. A line of captives straggling along, all roped together by the neck. Slaves for Glass Town.

The change in the landscape was abrupt, the country here painted with a different palette. Green hills gave way to pale fields of wheat, barley and rye; the soil milky sienna between rows of vines and small fruit trees. A wide, meandering river showed silver, its course marked by a dark-green line of willow, alder and ash. The people working in the fields were burnt brown and wore wide straw-brimmed hats against the sun. It was suddenly much hotter. Tom's shirt was sticking to his skin. He loosened the fastening and pulled his neckcloth higher against the dust being thrown up from the white road they were travelling. Its margins punctuated by tall pine and poplar, it crossed the plain, straight as an arrow, to a vanishing point on the horizon.

When the sun began to set, Rogue brought the column to a halt. They would camp here for the night.

Augusta was invited to dine in Rogue's pavilion. She was reluctant to go, preferring to stay with her own people, but she would learn more if she joined him and his officers. Tom wasn't invited; neither was Keeper. The dog stayed with Tom and both of them felt a pang of jealousy as Augusta strode off in her grey riding habit to Rogue's pavilion. It was more than a tent. Tom watched servants and soldiers unpacking wagons, running backwards and forwards, creating a home from home—if your home was a palace. Bare ground was covered in thickly patterned carpet. Canvas walls hung with tapestries. Big wooden chests, that took two men to carry them, were unpacked for plates and glasses, linen, lamps and candelabras. Batmen in white gloves set the polished mahogany table for a banquet; Rogue travelled with his own chef.

Tom and Keeper went off to collect firewood. Their meal would be a simple affair. Bread, cheese and bacon eaten round the campfire. He ate with Annie, Lizzie, Isaac and Amos from Augusta's household, who were friendly enough—Annie gave him a generous platter of food and Amos passed him a flagon of beer—but they seemed shy of him and talked together in a dialect that Tom found hard to understand. They didn't understand him too well, either. It was easier to keep quiet.

Tom drank deep when the flagon was passed to him. He was thirsty from the ride and hungry now, too, although he shared his food with Keeper. When the camp broke up to go to their tents, he stretched out by the fire, a blanket over him, his coat as a pillow. As the fire died to embers, the dog yawned and settled down next to him. He wondered what they thought of him. Perhaps they accepted that he was from the Fairish. Maybe that was why they were wary of him. That could be good. It would stop them asking questions he couldn't answer, like, where exactly *had* he come from and what was he doing here?

Tom woke later feeling cold. He threw more wood on the fire and sat watching the flames, the blanket round him. From somewhere came the fluttering hoot of an owl;

another answering. By his side, the big dog snuffled and whined softly, his long legs tensing, paws twitching as if he was dreaming of running, hunting or being hunted. Tom leant down and stroked his tawny fur until the dog quieted. He looked up at the sky. It was a mass of stars. No light pollution dimmed the thick diamond dusting; there were millions and billions, so many and so bright, giving off their own light, set in strange constellations he didn't recognize. Keeper's warm skin and smooth hair felt real enough but these were no stars that he'd ever seen.

LUCY WAITED OUTSIDE, her book gripped in her hand. Was there really any point in doing this? Was it pointless and futile, like Natalie said?

"I mean, you don't even know him." Natalie had added a scratchy creak to the drawly American accent that she'd picked up from her favourite YouTube channels and which made her voice even more irritating. "Now, if you don't mind?" She'd swept back her long blonde hair. "I'd like some alone time with *my* boyfriend."

Natalie had turned her back and begun checking her look in the mirror app on her phone, applying a fresh coating of candy-coloured lipstick. It wasn't for him. He slept on like some enchanted prince. It was for the selfies she was preparing to take to put up on her Instagram, Facebook and Twitter accounts. To feed her followers. Add more.

Lucy had let the door swing shut and left her to it. There was no love lost between them. Natalie thought Lucy was a nerd and a freak, while Lucy thought Natalie was a total airhead of the first order.

Natalie applied mascara with steady strokes. Interest was falling off, truth be told—numbers going down, *#boyinacoma* no longer trending, even *#heroinacoma* was getting fewer likes—but she had a secret plan. Well, not *so* secret—she'd told Milo, but then, why shouldn't she? He was her boyfriend now—unofficially, as she couldn't be seen to be two-timing Tom. If she was extra *specially* truthful, it was Milo's idea, but she preferred to think that they came up with it together. If *#boyinacoma* had trended—and *#heroinacoma* had gone even better—*#boyswitchedoff* "would go pandemic!" Milo had told her. "There must be a switch around there somewhere…" He'd grinned. "Only kidding!" Milo had a wicked sense of humour. "It's just a matter of time, babe," he'd said then. "Just a matter of time. But you've got to be ready, so keep feeding in the pix. I'll do the rest."

Natalie wasn't sure what "the rest" was but she'd leave that up to him. Milo was clever. And rich. Natalie didn't know how he made his money—something to do with the internet—but he had plenty of it. He was getting a Maserati as soon as he passed his driving test. He'd promised to fund *Vlogit*, the shopping and fashion vlog she planned to start sometime soon. She had such *great* taste—all her friends said so, online and in real life. She could have her own reality TV programme—*so* much to share, *so* much to offer—but that was for the future. "If you want to be an influencer, you gotta build a platform, babe," Milo had told her. "Create a presence."

Building a platform—that's what she was doing right now. She plumped Tom's pillow and put her head next to his, holding her phone at just the right angle to show her good side. Another of Tom on his own, eyes closed, tubes going in and out of him. She applied just a tiny hint of blusher to his cheeks. He looked so, so *alive*. So young, so beautiful, but doomed… She really did want to cry, so it wasn't hard to take the next set of selfies with tears just about to spill. Not too much, though. "*You don't want a red nose and mascara clown eyes*," Milo had advised. Just one last one. There, all done.

"He's all yours."

She was too busy sweeping back through the shots she'd taken to even look at Lucy. She went off down the corridor, scrutinizing each shot, binning the not so good. "*Better to have a few crackers than a load of duff stuff*," Milo had said. She took his advice; he knew tons about the "net". With a few pecks of her pink shellac nails, she uploaded her choices. She took a few shots of hospital signage, just for good measure, and popped the phone in her pocket. She smiled with satisfaction. The notifications were starting. She hadn't even left the hospital and she was already getting likes.

Lucy went back into Tom's room and resumed her seat. She found her place in the book and continued to read. There was no difference in Tom—there never was—but Lucy had the suspicion that Natalie's visits upset him in some way. It was nothing she could put her finger on, but the feeling in the room had changed from calm to agitation. His monitors showed nothing but she felt a subtle shift in him.

Lucy read on but her mind wasn't really on the book. She knew what Natalie was doing. She followed her on social media but it wasn't just that. Lucy was no slouch at the internet herself—not in Milo's class but way beyond Natalie's capabilities. Natalie always used the same password, glamgirl4luv. She was seeing Milo on the sly. Not in public, beyond the odd word in the sixth form common room, as she couldn't afford for them to be seen out together, but she was WhatsApping him and even emailing him from her school account—which was stupid, even for Natalie. Lucy didn't quite know what they were up to but neither of them had Tom's interests at heart—that was for sure.

"She gone?" Joe, the male nurse, popped his head round the door.

Lucy nodded.

"Good." He came in, shaking his head. "She's no good for him, that one." He went over to Tom, checking the readings from the machines, taking his temperature. "Gone down. That's better." He picked up the chart at the bottom of the bed. "Normal now. It was up yesterday. I was a bit worried. I was scared he might have got an infection. That would be dangerous for him." He pulled the gown aside and looked down at Tom's shoulder. "There's been some unusual brain activity on the EEG and I still don't know what to make of this."

"What?" Lucy got up from her seat and went over.

"There's a mark. Here. See?" He pointed to a small indentation, a slight discoloration. "It just appeared yesterday, with the temperature. I told the doctor."

"What did she say?"

He shrugged. "Didn't think it was significant. Thought he might have had it before but we hadn't noticed. Can't argue with the doctor." His smile was ironic. "But I *know* it wasn't there. I know his body as good as I know my own." He laughed, his eyes creasing. "Better." His round, smiling face grew serious. "And it looked like a bullet scar. An old one, long healed, but that's what it looked like. I've seen them before in my country. Almost gone now. It's faded some more." He gently readjusted Tom's gown. "You can hardly see it. That's another strange thing." He folded his arms, looking down at Tom. "Where do you go?" he said quietly. "Where did that come from?"

"Go?"

"Oh." Joe looked sheepish. "Where I come from they'd say he was travelling. In the spirit world, you know?" He gave a shrug. "It's just what my people believe. I better be getting on."

He left and Lucy settled back down with her reading, her quiet voice adding to the noises the machines made. Tom was thankful. There was no way that he could show it, but her voice and her presence soothed him. He'd come to hate Natalie's visits.

He knew this was life—his real life. He wasn't sure where the other place was. Something to do with that thing Milo had stuck in his ear, but how it worked and where it took him, he had no idea. He just knew he wanted to be back there. If he could, he would have shed real tears.

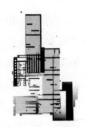

CHAPTER SIXTEEN
GLASS TOWN

HE WOKE SOBBING. Keeper was licking his face, whimpering concern for him. Tom wiped the sleep and tears from his eyes and struggled up, grateful for the dog's warmth in the predawn cold. The strange stars had faded; the eastern sky was lightening, turning pink and yellow. Tom stood and stretched; the dog got up with him, slowly, as if his legs were stiff also. He looked around at the rest of the camp sleeping. He could try to escape if he wanted to. But where would he go?

He squatted down, stirring the fire to find a few live embers. He threw on some kindling, waited for it to catch, added small sticks and then bigger branches until he had a decent blaze going.

Annie came up, yawning. "See you 'ad company." She scratched Keeper behind the ears. "Good lad." The dog whined and licked her hand. "I know what you want." She laughed. "Soon have a bit o' bacon cooking. Thanks for keeping the fire in," she said to Tom. "That warm in the day but starving cold at night. Eeh, day." She sighed, hands on the small of her back to ease the stiffness there. "Can't stand it down 'ere." She handed him a big iron kettle. "Fetch us some water, would you? Down at the stream yonder."

Tom went off, the dog following, the big kettle swinging from his hand. When he came back, kettle filled, Annie threw in a good handful of black tea and hung it over the fire. The brew was strong and tarry. Tom sipped the scalding liquid and felt the life come back into him. Annie soon had slices of thick bacon sizzling. She sawed bread from a big flat loaf to use as a platter. Bacon first, then the thick, greasy slice of bread. Tom didn't think he'd ever eaten anything so good. He fed rind and crusts to Keeper, and listened to the talk round the fire—of home, mostly; what might be happening there, and what might await them in the city.

"How about you, young man?" Amos asked him. "You ent from these parts."

"No," Tom replied.

"What are you, then?"

"A soldier."

They nodded. Soldiers could come from anywhere.

"Int' battle, were you?"

"Yes, I was there."

"Bad do. Heard you was winning when the Jinn come for you. We seen 'em. Int' distance, like, but near enough to feel their passing."

Annie shuddered. "How'd you escape? We watched and wondered."

"We found sanctuary."

"Wi't' Fairish?"

He nodded.

"Ent always to be trusted but they seem to have done right by you." Amos grinned, his weathered face creasing.

"They did for them murdering swine of soldiers," Isaac added.

"We keep the Fairish as friends," Annie said. "Leave milk out, butter and that."

Isaac laughed and spat into the fire. "Good thing we do."

Augusta joined them after breakfasting with Rogue and his officers. The long column was setting off early to avoid the heat of the day. The dust thrown up by the horses and wagons was choking. Tom pulled his neckcloth up, winding it round his face.

"That," Augusta pointed, "is Glass Town."

In the far distance, spires and slender towers gleamed and glittered in the rising sun. As they rode on, the city seemed to get no nearer; it appeared to float on a pool of quicksilver, receding in front of them, like a mirage. Then suddenly, as the sun rose towards its zenith, there it was, solidifying out of the plain. Tom stopped to gaze in wonder. Set on high cliffs, it thrust out like the prow of a ship. Crenellated walls, carved from the living rock, spiralled up and up to a great tower at the summit which seemed a miniature of the city that supported it. Other towers and spires soared above the winding walls. It was like Middle Earth's Minas Tirith before it was even imagined. The city shone a blinding white-gold in the sun. Maybe it was the glare from it, or the tricks that the light played, but something about it looked unreal, like a painting, or a backdrop, or a model made for a film or a game. It was a feeling that would stay with Tom, on and off, the entire time he was in the Great Glass Town.

They were riding through a rich land, with vineyards, olive and citrus groves on either side of the road. It grew ever more tropical as they approached the city, the road shaded by tall palms topped with great spreading fronds and laden with hanging clusters of dates. Tom wanted another look at that map. It didn't make sense for the climate to change as quickly as that.

Round the base of Glass Town, a slow-flowing river lay like a mirror, the city perfectly reflected in its glassy waters. A drowned city, that looked exactly like the one above but with everything reversed. It was impossible to tell which side was up.

"The city is surrounded on three sides by water," Augusta said. "On the north side, the harbour is famed for its depth and stillness. These mirror waters give Glass Town its name."

A many-arched bridge spanned the river. Small boats and skiffs looked like children's toys as they sculled beneath it. The centre arch was a drawbridge to allow taller ships through. On the other side of the bridge the banks were crowded with warehouses, fishing lofts, boathouses and the chimneys of factories and slow-turning water wheels. The entrance to the bridge was guarded by carved lions on tall pillars and soldiers at attention, rifles on their shoulders, their uniforms immaculate, standing so still that they looked like they'd been painted. They snapped to and presented arms as the column rode past.

They entered the city through a great gatehouse. High above them, soldiers marched to and fro with the precision of automata. They rode under the teeth of a huge portcullis. Great oak doors, studded and banded with iron, stood back against the rock. It was cool inside the thickness of the walls and smelt of stone. To left and right, arched doorways led to guardhouses. Off-duty soldiers sat in their shirtsleeves, reading newspapers, playing at cards and dice. Long pikes and halberds, rifles and muskets stood in racks against the walls.

"The city is well defended, as you see." Rogue had come to ride beside them. "The gates are closed at curfew. The walls patrolled day and night."

They took the wide street and began winding their way up into the city. Tom looked around, trying to get a measure of the place. They passed shops with goods of all kinds displayed on wide shelves in front of open windows. Inn signs swung above their heads. Street sellers shouted from stalls set up on corners. A great many people were about: men on business, women shopping accompanied by servants carrying parcels, servants running errands, tradesmen making deliveries. The men wore tricorne hats, their hair long, tied at the nape. They were dressed in knee breeches, velvet coats and waistcoats, high-collared shirts and neckcloths, despite the heat. The women wore long dresses of thin, floaty material, or brightly patterned cotton, with gloves above their elbows, their faces shaded by bonnets and parasols to protect them from the sun. The servants sweating after them were afforded no such luxury. Here and there, threaded through the crowds, were dark-skinned, dark-eyed people; the men in white tunics, with brass torques and armlets; the women in colourful robes and turbans, bundles perched on their heads. They looked comfortable in the heat, as though they were used to it, as if this was Africa—although where in Africa, he couldn't say. Maybe this was some kind of colony. The buildings and the people in charge were European but the temperature was decidedly tropical. Yet they were hardly more than two days' ride from somewhere that had looked and felt just like Yorkshire…

Their road took them past wide terraces, their squares cooled by gushing fountains, their piazzas shaded by awnings and the dark leaves of fig and palm. One of the secrets, within this city of many secrets, was the gardens that hid behind the high, blank walls that gave on to the streets. Glimpsed here and there, through a partially open door, hinted at by the trickle of running water, the sound of a playing fountain, by feathery fronds that topped the parapets. Beyond lay a hidden world, the air strong with the scent of lavender, myrtle and orange blossom. With walkways threaded through beds of herbs and flowers, leading to arbours and pergolas twisted with violet wisteria, pink and white oleander, bright papery purple bougainvillea, heavy vines. Apricots, peaches, purple figs ripened on honey-coloured stone; oranges and lemons glowed from glossy green leaves.

As they went higher, the people were fewer. The summit was deserted. The city levelled into a vast piazza, paved with different-coloured stone—pink, white and grey—set in geometric patterns. Tall colonnaded buildings lay to either side, built in white and grey marble. In the centre stood a white marble tower, spiralled like the city, a miniature version of it reaching up into the sky, its great domed roof gleaming gold. A wide flight of steps led to a porticoed entrance with beaten bronze doors.

"The Tower of All Nations," Augusta explained. "These are government buildings."

The sun glared off the marble frontages, filling the colonnades with deep shadow, rendering the windows black. Wide streets of tall buildings punctuated by square towers and rounded cupolas led off the piazza and diminished into the distance, giving an illusion that the city, endlessly repeated, was disappearing into infinity. The dizzying perspectives, the harsh light and sharp shadow reminded Tom of surrealist paintings.

"There don't seem to be many people about," he observed.

"Ordinary folk are not allowed up here," Augusta replied. "It would spoil the city's symmetry. Their commerce is underground. This whole area is supplied by passageways and tunnels. The hill is riddled with them. There is as much below ground as above it. Storehouses, wine cellars, workshops—and dungeons, of course."

"This is where I must leave you." Rogue reined in his horse. "I have business in the Tower of All Nations."

"So we are prisoners?" Augusta twisted in her saddle. "Do you plan to put us in your dungeons?"

"Don't be ridiculous, Augusta. Of course not. Don't be so histrionic. You are an honoured guest of His Grace." He turned to their escort. "Take the Lady Augusta to the Duke's Palace, see her safe to her apartments." He turned back to address Augusta. "You are free to go anywhere you like. You'll only be put in the dungeons if you try to leave the city."

They were taken to the Duke's Palace. In front of the building stood a colossal statue of the man on the back of a rearing horse, waving his sword. The great bronze doors of his palace were opened by two burly footmen and clanged shut behind them with an echoing finality that seemed to say that they were just as much prisoners here as the unfortunates in the cells below the Tower of All Nations.

They stepped into a cavernous, marble-floored atrium, dark after the brightness of the day outside. A huge bust of the Duke, many times life-sized, presented him laurel wreathed and at his most imperial, his aquiline nose high in the air, blank eyes fixed in a supercilious stare. Their footsteps echoed as they skirted round it to reach the wide twin stairways that led to the upper reaches of the house.

Everything about the Duke's Palace was at least three times the normal size, from the pillars of the porticoed entrance to reception rooms the length of a ballroom, to ballrooms as big as a ploughed field. The banqueting hall seated a hundred and fifty guests. All for show, like its owner. It lacked human dimensions or any sense that it was a home.

Augusta hated it here: the Duke's ludicrous palace, the stifling heat, the general somnambulance. She was shown to her own apartments. It was as though she'd never been away. The rooms were airless and smelt of dust. She felt as trapped as the flies that buzzed against the shutters and flew about in pointless, zigzagging patterns. She left Annie to air it out and went up to the loggia at the top of the palace.

The great bell of the cathedral boomed, deep and sonorous, sending pigeons skywards. Lesser bells sounded from all over the city. The streets were deserted; houses and shops shuttered. All work stopped at noon.

The loggia was open on three sides to catch the slightest breeze. Swifts screamed, darting in and out of the slender pillars on flashing scimitar wings. Below her lay the Palace Gardens. For the Duke's use only. The raked paths were perfect; low box hedges, clipped and barbered, bordered the formal beds; at the centre of each an orange or lemon tree, pruned into a perfect ball, the glowing fruit inspected every day, the imperfect discarded. A large aviary spanned the end of the garden, bright with exotic birds: finches and hummingbirds in jewelled flight among the bigger birds' scarlet, azure and emerald plumage. At a glance, it appeared that nothing confined them, but Augusta knew they were caged within a fine mesh that disappeared at a distance, so that they looked to be flying free.

She moved her gaze to the glitter of the town's many towers, the glare of the marble palaces blinding under the whiteness of the afternoon sky, the terracotta roofs baking in the lesser town. She longed for grey skies, grey stone walls, drab little hedgerow sparrows, the lonely curlew's call, the cool bite of a wind that held the promise of rain. Her country was near. Near enough to see it from this high point in the town, but when she looked in that direction, her hills and mountains seemed insubstantial, clouds within clouds, grown even hazier from the tears of anger and frustration filling her eyes. They had no right to keep her here.

Augusta looked beyond the city walls to the glassy, still waters of the Great Harbour, hoping to see John Ross's brig *Alexander* or William Parry's *Hecla* and *Griper* returned from their Northern voyaging, triumphant at finding the elusive North-west Passage that led into the Pacific Ocean. They would then set sail, taking her with them to found her own land of Gondal... But there was no sign of them. Instead, the harbour was filled with black hulls, black sails flying the Red Rover. Rogue's flag.

A dart and heart dripping blood. Just offshore lurked a black freighter, also flying the Rover, the guns on her deck trained on the town.

What is that doing there? Is Rogue holding Glass Town to ransom?

Augusta turned for the stair, Keeper at her heels. She may have been confined by the city walls, like the birds within their aviary cage, but she had to find out what was happening here.

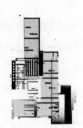

CHAPTER SEVENTEEN
BRAVEY'S INN

SHE TOLD ANNIE to say that she was resting and not to be disturbed, should anyone enquire, and went to find Tom. He was up in the servants' quarters, which made it quite a lot easier to get out undetected.

"Where are we going?" Tom asked, as Augusta led him down a little-used, circular stairway. She'd stayed in the palace since she was a small child, sometimes willingly, sometimes not. She knew all its secret panels and passages, exits and entrances. She might not be a prisoner but there was no need to advertise what she was about.

"Bravey's Inn," Augusta replied, as she opened a small doorway at the bottom of the stone steps. "I want to know what's going on. We should find Wellesley there."

The door led into an internal courtyard, which was why it was not locked. Augusta went through a door on the other side and into a wide stone passageway used for deliveries. It led past the kitchens and buttery, through an archway and out.

Augusta stopped and looked up and down the street. It was deserted. She leant against the wall for a moment. Now she was outside, now she could breathe.

"Who's Wellesley?" Tom asked.

125

"Lord Charles Wellesley is the Duke's other son. Unlike his father and brother, he's not a military man. He edits a magazine."

Bravey's was like no inn that Tom had ever seen. They went in through an entrance nearly as grand as the Duke's Palace. The light from a great glass dome set into the ceiling was broken into shafts by drifting tobacco smoke. Logs burned in a wide fireplace, despite the heat.

"That's Bravey."

The man behind the bar was huge, his coat stretched tight over his shoulders, his belly bursting from his straining waistcoat, his features made small by his jowls and mutton-chop whiskers. His little hands poured ale and cider into crockery pots and pewter tankards, filled thick glasses with wine and spirits. Serving girls whisked away trays to be conveyed to the various tables that crowded the wood-panelled room.

The serving girls were the only women there, as far as Tom could see, apart from Augusta. By the window, gentlemen sat in earnest conversation or reading the newspapers and periodicals kept on poles for common reading. Many of them were drinking dishes of coffee or tea dispensed by a serving woman from a pot and a kettle hanging over the fire.

That didn't seem to be the beverage of choice for the young men at a long table at the far end of the room, their noisy discussion dominated by a skinny young man with a thatch of bright red hair and milky pale skin. His rusty black suit looked a size too small; his bony wrists stuck out from his frayed shirt cuffs. He was on his feet, his thin-fingered hands weaving his words in the air.

Charles Wellesley folded his copy of the *Young Men's Magazine*.

"Augusta!" He rose to meet her, kissing her on both cheeks. "How delightful. I heard you'd come back to us."

"Not willingly, I assure you."

"I heard that, too. And who is this?" Wellesley looked enquiringly at her companion.

"This is Tom."

"And who might Tom be?" he went on. "One of Parry's, are you? Or perhaps you serve with our brave Commander Ross?"

"He's with me," Augusta supplied.

Lord Charles's look of enquiry remained but Augusta gave no further explanation.

"Whether or no, I'm pleased to meet you… Tom." He offered his hand. "I am Lord Charles Wellesley. Son of the Duke, brother to Douro, although they rarely claim me. Call me Charles or Wellesley. I find Lord a little too… formal."

"Reading your own magazine, I see." Augusta picked up the folded copy.

Tom glanced at the front page. It looked handprinted.

"And enthralling it is, too. All the gossip, the scandals, who's in love with whom, who is plotting against whom. There's an entertaining account of a recent bout of body-snatching…" He glanced sideways to a white-haired old fellow sitting on an adjacent table. "Dr Bady up to his tricks again."

The old man at the adjacent table rattled his copy of *The Intelligencer*. It had the same kind of print and weird font.

"I heard that, Wellesley," he said. "All in the pursuance of knowledge and science, I may assure you."

"All written by me, so, of course, everything in it is true." Wellesley steepled his manicured fingers. "Within the bounds of what is *possible* to be true. *Allowed* truth, if you follow. I have no desire to pine my life away as an unwilling guest of my father, the Duke, in the commodious accommodation he keeps under the Tower of All Nations. I print what is politic to print. Other messages are there for anyone who has the wit to see them."

Lord Charles Wellesley seemed harmless enough. An affable fellow, bland and cheerful, with curling, light brown hair, but his pale blue eyes were lit with a shrewd intelligence that said he was not to be underestimated.

"All peppered with a seasoning of poetry," he added, looking towards the table in the corner. "Some of it of questionable quality."

"How would you know, Wellesley?" the pale young man with the red hair shouted across the room. "D'you know what I think of the rag you write? I wouldn't wipe my arse with it. I'm starting my own magazine," he added, to a roar of support from his friends. "See how you like what I'll write about you!"

"That is Young Soult," Wellesley said for Tom's benefit. "A poet—of sorts. A poetaster, a rhymer. Very thick with Rogue." He dropped his voice to a theatrical whisper. "I hear they've formed a secret society to plot *revolution*!"

The doctor snorted. "They are always plotting revolution."

"We're past the plotting." Soult was approaching them. "This time it's going to happen."

"Oh, really? You and who?" Wellesley nodded towards the table Soult had just left. "Petty thieves, poachers and brawlers, hot bloods and rare lads, pugilists and dog fighters—sots like yourself? I hope Rogue, or Northangerland as he now calls himself, is not relying on the likes of you."

"We have the support of the people. Dark Lantern Men." Soult looked down at Augusta. "You'd know all about them." He turned to Lord Charles. "We'll give you something to write about, you see if we don't. That's if you've still got a press to print on. That's if it hasn't been burnt down!" He spoke slowly, anger and passion replaced by the hiss of cold menace. "It. Will. Be. Soon."

"What is he saying?" Augusta leant forward. "Could it be true?"

They'd seen those words, *It Will Be Soon*, on the way here, scrawled on walls, on doors: ghost letters painted over, repainted and painted over again.

"Anyone can daub on walls." Lord Charles was inclined to be dismissive. "There has been unrest in the city. Mostly calm on the surface but the dungeons are full to bursting. The city is ripe for revolution. The Duke runs it like his own personal fiefdom and he is unpopular. They've begun throwing brickbats at his carriage. Douro's just as bad. The people see him as weak and vain, and I wouldn't disagree. But is *Rogue* the right person to lead them? He's been getting bolder, stirring the people up with his speeches while his rare lads go about the streets, cudgels at the ready, fomenting trouble and inciting rebellion—and the Watch finds urgent business elsewhere."

Augusta was frowning. "But that would just replace one tyranny with another…"

"Indeed. You took my very words. A merry band of rebels and regicides threaded through with the Duke's spies, all changing sides in a bewildering kaleidoscope of intrigue and plotting." Wellesley turned to Tom. "Welcome to Verdopolis, young man."

"*Verdopolis?*" Augusta frowned.

"That's what it is to be called from now on, by the Duke's decree. He thinks it has a better ring. Mixture of French and Greek. A more fitting name for what he now calls the Great Glass Town. It's all to do with the Duke's pretensions, his grasping after grandeur." He turned to Augusta. "Shouldn't you be at the palace? Shouldn't you be getting ready?"

"For what?"

"The reception before the Grand Ball that is to be held in honour and celebration of your betrothal."

"I have no intention of attending. The very idea is absurd. I'm not going to marry Rogue or Douro, or anyone. Why me? There must be any number who'd jump at the chance."

"Tripping over each other in the rush to the altar, I shouldn't wonder." Lord Charles laughed. "But only you will do. Which one of your suitors will it be?" He narrowed his eyes, his head to one side in pantomime speculation. "My money's on Rogue."

"People are *betting* on this?" Augusta looked outraged.

"Most certainly. The odds are brisk and shortening among the sporting fraternity."

"Why Rogue? Pray tell me."

"Well, let me see…" Lord Charles marked the points off on his fingers. "He likes to win. He likes a challenge—and you *are* a challenge—plus he wants your lands."

"Doesn't Douro want the same thing?"

"Not as much. And what Rogue wants, Rogue gets, in the general way of things. Besides…" Lord Charles shrugged. "He has his guns trained on the town. If we want peace… If we want to avoid *unrest*, shall we say? You are the price to be paid. The hope is that, once he has what he wants, he will go away."

"Taking me with him like a prize pig at a country show?"

"I wouldn't quite have put it like *that*." Lord Charles looked down at the toe of his highly polished boot. "A filly, maybe."

Augusta wasn't laughing.

"I like it no better than you do…" Lord Charles went on.

"But you're not prepared to do anything about it." She turned to confront him. "What about Douro? The Duke?"

"The people hate both of them, I told you. They'll be lucky to get away with their lives."

"If Rogue isn't stopped?"

"Quite so."

"And I'm to do the stopping?"

"That's the sum of it."

"And if I refuse him?"

"All hell will break loose."

As if his words were prophecy, glass showered over a startled gentleman sitting in the window and a cobblestone bounced across the floor.

Wellesley brushed shards from his shoulder. "Perhaps it has already."

There was a rush to the street outside. Soult's table rose with a great roar, some to hurl insults and pint pots, others to join the march outside with cries of "Insurrection!"

Men and women were filling the street, workers carrying banners and the tools of their trade. The march was for the most part peaceful, although a few hotheads were running up and down the sides of the crowd like harrying dogs, shouting slogans, cobblestones ready for throwing.

Lord Charles watched from Bravey's door, his mild blue eyes suddenly sharp and darting, assessing, taking note of everything.

"Ah, Bud!" he hailed a tall, bony, muscular fellow, following the crowd with a shambling gait, notebook in hand. "What the devil is going on?"

"As if I'd tell you!" he snarled.

"Captain Bud's manners don't change, I see," Augusta remarked as he lurched off.

"Rival scribe," Wellesley explained. "He writes for the *Intelligencer*. No love lost between our publications, you might say."

Tom nodded. No change there, then.

"There's Johnny Lockhart." Augusta pointed. "He's likely to be a little more forthcoming."

A fresh-faced, fair-haired young man came running over, his stockings torn, with what looked like fresh blood spattered across his shirt.

"You're hurt!"

"Don't fuss, Augusta." Johnny Lockhart sniffed at the blood dribbling out of one nostril. "A bloody nose, that's all."

Lord Charles proffered a handkerchief to staunch the flow. "What's happening, Johnny?" he asked, taking pencil and notebook from his pocket. "Care to comment?"

"Yes, I would." He blew his nose copiously and handed back Wellesley's kerchief, now bloodied.

"Oh, do keep it." Lord Charles opened his notebook. "Now, what is this all about?"

"This is a peaceful march. Mill workers protesting about wages and working conditions; hand weavers unable to feed their wives and children on account of those very mills and factories. All demanding no more than fairness and a say in the government of our city." He pushed his long curly hair back and looked at the passing crowd. "Their purpose is to present a petition but I fear they will not get as far as the Tower of All Nations. There has already been trouble. Rogue's rare lads and bully boys have come pouring out of the alleys and the pot-houses intent on causing trouble, starting fights and smashing windows, doing everything they can to provoke the Duke. He'll have the Guard out—and that's what they want. It'll play right into Rogue's hands. What started as a peaceful march will end in massacre, and there's nothing stirs the people like a field of innocent dead."

"Do you think that is his purpose?" Lord Charles looked up from his scribbling.

"Undoubtedly. His ruffians are everywhere. I've seen Scroven, Laury, Poacher and here come two more. Naughty! Pigtail! Care to tell us what you're up to?"

The two men slouching past turned to scowl at him. Naughty was on the skinny side, his small eyes as dull as the steel axe that he wore in his belt. He was dwarfed by Pigtail. Getting on for seven-foot tall, and ugly with it, with a big shapeless nose, a mass of black beard and a greasy cue of hair hanging down his back. The cudgel looked like a toothpick in his huge hands.

"Careful," Wellesley breathed. "Either one would cleave your skull as soon as look at you."

"Let them try!" Johnny Lockhart patted the pistol at his side. "I'm not afraid of Naughty and his kind."

"I'll come with you," Lord Charles said, as Lockhart made to rejoin the crowd.

"We're coming, too." Augusta seized Tom's hand.

"No." Johnny shook his head. "It's too dangerous—did you not hear what I said?"

"Since when did danger bother me? I'm as brave as you are, Johnny Lockhart."

"You won't keep her out of it." Lord Charles grinned.

"Very well. Stay with me. First sign of trouble—who's this fellow?" Johnny frowned at Tom, as if seeing him for the first time.

"Tom. A friend."

"Is he?" Johnny Lockhart narrowed his eyes. Then his face relaxed into a smile. "Pleased to meet you, Tom." His strong grip tightened on Tom's hand. "You look after her or you will answer to me."

"I've been friends with Johnny since school days," Augusta said, as Johnny led them into the crowd. "He's one of the few I trust."

"What about Lord Charles?" Tom asked.

"I'd rather trust an adder. I'm going to catch up with Johnny. Find out what's happening."

She ran on while Tom lagged a bit behind, marching along with men, women, even children; respectable folk but poorly dressed, clothes well worn and well darned, some little more than rags sewn together. Hunger showed in some. Gaunt, hollow-eyed men trudged silently; their women pale, yellowish; their children barefoot and ragged, their limbs stick thin or bent with rickets.

"Hand weavers," Augusta said on rejoining him. "They carry their tools. Temple, reed, shuttle and heddle. Proud of their trade. They did well once, very well, but they've fallen on hard times. Been replaced by steam weaving. They took to smashing the machines—"

"Not marching just for us, lass." One of their number turned around. "But for them poor buggers as have to work 'em, choking on lint day and night. Them looms'll have yer arm off easy as tearing paper and then what d'yer get? Nowt. Out on t' road. We're off to that parliament to present our grievances."

"The Duke'll do summat about it," a woman said. "Soon as he knows."

Someone had started a hymn. The man and the woman joined in. "To Be a Pilgrim."

Augusta shook her head. "The Duke won't do anything. He owns the factories and mills."

A man came up alongside them. A horn lantern swung from a long pole he carried on his shoulder. His face painted black, green and brown. The men about him were similarly disguised.

"Lady Augusta. Well met." He nodded to Tom. "And you, young sir."

"Tom, this is Jethro, Isaac's brother."

Tom could see the resemblance. The same blue eyes,

high cheekbones and craggy features, although his face was thinner and showed marks of hardship under the camo paint.

"We're grateful for your sanctuary when we had nowhere to go, hounded from our homes for defending our livelihood, our way of life." He swung his lantern. "You have been a good friend to those who follow Ned Ludd."

"What brings you to the city?" Augusta asked.

"What brings everybody? The need for bread. We can't break all the machines. They's too many. We're here to spread the word to unite. Together we are stronger." He looked back at the marching column. "General Ludd will lead a different army."

"Who's General Ludd?" Tom asked. "Is he here?"

"He's not a real person," Augusta explained. "He's…" she thought for a moment, "a mythical leader, a shadowy figure, the first to break the machines that deprived the hand weavers of their living."

"She's right, young sir." Jethro smiled, teeth white against the masking face paint. "Machines that do the work of twenty men, minded by bairns, taking away the livelihood of honest, skilled workers, so they can no longer feed their families, taking the bread from their mouths to feed the maws of those who have plenty already. We are his followers. We meet in secret, the light from our lanterns blackened, our faces too, as you see, so we cannot be recognized and persecuted. More are joining us every day," he said, his eyes shining with pride and belief. "Now it's not just us weavers. Lads and lasses from mill and factory. Together we will conquer the world."

"Not if I 'ave my way," a thin, harsh voice hissed. "We're 'ere to weed out troublemakers and looks like we found one."

"S'death. It sounds like a curse," Augusta whispered to Tom. "But it's his name."

The man who had stepped out to bar their way was tall and thin, dressed like an undertaker, his face pale and cadaverous, with pale eyes set deep in his head; the only colour about him, his shock of red hair. The name suited him.

His men had caught hold of Jethro.

"Unhand me." Jethro raised his arms above his head. "I'll not fight. Not with women and bairns about."

"Keep a tight hold, me boys," S'death ordered. "We don't want this 'un getting away." He came up close to Jethro. "You can blacken up yer faces as much as you like and go to yer daft meetings, waving yon dark lanterns, but we know who you are."

"Where are you taking him?" Augusta demanded.

"Somewhere he'll be doing no harm for a good long while, milady—as if it had owt to do wi' you. Who's yer chitty-faced friend?"

"This is Tom."

S'death looked him up and down with sneering contempt. "Make yer sens scarce, the both on you. Get back up to the palace. Tha's no business here. Hear that 'larum?" A bell clanged an insistent warning. "This lot's about to get a lacing. Come on, me boys. We're off to clatter a few heads."

He left them, striding off on long, thin legs, making free with the truncheon he was carrying, his bully-boy snatch squad followed with the wide-legged, rolling gait of lads looking for a fight.

The feeling in the crowd was changing. From up ahead and behind came the sound of angry shouting; a woman's scream ripped through the air like tearing silk. There was pushing and jostling; a surging movement bunched people closer together.

Tom was beginning to sweat. In a minute, less, a crush formed; the crowd no longer individual people, but a liquid, moving mass. So strong. Inexorable, never stopping. He was being dragged off his feet. He was being squeezed so hard he couldn't breathe, couldn't move his arms; no matter what he did, it was impossible to break the python grip.

Right in front of him, a boy was stumbling. He'd lost his trainer. There was a hole in the heel of his sock. A white sock, grubby, a claret and blue stripe round the top. An away fan caught in the crush that had formed in the tunnel. If he fell, he'd be trampled. The crowd was already closing in. Tom managed to free his arm enough to reach him. He made a grab for the boy's T-shirt, pulled him up, but then he himself was falling...

"Are you all right?" Augusta's voice was close but seemed to come from an impossible distance. "You've gone awfully white."

"I'm... I'm..." Tom looked round, not sure where he was. The crush was the same, but the crowd was different.

"We have to get out of here."

"Not that way. This." She gripped his hand so hard it hurt. She felt the danger, too.

They fought their way into a side street, leaning against a wall as the crowd went on past them like a river in spate. In the distance, Tom could hear the rumble of heavy wheels on cobbles, the clop of horses' hooves, the chink of headgear. A glance to the end of the street answered the question. Horse artillery moving from a cross street, one gun followed by another, accompanied by soldiers on horseback.

"My God, they're moving guns up from Iron Forge." Augusta gripped Tom's hand tighter. "We have to get to the Duke. We have to stop this."

CHAPTER EIGHTEEN
THE DUKE'S PALACE

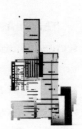

THEY TOOK BACK WAYS to the Duke's Palace. The streets were empty, the houses and shops shuttered, the piazzas and squares deserted. Even the cats had crept indoors.

They ran into the palace through a side entrance, up flights of stairs and into a long corridor, past startled footmen and into the Grand Salon, where the reception had already begun.

The salon was stuffy and stiflingly hot. Although it was full daylight outside, the room was lit by candelabras, the shutters closed, heavy velvet curtains drawn across. A small orchestra played in the corner as those assembled moved in a clockwise direction. The slow, stately pace halted in confusion as Augusta and Tom forced their way, pushing past officers in blue and scarlet uniform, and gentlemen in wigs, curled and powdered, and court dress of velvet and brocade. The ladies on their arms gasped at this sudden and violent intrusion, stepping back in a rustle of silk and satin, fans beating with alarm.

Augusta skidded to a halt in front of the Duke. She even curtsied. *When in Rome…*

Tom stood next to her, arms folded. He wouldn't bow.

"Your grace," she started. "Your grace, I…"

The Duke raised an arm that had been resting on a winged chimera. His hand commanded silence.

The fans stopped. The chamber music ended with a screech and a squeak. Every eye turned to the Duke on his gilt and oversized throne. He squinted down, his head tilted back on to the ducal coronet behind him, resting on the letter "A" with its framing of laurel and the motto *Virtutis fortuna comes—Fortune is the companion of virtue.*

"What is the meaning of this interruption?" he roared, his other hand curled into a fist, pounding on the golden lion's head.

Tom met his gaze. Like the statue outside, the bust in the hallway, the throne was there to add power and authority but the Duke himself lacked a little in the imperial dignity department. His clothes were splendid enough, his uniform badged with the stars, crusted and braided with gold brocade, but it looked several sizes too small. His head resembled a pineapple: wider at the neck than the crown and topped with a crest of suspiciously jet-black curls. More curls were teased down, artfully arranged across his noble brow to disguise his receding hairline. A high collar and carefully wound neckcloth failed to hide his double chins. His long nose was pointed and slightly tilted; the mouth beneath it twisted like a holly leaf. Rather than commanding and lordly, he appeared to be weak, vain and cruel.

The Duke looked to his son, the Marquis of Douro, who stood at his side. Douro was youthful-looking, with a mass of curling auburn hair and fine, almost feminine features. He might have looked young, but he had the same twisted mouth as his father and a hardness about the eyes. The same vanity, too, and sense of his own importance. His uniform was tailored to flatter his youthful figure, the short red jacket to show off his slender waist and narrow hips, the high standing collar to emphasize the supercilious tilt of his head. Gold tassels at each shoulder, braids draped across facings studded with medals and badges to demonstrate his rank and distinction. His ready colour was heightened with indignation; his near-violet eyes darkening to purple.

Tom tensed as Douro moved towards Augusta, his hand on the sabre that dangled from the wide sash he wore.

"That will do." The Duke waved him away. He looked down at Augusta, his prominent eyes bulging with petulant anger that could easily tip into rage. "What *is* the meaning of this? Bursting in here, causing a to-do? Dressed in *riding* habit. Where is your court dress? Go and change immediately!"

"Your grace," Augusta started again, "you must hear me! You must stop this! Your soldiers are turning their guns on your people. Do you not hear their cries and distress?"

From outside, the sound of shouting and screaming came thinned and muffled but still audible and unmistakable. Distant small-arms fire was reduced to popgun percussion, but there was no denying the boom of artillery.

"You cannot allow this… this slaughter to go on, my lord. In your name! In *your* name!"

The Duke turned to his son, who whispered in his ear.

"A little local difficulty, I'm assured. Hotheads and ne'er-do-wells. We can't let the mob take over." He looked around the room, garnering nods of approval. "A firm hand is needed or we'll end up like the French."

He said this to enthusiastic nods and even a scattering of applause and one or two "Bravos".

"They are not a mob of hotheads and ne'er-do-wells," Augusta insisted. "They are ordinary men and women. Your loyal subjects. They're coming to present a petition at the Tower of All Nations. All they want is for their grievances to be heard."

"That is not what I am being told. Troublemakers to a man and woman."

"There are troublemakers out there—troublemakers aplenty. Supplied by the man standing at your left shoulder, sir."

"Your grace." Rogue strode out, splendid in a uniform of black and gold. "I really must protest this… this calumny. My men are trying to bring *order*."

"Is that what you call it?" Augusta spat the words out.

"Enough! Enough!" The Duke held up his hand. "All this… disruption… is most tiresome. My guests can't get into the city. The Grand Ball will have to be postponed because of it. And you, madam…" his eyes turned to Augusta, "take yourself in hand. Better than that—let someone do it for you, since you seem incapable of proper behaviour. I'm sure Lady Zenobia will oblige." He nodded and a tall, dark-haired woman stepped from the crowd with a smile and curtsied low. "I cannot have you running around like this when you are to be married to my son!"

A collective gasp swept the room. Lady Zenobia stayed frozen in her low curtsey. Douro stepped forward, his small mouth opening to protest. Rogue appeared unmoved but his jaw tensed and his hand tightened on his sword.

No one was expecting this. Lord Charles had lost his bet.

"I was going to announce the engagement at the ball," the Duke went on, seemingly oblivious to the spreading consternation. "But since that is postponed, now is as good a time as ever. I have decided. The Lady Augusta will marry my son. It's best for everyone, I'm sure you'll all agree."

It was clear that almost nobody agreed. Lady Zenobia least of all. She kept her head bowed so the Duke would not see her fury.

"The formal announcement will be at the ball tomorrow. Until then, Augusta will be in the care of Lady Zenobia."

"It will be my pleasure, your grace." The lady rose with a slight stagger but her smile was back in place.

"And whoever is this fellow?" The Duke gestured towards Tom with a petulant twitch of his ringed fingers. "Yes, you, sir!"

"He's my equerry." Augusta spoke while Tom was framing an explanation.

"Well, make sure he looks like one the next time I see him. And teach him some manners or I'll clap him in irons. Now, play up, play up!" the Duke shouted to the orchestra. "And dance, damn you! I will have dancing!" The Duke's right hand beat out a staccato rhythm on the lion's head and the crowd broke into couples. "Louder, I say. Louder! And something lively!"

The orchestra dutifully struck up a spirited tune to hide the cries that continued to filter in from outside.

"My congratulations on that performance," Lady Zenobia said as she approached them. "*Spectacular*, even for you. I can't imagine why you even bother to come to court."

Zenobia undulated—that was the only word for it—moving at a stately, measured pace. Overdressed, as usual, in a robe of dark red velvet worn to complement her dark beauty. Augusta sometimes wondered if she had legs under there, or ran on castors. The ostrich plumes on her elaborate headdress nodded and long gold earrings, dropping like chandeliers, swung from her ears. Her heavy garnet necklace had the letter "Z" in bright coral at its centre: theatric jewellery worn to make her seem exotic and to show off her long neck. Her hair cascaded in curls, as glossy as grapes, as black as her eyes and thick arching brows.

"I'm not here by choice," Augusta replied. "Douro is in want of a wife and I am to supply the deficit, it appears."

Zenobia had no ready answer to that. She deployed her fan to hide her lack. She was an artist with the fan, using it as a weapon, a disguise, an instrument of flirtation. At present, she was using it to cool the colour rising in her cheeks.

"I'd have thought that *you* were the obvious candidate. But…" Augusta shrugged, with a show of innocence. "It seems not."

Zenobia's colour heightened further. Her dislike of Augusta almost rivalled her love for the Duke's son. She had been hopelessly in love with him since they were children. She looked down her thin, finely modelled nose, delicate nostrils flaring. Her small mouth pursed. The dimple in chin and cheek did little to detract from her imperious manner and those black eyes could flash fury in an instant. They were flashing now.

"I like it no more than you do," Augusta said. "Let us not quarrel." She paused. "There is a way out of this, though…"

Zenobia shut her fan. "Oh? What is that?"

"You help me escape. From the Duke's Palace. From Glass Town. With me gone, you'll be free to marry Douro."

Zenobia frowned, considering. Augusta watched the changes in her face as she weighed risk against temptation. It would mean going against the Duke's express wish. The Duke's word ruled here and Zenobia never broke the rules. Well, almost never, and that one time Augusta had got the blame.

"Where would you go?" she asked.

"What does it matter?" Augusta quelled her impatience. "A long way from here, I promise. Just say you will!"

"I'll think about it." Zenobia still looked torn and not a little doubtful, but she hadn't rejected the idea out of hand. "I'll send my ladies to attend to you—I don't suppose you've brought anyone *suitable* with you. As for this fellow…" She eyed Tom with distaste and disapproval. "I'm sure your *betrothed* can spare a gentleman to attend to him."

"There's no need—I have Annie, and Isaac can attend to Tom."

Zenobia gave a sarcastic laugh, equilibrium restored. "Someone *suitable*, I said. Go to your rooms. Two of my ladies will be with you directly." She nodded to the attendant footmen. "Look after this *gentleman*, would you? Find him quarters and stay with him until the Marquis's man arrives."

"Of course, my lady."

The footmen took Tom's arm none too gently.

"No need." Lord Charles Wellesley pushed himself off the wall, where he had been closely following the whole encounter. "I'll look after this young chap." He laughed as he steered Tom by the elbow. "Lost my bet, it seems. Come to my rooms. You'll be comfortable there. My man, Henry, will look after you. Find you some clothes to wear."

Augusta had no intention of going to her rooms—not yet, anyway. Zenobia's "ladies" would be no better than prison warders. They'd have to find her first. The Duke might have closed his ears as tightly as the palace shutters but she had to know what was happening outside the charmed world of the court.

She went up to the loggia. A hot wind, blowing from the east, was dropping a fine, red desert dust on the city, like powdered blood. Far below, she could see that the march had reached the Great Piazza. A crowd was there, dense at the centre, scattered towards the edges. Troops blocked the exits to the piazza. Soldiers were lined up in front of the Tower of All Nations, guns trained on the crowd. They looked like models from this distance, the officer's raised sabre like a silver toothpick. People were running, some falling, but they looked no more real than pieces on a chessboard, their cries like bird calls, the gunshots a sudden, percussive *rat-a-tat-tat* on a drum.

Again it happened, and again. Augusta looked away.

When she finally looked back, the square had emptied, except for the soldiers and the dead.

CHAPTER NINETEEN

GLASS TOWN INTRIGUES

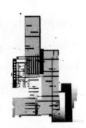

THE NEXT DAY, all that was left to show was a faint staining on the marble of the piazza, pink on grey. Soldiers had been out there all night, according to Annie, scrubbing away the bloodstains, putting all to rights. The city was quiet, under strict curfew. Anyone venturing out was subject to instant arrest. Meanwhile, the whole garrison was sanding the streets, putting down sawdust to soak up the blood.

"They're even putting out flowers, potted trees and that, to make it all look pretty," Annie went on. "Pretending nowt happened. But it did. Untold dead. God knows how many injured, jails full to bursting. It were worse in the Lower Town. Used cannon down there, they did. Not up here. Might damage the buildings. Buildings matter more than people. They was marching for justice and all they got was grapeshot. Duke's declared a Fiesta, is what I'm hearing. Fountains to run with wine. There's going to be tables set out all over the city, food from the Duke's own kitchens. A reward for his loyal citizens, he's calling it. I got another name for it. Bribery, pure and simple."

Riots one night, Fiesta the next. How very Glass Town.

"Now, come on," Annie chivvied. "Frame yourself before them snooty cows get 'ere. Put yer mitts in this."

"What is it?"

"Lemon juice. I got more for yer face. It's sovereign for skin lightening."

A pale complexion was prized at court. The ladies all shaded their faces with hats or parasols and wore long white gloves.

"My skin is fine as it is."

"Not according to Lady Zenobia. She's sent salts for yer bath, an' all. Special ingredients from the desert brought in by Arab traders. I've been instructed to give you a good scrubbing. I've drawn yer bath. You can soak yer fingers while you're in it."

The bathroom was marble floored. The bathtub was fed with hot and cold water running from a great brass tap. Augusta stepped into the tub and wondered if this was one of Zenobia's jokes. Her "special ingredients" stung the skin, smelt repulsive and turned the water black. Annie emptied that and ran more water, adding lemon and bags of lavender. Augusta settled down to a good soak while Annie busied herself with lotions, also sent by Zenobia. More special ingredients with whitening properties, also from the desert, but these were soothing on the skin and didn't smell so bad. A bath meant a door locked against Zenobia's ladies.

She and Zenobia should have been friends, but they were not. Too alike, in some ways; in others, polar opposites. They were never destined to be close. They had always been wary of each other, even at school.

Zenobia was no silly miss like the other girls who had spent their time in ladylike pursuits, such as drawing and embroidery and perfecting their French, when they weren't perfecting the arts of flirtation: smiling at the young lords, simpering at the masters, giggling in corners about one beau or another. Zenobia was clever and she took her studies seriously. Augusta had found the classroom restricting, airless and stuffy; she had longed to be out of doors and had wanted to learn what the boys were learning: the art of war, tactics and weaponry, how to be a ruler one day. She'd begged and pleaded to be allowed to join them on the firing range and the fencing floor. She was an excellent shot and fencing was not so very different from dancing. She was tall for her age, with a long reach, slight, lithe and quick on her feet. Of course, such masculine pursuits were forbidden to her.

Whenever she could, she would slip away to watch the boys at their practice. Fencing fascinated her and she was determined to learn. Rogue offered to give her lessons. Not to please her but because it amused him. He would do anything to challenge the rules and he had an excuse to beat her—and beat her he did. They practised with wooden sticks at first, and he hit her black and blue. They advanced to rebated swords, the kind the boys used in practice. Then one day, they did not. She still had the scar. So had he.

Not long after that, she was sent away from Scholars' Island for good, although the reason was nothing to do with Rogue.

Zenobia was most often to be found in the Masters' Library, translating works from Greek or Latin. Augusta had no interest in dead languages and thought her reading dry. She preferred stories, histories, books about the world and the birds and animals to be found in the different regions of the earth. She liked to study the maps of the explorers, to turn the great globe that stood in its frame of shining brass and polished mahogany, tracing the black broken lines that spread like a spider's web over the oceans to show the voyages of the Founding Twelve. She would dream of her own voyages, standing on tiptoe, following the sea road to the Northern oceans, the whale road that led through the fields of ice where the Esquimaux lived and great white bears roamed, where seals and walrus floated on ice islands and whales, as big as ships, blew rainbow plumes into the frozen air from holes on top of their great bowed heads…

One day, she made the mistake of telling Zenobia what she dreamt about. Zenobia had come over in apparent innocence and asked her what she was doing, what was she thinking as she turned the globe. So Augusta told her about the journey she meant to take to see the great white bears on their ice floes, the Esquimaux in their skin canoes.

"How do you know about all this?" Zenobia asked.

"Ross and Parry. They've been there."

"Oh, have they? And I suppose they are going to take you with them?"

"One day." Augusta's fingers spanned the Arctic seas. "One day they will." They would go in the ships, *Hecla* and *Griper*. Ships with thick oaken hulls, re-enforcing cross-beams and iron-plated bows to withstand the ice's crushing embrace. They would find the secret passage that would take them through the ice-bound seas and out into the ocean beyond. She'd been about to tell Zenobia of the wonders they would see on their journey: whales with a single horn, like the fabled unicorn; great leviathans rising up from the deep, all glistening black and walking on their tails.

"Isn't it time you said farewell to such ridiculous ideas?" Zenobia had set the globe spinning away from her. "You will *never* get away from here. Isn't it time you grew up?"

When they grew older, things got worse, not better. Zenobia had always been in love with Douro but he took no notice of her. When Douro started noticing Augusta, that was when the trouble really started. The Masters' Library was a well-known place for trysts and Zenobia had found them there, on the upper gallery, looking at a book of birds together. Perfectly innocent, Augusta had thought, except it wasn't—on his side anyway. His interest in the birds was feigned and he was standing a little too close, leaning over her shoulder to turn the big heavy pages, their fingers touching; she could feel his breath on her cheek, smell his cologne, the pomade in his hair. Zenobia flew at her. Knocking the book out of her hands, pinning her against the shelves, pulling at her hair, scratching at her face. Augusta fought back but Zenobia was bigger than her and much stronger. Douro disappeared. It was Rogue who pulled them apart, laughing. He'd seen the whole thing.

Augusta had been expelled, blamed for everything. Zenobia stayed, still hankering after Douro. She'd been hankering ever since. He was her only weakness. Douro had always rejected her, preferring his adoring mistresses, like poor, unfortunate Sofala or long-suffering Mina Laury, too low-born to be taken as wives, or the hopelessly besotted Rosamund Wellesley. *What do women see in him?* He treated them all appallingly. Zenobia was intelligent enough to know better…

Augusta's reverie was interrupted by a violent banging on the door.

Annie looked up in alarm.

Not Zenobia's ladies, surely?

A rough male voice said, "Open this door, or we'll break it down!"

"Just a minute!" Augusta stood up quickly, stepping into the towel Annie was holding for her. "What is the meaning of this—this intrusion?" she shouted through the door.

"We've got orders to keep you under close guard."

There was the rap of rifle butts on the floor.

Augusta pulled the towel round her. Zenobia's ladies were one thing, armed guards quite another. Zenobia must have betrayed her at the first chance. Gone straight to the Duke, in the forlorn hope that he would change his mind and favour *her*, no doubt. *Why does she not see?* The Duke would never allow the marriage. The Duke and his son were in need of money. The building of Great Glass Town had proved expensive—ruinously so, some said. Coffers needed replenishing. For all her blue blood and breeding, Zenobia was lacking in fortune and land, while Augusta's fortune was great and her estates went back to the Founding Twelve. Once they had their hands on her wealth, they would squander it all and bleed her lands and her people dry…

The banging started again.

"Right!" Annie headed for the door. "They're getting a piece of my mind!"

The soldiers retreated under Annie's blistering tongue, but only as far as the outer chamber.

"They're still there, milady, and now Lady Zenobia's ladies have arrived."

Annie looked flustered and thoroughly out of temper.

"Well, we must make them welcome, Annie. Tell them I'm dressing."

Augusta sat on her bed in her shift and tried to compose herself. It was important to appear cool, not to show the least agitation, even though it was already hot, her rooms were stifling, and she was now doubly a prisoner. Something close to panic was rising, frothing up like yeast inside her. *What am I to do?*

CHAPTER TWENTY

EACH STITCH
A THOUGHT

ALL THESE GLASS TOWN INTRIGUES. No matter how long you'd been absent, how far you'd travelled, once you were back, it was as though you had never been away...

It might have been hot in Glass Town but here it was raining; a heavy, penetrating rain. Not that a bit of weather would keep Emily inside, but there was a mountain of work to do. Keeper was stretched out in front of the fire, his paws twitching as if he, too, dreamt of running free across the moors. There was a good blaze in the grate; they might have lacked for funds but they seldom lacked for peat. She was supposed to be sewing a shirt, the seams long, the stitches small and all of a size. She turned one selvedged seam and started up the other way. She didn't mind sewing so much, although she was often scolded for slapdash work and carelessness. She could think while she sewed—think and reflect. Thought runs faster than quicksilver, so she pinned, tacked, stitched it down as she worked.

She began on the other sleeve, brooding about Glass Town. *They* had buried their differences, which were trivial anyway, and had joined forces. They were playing with her, trapping her between them like the cats, Tiger and little black Tom, might play with a mouse. They had evoked the Jinn, the Genii, the terrifying physical manifestation of powers created in childhood, used now to herd and harry, to force her back to Glass Town where they were all powerful, where they dictated everything. Glass Town was *their* world. Going back was a trap, she could see now. They *allowed* her to escape, of course they did. They were there waiting for her. Rogue and Lord Charles Wellesley. A deadly combination. Rogue's brute force and Wellesley's subtlety. Separately, she could take them; outwit one, overpower the other. But together? She could feel cold doubt seeping into her, behind it the icy swell of fear. The Jinn were not just columns of fire and smoke; they could take other forms, manifesting in the mind…

A miss stitch drew blood. She watched it beading then sucked her thumb. She mustn't think like that.

What did she have in answer? She matched the sleeve to the cuff. The boy, Tom. Brave, strong—and different. Neither theirs, nor hers. The unknown piece on the board. Like the Fool, Matto, in the Tarocchini, a card with no value, no number, but which could beat any other. He could make a difference but how? She didn't know yet.

Meanwhile, she must do the unexpected. Yes. That was the key to this.

She worked on, quickly, methodically: each stitch a thought, each thought a stitch. When she finished one seam, she started on the next. At length, she ended with a double stitch and a French knot, biting off the cotton; someone had taken the scissors from her workbox. She put the needle safe in her needle booklet, her silver thimble into its holder. Then she shook out the shirt, examining her work for that day. A tiny spot of blood, already darkening to rust, on the inside of the sleeve, where no one would notice, but she knew it was there. She knew every inch. She smiled to herself, imagining him wearing it, her words running up and over, round and about him, encasing him like an invisible spell.

She put the work aside for the day and removed the tray from her workbox, moving the silks and swatches, ribbons and snippets, and took out a small sheaf of paper. She went to the parlour. It was colder in here, but she was in need of pen and ink. She intended to write.

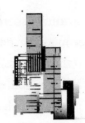

CHAPTER TWENTY-ONE
THE
UNEXPECTED

AUGUSTA WAS STILL in her petticoats, still debating what to do. The clock was chiming the hour. The soldiers might have been banished to the corridor but Zenobia's ladies were still there, her secondary jailers. She'd tried to persuade them to leave her, that their own mistress would be needing them and she had Annie, but they had no intention of going anywhere. She could hear them chattering through the door, ordering Annie to bring them this and that. They'd even banished Keeper. He made them nervous, so he'd been removed to the servants' hall.

"He'll be all right down there—the kitchen boys are making a fuss of him," Annie had told her. "Giving him bones. He's quite happy."

How simple life was for dogs.

"I haven't had a minute," Annie said as she came in, carrying the dress that had been delivered for Augusta.

She laid it on the bed, smoothing out the pale lilac organza. The high bodice was sewn with seed pearls, the hem embellished with roses. Lilac didn't suit her, draining the colour from her face. Besides, it was a colour she loathed. Zenobia would have chosen it especially. It was perfectly hideous. Not something she'd wear at all. A stand on the dressing table held the diamond tiara, too like a crown, the necklace of sickly yellow topaz that clashed with the dress and earrings of the kind Zenobia favoured, long and dangling.

Augusta frowned and bit her lip. She couldn't see herself in any of this. A petty war within the greater. *Who knows what is happening outside?* Confined within these walls, she'd had no news.

"That shade won't do owt for you." Annie looked down critically. "Tack every bit o' colour."

"Where's Tom?" Augusta asked quietly. Zenobia's ladies' hearing was acute.

"Don't know, milady," Annie whispered back. "Ent seen 'em."

"Go and find out, would you?"

"What about this?" Annie picked up the dress. "And yer hair, and that? Do you want Lady Zenobia's ladies to do it?"

"God forbid! It's not as if I've never dressed myself, is it?" Augusta despised the helplessness of court ladies, their dependence on others to do every little thing for them. "You can do my hair when you get back."

Annie returned, breathless. "Tom went off wi' Lord Charles. That was this morning. No one's seen him since."

That was worrying news. Augusta didn't trust Lord Charles Wellesley. He might have had more wit than Douro and more charm than Rogue but he was just as dangerous. Even more so. He was subtle and clever and had doubtless set himself the task of finding out as much as he possibly could about this new player. Augusta had deflected his curiosity at Bravey's Inn, but without her presence, he would be free to question, cozen and wheedle. Cozening and wheedling were his specialities. And if those didn't work? There were other methods. What Rogue's rare lads lacked in subtlety they made up for in violence and brutality. Augusta felt a prickle of fear. She could feel a trap closing. What if they were working together and it wasn't *she* who was the focus of their attention but Tom?

"Send Isaac and Amos," she said to Annie. "Tell them to comb the city. Tom must be found. I can do the rest of this myself."

Augusta finished her toilette and examined herself in the mirror. It wasn't only the lilac bleaching her of colour.

CHAPTER TWENTY-TWO

AT THE SIGN OF THE CROSSED HANDS

"How are you, young fellow? Rooms to your liking? Henry looking after you? Sleep all right?" Lord Charles came in without knocking and paced about Tom's room. "Good, good. Sorry I had to leave you last night. Had to write up yesterday's events and get the paper out. Breakfasted? Excellent." He smiled. "What have you been doing with yourself?"

"I've been reading this." Tom held up a book that he'd found on the shelf next to his bed.

THE HISTORY OF THE YOUNG MEN

From Their First Settlement to the Present Time

by JOHN BUD, ESQ.

He'd started reading, hoping to find out more about this place and how it had come about, but he'd just become more and more confused.

"What do you make of it?" Lord Charles asked.

"Not a lot, to be honest." Tom frowned.

"That's because Bud wrote it. Can't write for toffee. My own volume will be *far* better—when it's finished, that is." Lord Charles sat down. "What do you want to know? The Founding Story changes depending on who is doing the telling," he went on before Tom could answer. "But all agree that Glass Town was founded by the Twelve, a group of bold military men who sailed from England to establish a new land. After many adventures, they ended up here. Conquered the natives hereabouts and established the Glass Town Federation. They divided the territory between them into different kingdoms: the Duke, of course, in Wellingtonsland; Sneachie in Sneachiesland; Ross and Parry in Rossland and Parrysland. Together, they built the Great Glass Town where we are now."

"And where exactly is that?" Tom asked.

"Why, Africa!" Lord Charles exclaimed, as though that was obvious. "We are at the mouth of the Niger River."

That explained the heat and humidity, the tropical plants and trees. It did not explain why not more than two days' ride from here you could be in Yorkshire.

"What about Parrysland? That's nothing like Africa."

"Ah, no. That's true. The different lands take after their Founders and that's what Parry prefers. I spent a week there once. Cold and damp. Utterly dreary." Lord Charles shuddered. "Never again. Sneachiesland is even worse. Something of the Highlands about it. All mountains and moors."

None of it made any sense. Even the bit that was supposed to be like Africa wasn't *really* like Africa; it was like someone's *idea* of Africa. As for the rest—that must be someone else's idea…

"Don't worry." Lord Charles smiled. "All fearfully complicated. Our history is always changing. Facts and dates, people and places have ways of mutating so even I find it hard to understand. You know…" He leant forward, his blue eyes clouded with sudden doubt. His customary poise gone. "I sometimes think that none of it is, well, *real*. Glass Town and all of its people, myself included—we're mere ideas in someone else's brain. Part of some other creature's game…" He looked up with a sheepish smile. "I dare say you think that nonsense."

"No. Not at all." Tom wouldn't say that. He understood exactly. That was how he felt himself.

"Enough wool-gathering." Lord Charles stood up, suddenly anxious to get going, confidence returning. "Time I was on my rounds. Come on, young fellow. I'll show you something of the town."

"I was planning to go and see Augusta," Tom said. He might get more sense out of her.

"I wouldn't do that." Lord Charles shook his head. "Augusta is in purdah. Armed guards outside her door."

They left the palace and crossed the wide piazza. The tall buildings, blinding white in the morning sunlight, the colonnaded walkways, doors and windows in sharp shadow.

"How did they build all this?" Tom asked.

"With the help of the Genii," Lord Charles said, as if that actually explained anything. "The Jinn. They can be forces for good as well as bad. Build as well as destroy."

"What about the other people—the ordinary people? Where did they come from?"

"Some came with the Twelve," Lord Charles said vaguely. "Others came later, as colonists and settlers. The Duke brought thirty thousand veterans with him after he defeated Napoleon."

"Right." Tom nodded. "I see."

Thirty thousand seemed an awful lot, and defeating Napoleon—did the Duke sail back to do that? But there was no point in questioning. This was a fantasy and Tom was in it. He had no choice but to accept it, to play his role.

He looked around for something else to talk about. They were walking through one of the lesser squares. Men in livery were setting out tables, stringing flags and bunting. There appeared to be no trace of the recent disturbances. Everything was swept clean.

When he remarked upon it, Lord Charles shrugged.

"This is Glass Town. The Duke likes to look out at an Ideal City. Now it's Fiesta. He wants the people to join him in celebrating the coming betrothal of his firstborn to the lovely Lady Augusta. To share in his joy—as I'm sure we all do." The look he gave Tom was sharp and amused. "I see you don't approve. She must marry. It's been her destiny since childhood." He clapped Tom on the shoulder. "This is Glass Town—it's how things are done."

Tom shook his head. It might have been how things were done here, like in the old days with arranged marriages, but it still seemed wrong to him. She should have been free to choose.

"Who she marries should be her decision," he said. "If she marries anyone."

"I dare say that's so where *you* come from." Lord Charles's look became sharper. "Where *do* you come from? I am a man of great curiosity—you may well have noticed. Us newspapermen have to be. So I am bound to wonder where you were and what you were before you came to our dear Augusta. Are you her creature? You certainly are not one of ours. Did she conjure you, I wonder? And, if so, how did she do it? Where *did* you spring from?"

Tom didn't answer, just smiled.

"America, we were thinking," Lord Charles probed further. "By your way of speaking. Or perhaps the Colonies?"

Tom kept his smile non-committal. That would do. "We?" he questioned.

"Johnny Lockhart and I. We are journalists. Inquisitiveness runs in our blood, along with printers' ink. He's waiting for us at Bravey's."

They were approaching the inn now.

"Bud, Tree," Lord Charles greeted two acquaintances as they entered. "Author and publisher of that history you were reading, and rivals to me," he whispered to Tom. "Best to keep a wide berth. Ah, the good doctor. Mind if we join you?"

Dr Bady grunted without looking up from his copy of the *Young Men's Magazine*.

"Busy night?" Lord Charles enquired.

The doctor grunted again. "Morgue's full to bursting. Sit down, if you're going to. Brandy." He nodded to his empty glass.

"A large brandy for the doctor," Lord Charles said to the girl who came to serve them. "A jug of punch for me and my young friend here."

He sat down and took out his notebook. "These unfortunates in the mortuary. Of what kind? What ilk?"

"Working men. Women, too." The doctor showed no hint of sentiment. "Won't be needing the resurrectionists for a good long while." He went back to his paper as the drinks arrived.

"Rum punch!" Lord Charles poured two glasses. "Just the thing to set you up in the morning. Drink up, young fellow. Drink up!" He drained his glass and poured them both another. "Now, young sir, you were just about to tell me all about yourself."

"That punch is strong." Tom looked up to see Johnny Lockhart. He put a hand over Tom's glass. "Designed to loosen tongues."

"Johnny!" Lord Charles did his best not to seem put out. "Didn't see you come in."

Lockhart sat down. "I was at the bar."

"Ah, I was just making some enquiries of this young man: his origins, his country, the nature of his involvement with the lovely Augusta—"

"I dare say you were." He turned to Tom. "Be careful what you say to Lord Charles. Even he doesn't know what side he's on."

The words were light but Johnny Lockhart wasn't smiling. He was delivering a warning.

Tom passed on the punch.

"I say, Johnny! That's unfair! Who's talking of sides here? What's this I'm hearing?" he added, quick to change to subject. "Carnage on the streets of Glass Town?"

"I've just finished my piece for the *Intelligencer.* I dropped in to see who might be about."

Lord Charles looked around, reading the room. "Or not?"

"My thinking exactly." Johnny Lockhart nodded to an empty corner. "No Young Soult and his cronies." He glanced towards the bar, where Bravey was polishing glasses. "None of Rogue's rare lads."

"Probably plotting elsewhere," Lord Charles supplied.

"My very thought." He got up and turned for the door.

"Come, young fellow." Lord Charles drained his glass and they followed him out.

Johnny sniffed the air. "I can smell it. The tension." His fine nostrils flared. "Hot and dry. Like the air when the wind comes from the desert."

Lord Charles nodded his vigorous agreement. "The place is asmoulder. The fire still there but under the surface." He spoke with excitement and anticipation, making a running motion with his fingers. "Stamp it out in one place and it'll break out somewhere else in even greater conflagration."

Johnny Lockhart looked at him quizzically. "You sound as if you almost *want* it to happen." He laughed. "As long as you can watch from the sidelines making notes, eh, Charles?"

"Of course not." Lord Charles looked affronted. "Where are we going, by the way?"

They were heading down, away from the Duke's Ideal City to a different part of town altogether. Away from the main thoroughfare, into crooked alleys hung across with washing, with pavings broken, cobbles uneven, the central gutters clogged and littered with rubbish. There were more people here: poor people who walked warily, heads bent, as though afraid to look at those passing. Beggars stood on street corners or sat, slumped in doorways; among them were soldiers in dirty uniforms, some on crutches, or sporting filthy bandages.

They came to a crossroads and Lord Charles peered about warily as noise and shouting gusted from a nearby tavern.

"This is Rogue territory."

"Indeed it is." Johnny Lockhart didn't seem the least bit apprehensive. "Rogue's men, his 'rare lads', have clubs here, places of assembly," he said to Tom. "That inn, the Crossed Hands, is one of their places." He pointed to a crude sign: two hands making one fist. "The Duke has banned them, ordered their premises closed, but to little effect."

"What are we doing here?" Lord Charles asked.

"I have something in mind. A plan," Johnny answered. "We're known but Tom is not. He can find out what's going on."

A group of men came past, bottles swinging, and armed to the teeth. They looked like Scotsmen in belted plaids, dirks in their hose, long knives and basket-hilted swords swinging from their belts.

"Sneachieslanders!" Lord Charles said, aghast. "What are they doing here?"

"Arrived with their lairds to celebrate the coming nuptials," Johnny answered. "There's a whole swarm of them camped outside the northern gate."

Lord Charles shrank back as more of them reeled past. He took out his pocket watch. "Good Heavens, is that the time? I really must be off. Articles to write. A newspaper to get out." He caught hold of Tom's sleeve. "Think twice before you consent to one of Johnny's madcap schemes."

With that, he was gone.

"Madcap schemes?"

Johnny laughed. "Oh. I'm famous for them." He looked after Lord Charles hurrying away. "He ever was a coward—he rarely ventures down to the Lower Town. It's good he's gone. He likes to be on the winning side. The difficulty is: which side will that be? The city is on a knife's edge. You are a soldier, I understand. A military man?"

Tom nodded.

"Good, then you will be perfect."

"For your madcap scheme?"

"Oh, it's worse than that." Johnny laughed again. "What I'm about to propose is foolhardy, dangerous and possibly suicidal." He fixed Tom with his ice-blue eyes. "Augusta thinks you brave and trustworthy. That's what she said to me. 'I'd trust him with my life, Johnny. My life.'" His eyes grew darker, drained of their usual bright humour. "And it may come to that." He frowned. "Indeed, it might. And not just *her* life. Many others, besides. There's a deadly game being played here and I fear Augusta is the prize."

Put like that, how could Tom refuse? Besides, the faith she'd put in him made him stand taller. He would live up to that, whatever was asked of him.

"What do you want me to do?"

"Good man." Johnny clapped him on the shoulder. "See him?" He pointed to a man in a stained uniform, leaning on makeshift crutches, dirty hand cupped to catch the begging money. "There are many of his kind down here. You've seen them. Turned off from the Duke's army. Surplus to requirements now the war is over. Forced to beg. But a soldier is still a soldier—all the more dangerous if he's not being paid. Here." He dug in his pocket. "Give him five guineas and swap your coat with him."

The old soldier was already struggling out of his red jacket. He grabbed Tom's coat and the money then dropped his crutch and ran before they changed their minds.

"Put it on," Johnny Lockhart instructed.

It was none too clean; stained and tattered, the armpits bleached pink and stiff with sweat. Nevertheless, Tom did as he was told.

"I can't go much further." Johnny drew him into a doorway. "But you can go freely, just another soldier. Follow the Sneachieslanders into the Crossed Hands. Find out what they are about. Find out what you can. You better have some money." Lockhart took out more coins. "And this." He handed Tom his pistol. "Double-barrelled Blissett. The very latest model. Primed and ready. Do your best. Anything you find out will help Augusta. I'll see you back at Bravey's."

"How do I find my way back?" Tom asked. Glass Town was like a maze.

"Keep going up and you won't go far wrong. Good luck."

Tom stuck the pistol into the waistband of his trousers, at the small of his back under his jacket. He was being used as a spy, a clean skin, but he was OK with that. It was good to be doing something. Foolhardy, dangerous and possibly suicidal? Bring it on.

The Sneachieslanders had turned in at the Crossed Hands. Tom followed, head down, heart beating faster.

The inn was crowded, noisy and smelt of spilt beer, sweat and tobacco smoke. The Sneachieslanders were at the bar being welcomed like old friends. Tom elbowed his way closer. The chief among them, a big man with shaggy red hair, finished his pint in one gulp and whipped his hand across his bushy beard.

"Call that pish ale? Gis another."

"You with us?" The man next to him signalled for the barman to fill his tankard.

"That we are and there's more tae come. Our laird may be up with the Duke in his palace but he's pledged his allegiance." He raised his filled tankard. "Tae Rogue and revolution!"

"To Rogue and revolution!" All around him men raised tankard and glass and roared out the toast.

Tom had seen enough. He began to shoulder his way to the door.

"Where are you going?" A burly man grabbed him by the arm. "Don't look like any Sneachieslander. Soldier, are you?"

"Aye." Tom nodded. "With the Duke's army until I got a ball in the shoulder. Then he had no use for me." He spat to show his contempt.

The man's broad face creased with sympathy. "You ain't the only one. Many a good lad turned off wi' nowt. Crying shame the way you was turned off. Come wi' me. We're offering free drink and regular pay to any who join the Revolutionary Guard."

Tom followed him along a narrow passage pungent with urine and out into a large yard full of men lining up, ready to sign their name or make their mark. Once signed, they were marshalled into rough lines. Boxes of guns and ammunition and crates of cutlasses stood stacked next to the barrels along the wall.

Tom signed with an "X", like most of the rest. He collected his shilling and stood with the others at a rough approximation of attention, eyes front.

The monstrous bulk of Pigtail stepped out to address them. "Whatever ye was before…" he looked them up and down, "ye're now members of the Revolutionary Guard!"

A ragged cheer went up, led by the Sneachieslanders.

Pigtail raised his lead-weighted blackjack. "That's enough." He began to walk up and down the lines, beating the blackjack into his palm. "We'll have discipline here. We'll be moving shortly to a place of assembly. Ye'll stay there until the order comes through. That won't be 'til tonight. Once in place, there'll be no more drinking!"

A groan went up, spreading through the ranks.

"We were promised drink aplenty," one of the Sneachieslanders shouted, to a disgruntled mutter of agreement.

"After, milads. Afterwards. You'll be drinking the Duke's best claret and fine brandy in his very own palace."

A cheer went up.

"And think of all them pretty ladies!" Pigtail grinned, revealing a mouth full of blackened stumps and empty spaces. "It'll be worth the wait!" As he spoke, he paced the lines. One of his men walked behind him handing out blue jackets and tricolor cockades.

Tom kept his eyes averted, hoping the big man would not stop at him—that he wouldn't recognize him from yesterday. He was just thinking that maybe he'd got away with it, when Pigtail turned.

"Don't I know you?" he said. "Ain't I seen you before?"

"Who, me?" The man next to Tom looked up, terrified. Tom could feel him shaking.

"Not you." Pigtail brought the blackjack up under Tom's chin. "You."

"Not me, Cap'n," Tom said. "Only just got 'ere."

"That so? I could've sworn I seen you, keeping fancy company, and you weren't in no poor soldier's rig." He turned to the assembly at large. "We got a spy, boys! Impersonating one of yer own! What shall I do wi' him?"

"Shoot him!" Shouts rang out all round. "String 'im up!"

"There. The citizen comrades have spoken. Either one more 'n you deserve. I got something special in mind for you." Pigtail jabbed the blackjack up harder. "But that will have to wait 'til later. Now we got other business. Scroven, Laury, take 'im to the vaults."

Tom was hauled out of the line by two of Pigtail's cronies.

"Have fun," Pigtail called after them. "But not too much. I want 'im living and breathing come tonight."

Tom felt the point of a cutlass dig into his side.

"Hands behind!"

He was roughly tied and pulled into the back alley that ran behind the inn, then marched along by the two men, one in front and one behind.

"Make way!"

The main body of the Revolutionary Guard was wheeling right out of the yard. The way was narrow. Tom and his captors had to flatten themselves against the wall as line after line of men filed past.

"Where are they all going?"

"Cox's Yard," the smaller of the two men told him.

"Don't tell 'im!" the other snarled. "'E's a spy! Didn't you hear 'tail say?" He shook his head. "You got cloth ears and nowt between 'em."

"Who are you calling cloth ears?" the little one objected.

"What's the difference? He ain't going to be telling anybody, is he? Like as not he'll have no tongue!"

They both laughed.

Still the men were marching past. Tom didn't need to count them. He'd already made a rough estimation. He had his back against the wall, hands hidden. The knot was badly tied; he already had one hand loose. They hadn't bothered to search him. Johnny Lockhart's gun had two barrels, both of them primed.

"C'mon."

Once the last of the marchers had passed, the taller man prodded him on.

"Wait a minute." Tom's head fell forward. "I don't feel so well."

"We ain't got time for the vapours." He pushed Tom harder.

Tom lurched, retching, as if he was about to spew.

Both men instinctively took a step back. By then, the pistol was in Tom's hand.

The two men looked at each other, as if sizing up whether to rush him.

"I wouldn't advise it. Two barrels, see?" Tom pulled back the hammers. "One each. Walk in front of me."

There was an outhouse across the way. Tom directed them towards it. "Open the door."

The small shed smelt like it had once housed a pig.

"Inside, both of you."

Tom dropped the outside bar on them and ran.

"*Keep going up and you won't go far wrong.*" Johnny Lockhart's words rang in Tom's head as he took worn and narrow steps two at a time.

Every now and then, he stopped to rest, hands on knees, and to listen, but there was no hue and cry. His captors must still have been in the pigsty. Tom slowed his pace. He was leaving the crowded houses and crooked alleys. A turn to the right took him to a street he recognized. Bravey's Inn was just up ahead.

Johnny Lockhart was sitting by the window, anxiously scanning the street.

"Glad to see you safe." Lockhart put a brotherly arm round his shoulder.

"Indeed!" Lord Charles stood to welcome him. "Bravey! A jug of your very special punch over here."

"We don't serve soldiers."

"Since when?" Johnny Lockhart demanded. "That's Douro's regiment. This man and others like him were wounded in the late wars. Is this any way to treat men who have served loyally?"

"We don't want a row." Lord Charles put a placating hand on Johnny's arm. "Nonsense, Bravey," he called to the landlord. "You've served him before." He turned to Tom. "Perhaps remove the jacket?"

Tom looked down. He'd forgotten he was still wearing it. He felt a surge of sympathy for the man whose coat he wore. He was a soldier, after all. Why should he take it off? He kept it on.

He was glad of the punch, hot and very strong. The fumes were enough to make you light-headed. Tom drank deep.

"Now, tell us all."

Lord Charles and Johnny Lockhart listened carefully to what he had discovered about the recruiting of the Sneachieslanders and others to the Revolutionary Guard.

"They are being mustered at a place called Cox's Yard."

"Cox's Yard?" Johnny Lockhart frowned. "I know it. Down by the docks. A big place. Room for hundreds. What then?"

"They are to wait for a signal. It'll be tonight."

"Well done, my boy." Lord Charles clapped him on the shoulder. "More punch?"

"Not at the moment." Tom looked round in some discomfort. "I need…" He didn't quite know the word for it.

"The jakes." Johnny Lockhart grinned. "Out back."

Tom found the outhouse with some relief.

"Now it's our turn, soldier boy." Strong hands seized Tom by the shoulders. "See how you like this."

Tom felt a sharp blow to the side of his head. He was hauled away, half stunned, legs buckling. Up steps and down steps, passed off as a drunk as he dangled between the two men like a string-cut puppet. They halted at one of the fountains and pushed his head under until he was nearly drowning, before dragging him out and pushing his head under again.

Scroven laughed. "That ought to wake him up a bit."

Tom shook the water from his eyes, his head clearing.

He was marched on across the square and down a side alley. The men stopped in front of a low, iron-studded door. Laury took out a big bunch of keys and unlocked it. Steep stone steps led down into darkness.

Scroven pushed him and Tom fell forward. He was picked up at the bottom and dragged along a stone passageway lit with flickering torches set in sconces, barred cells on either side. Tom caught glimpses of ragged, skeletal bodies chained to walls. The stench had him gagging: clogged drains, rotten rushes, human excrement added to the onion stink of his captors' sweat.

"Gipping like a maid, are we?" Scroven jeered. "You ain't had anything to puke about yet."

An iron door creaked open and Pigtail threw him through it. Tom landed in a heap of filth and looked up at the tall, spare, black-clad figure of S'death.

"Chain 'im up."

Iron manacles snapped round Tom's wrists and ankles and round his neck.

He was in a proper torture chamber; chains hung on the walls and from the ceiling. A brazier glowed in the corner, presided over by a big man, his upper face obscured by a leather flap with two rough eye holes cut into it. He wore a greasy jerkin and a thick apron over his breeches, the various pockets filled with hammers and pliers. Sweat gleamed on his bald head and the thick rolls of fat on his neck as he stirred and adjusted the various irons protruding from the coals.

S'death stepped forward. "Meet my man, Gregory."

The man looked up and grinned, revealing a gaping hole where his teeth should have been.

"He don't talk. Tongue ripped out for a previous transgression but he's learnt the error of his ways. Ent that right, Gregory?"

The big man grunted and nodded his head.

S'death went over to the brazier and selected an iron with his gloved hand. The letter "R" at the tip glowed deep ruby red as he brought it close to Tom, then closer. Tom could feel the heat on his cheek. He flinched away but his head was held fast by the iron clasped round his neck.

"We have other instruments—other irons in the fire, shall we say."

Gregory grinned his black grin and S'death snickered slightly at his own joke.

"Even the humble poker has its uses. Gregory is inventive. Ain't that so, Gregory? And he do love his work."

The big man gave a leering laugh and nodded vigorously.

"You can't imagine what he'd do with it."

S'death smiled as Tom struggled against his fetters—he could imagine it only too well.

Struggling was futile but Tom couldn't help it. It was an automatic response.

"Or maybe you can. Eyes for a start, and other tender parts."

S'death returned the branding iron to the brazier and selected a long, smooth iron instead. Tiny red and gold sparks ran up and down the shaft as he walked round Tom, feinting towards him, like a fencer.

"So, where to begin? Why don't we start by you telling me everything you know. Then maybe we won't need to use any of these things."

Gregory's face fell at the prospect.

"Ne'er mind, Gregory. There'll be others. Dungeons are filling by the minute. We'll soon have more than even you can handle."

S'death waved the iron under Tom's nose, the cherry-pink tip so close he could smell singeing.

"I don't know anything!"

"No! *Don't know* ain't good enough. We know you been spying. And who for. What we don't know is what you been telling 'em. Gregory, gimme the branding iron again. It should be good and hot."

"Enough." Pigtail came into the chamber. "He ain't to be damaged."

"Who says?"

"Orders." Pigtail showed him a paper.

"Whose orders?"

"My orders." Johnny Lockhart stepped into the room, a pair of pistols trained upon them, with more in his belt. "Release him."

Gregory released Tom's manacles, whimpering his reluctance.

"Hurry up, or I'll blow your head off!" Lockhart demanded.

"No hard feelings, young fellow." Pigtail hauled Tom to his feet. "We'll meet again later," he whispered in a gust of foul breath. "We've got something very special in mind for you."

Once Tom was free, Johnny slammed the cell door on them and locked it.

"Very special," Pigtail was shouting. "An honour, you might say!"

The accompanying laughter echoing after them suggested that it would be anything but.

CHAPTER TWENTY-THREE

FIESTA

THERE WAS NO SIGN OF TOM. No word from Isaac and Amos, who'd been sent out to search for him. No sign of *them*, either. Annie was worried but Augusta could delay no longer. Zenobia was outside.

"What are you doing in there?" She rapped on the door. "We will be late."

"Carry on searching," Augusta whispered to Annie. "If there is any news, find a way to let me know."

Augusta took a deep breath as Annie opened the door. Zenobia was waiting, resplendent in a plumed headdress. Her gown of blood-red silk was low-cut across her creamy bosom; she wore rubies of the exact same shade round her neck and dangling from her ears.

"Let me see…" She circled Augusta. "Hmm, not too bad. You'll never have my presence, of course. Oh." She shied away with a mew of disgust. "What's that ugly thing on your wrist? Take it off immediately."

Augusta looked at the silver band with its black stone. She turned it. "I can't—it won't come off."

"We'll be late, my lady," one of her women whispered.

"Leave it, then. It is the Duke's wish that we should enter together."

Zenobia took Augusta's arm. Her women fell in behind them like a guard.

The doors of the ballroom opened before them and the crowd parted as they entered, making a long corridor for them to pass. Zenobia nodded from side to side, flicking her closed fan towards this one or that one as if dispensing blessings. Augusta held her head high as she ran the gauntlet of looks, glances and whispered comments.

The Duke was sitting on his gilt throne, high on his podium. Douro stood on one side of him and Rogue on the other.

Zenobia smiled up at Douro. *Whatever happens this evening*, her look seemed to say, *you will be mine.* She lowered her gaze, veiling the stark challenge in her dark eyes as she bowed to the Duke. The ostrich feathers in her headdress dipped and bobbed as she dropped into a low curtsy, tugging Augusta down with her.

"Tonight we have a double celebration," the Duke announced.

At a clap of his hands, phalanxes of footmen came out from left and right, each bearing trays carrying coupes of champagne. At another signal from the Duke, Douro and Rogue stepped down from their places. Douro splendid in scarlet and swathed with gold braid, spurs clicking on the marble; Rogue all in black. Douro took Augusta's hand in his sweaty, flaccid grip. Rogue moved to Zenobia's side.

Augusta heard the hissed intake of her breath. Whatever she'd been expecting, this wasn't it.

"The Duke is always full of surprises," Rogue whispered as the couples turned to face the assembly.

"We are here to celebrate the betrothal of my beloved son, Arthur Augustus Adrian Wellesley, Marquis of Douro to the Lady Augusta Geraldine Almeida."

Douro's grip tightened and he tugged her forward.

"And my dear friend's son, Alexander Augustus Percy, Duke of Northangerland to Lady Zenobia Ellrington. So, raise your glasses. A toast to the happy couples!"

Glasses were dutifully raised; the toast made.

"To the happy couples!"

The orchestra struck up and Douro took Augusta into his arms. He was careful to hold her well away from him. As the couples turned and turned about each other, Augusta glimpsed Zenobia scowling and Rogue smiling. The deeper her scowl, the wider his smile. He was the only one enjoying this the least bit.

Douro leant towards her, whispering into her ear. "You are my lady now and I will expect you to behave as such. No more escapades, no more running wild. You will stay here, by my side. You will have little choice in that. All you have will be mine. You have been given your head for too long. It's time you were curbed. Since you cannot discipline yourself, I will do it for you. From now on, who you speak to, who your friends are, what you do, every moment of your day, I will decide. Once we are married you will do your duty. You can be sure I'll do mine. I'll take pleasure in it."

"I loathe you."

"That will only add to it." He laughed as he pressed her closer.

She had been wondering how things could get any worse. They just had. Well, she'd see about that.

"I have great plans," he went on as he steered her round, "and you could be part of it. The Duke, my father, can't rule for ever. When he dies, or decides to abdicate, whichever is the sooner, I will take over. I will make a new kingdom, Angria."

Angria? Augusta hid her grimace in his shoulder. The name was worse than Verdopolis.

"Whose idea was that?"

"Mine, of course. What think you of it?"

Augusta didn't reply; she concentrated on following his lead, jammed to him in a rigid embrace. He guided her through and around the other dancers with all the natural grace of clockwork. Augusta smothered a shudder. If his dancing was anything to go by, it didn't augur well for their marriage.

"You can be part of it, at my side as my dutiful and obedient queen. Or…"

"Or what?"

"You will be banished to the furthest castle on the furthest estate, where you will sigh out the rest of your life. There will be no escape. It is your choice. Now, if you will excuse me."

He released her with a bow and was soon in the arms of

Mina Laury, his faithful, long-suffering mistress. Augusta didn't expect *that* would change.

Augusta did not lack for partners long; she was whisked from one young lord to another. She excused herself and stood watching the dancers; the Sneachiesland lairds in their swirling kilts and black and silver jackets cut quite a dash among the young officers.

A footman glided up to her with a note on a silver salver. It was from Annie: *No sign yet.*

"What is that? A billet-doux?" Zenobia was suddenly next to her, peering over her shoulder.

"Nothing." Augusta tucked the note into her reticule.

Zenobia watched the dancers, glowering as Douro and Mina Laury swept past in each other's arms. "Happy now?"

"Not at all. I don't want to marry."

Zenobia looked at her. "Not ever?"

"Not ever. You've come off better. You and Rogue are made for each other."

"Speak of the devil…"

The devil, indeed.

"Would either of you ladies?…" Rogue started. Zenobia turned her back with an exaggerated shiver. "Augusta?" He held his hand out to her. "Shall we join the dance?"

Rogue led her on to the floor.

"It's not quite what anyone wants, to be sure," he said as he took her into his arms. "Zenobia least of all. She hasn't ceased scowling since the Duke's announcement."

Zenobia was leaning against a column, glaring at them. "But the Duke wills it and his will be done. He rules here with absolute authority. What was Douro whispering to you about? His great plans, no doubt. They will come to nothing. You have my word on that."

Rogue danced well, without Douro's stiffness. Although he held her more tightly than she would have liked, she'd had worse partners. He was a good height and at least his hands were dry. He had none of Douro's girlish prettiness. His skin was swarthy, slightly pitted; his looks less than perfect. The scar on his left cheek, the ruggedness of his strong features, gave his countenance interest. His eyes were large and deep-set, a blue so dark as to be almost black, with no difference in shade between iris and pupil.

His hold on her tightened. "Look at me like that and I'd think you really would like to marry me."

"I was merely thinking I've never seen eyes like yours. They are almost black."

"Black eyes, black heart. Is that what you think?"

Augusta didn't answer.

"That's enough dancing." He released her from his arms but did not let go of her hand. "Come. There's food, I hear. I'm ravenous."

He led her to the adjoining room. A long table was set out with all kinds of food. The centrepiece was a swan carved from ice, heaped about with lobsters and oysters. There were huge hams and pies. Mousses of various kinds, a salmon and capons in aspic. At the other end of the table was a model of Glass Town made from spun sugar, wobbling castles of jellies and blancmange, and silver dishes piled high with peaches and grapes, pineapples from the Duke's hothouses. Men and women grazed along the table, piling their plates high.

"Larks' tongues." Rogue seized a tiny triangle of toast from a silver salver. He crammed one into his mouth and then another. "My favourite."

"There you have it," Augusta said. "I could never marry a man who enjoyed larks' tongues."

"I like the birds, too," he said. "All songbirds, in fact. The innards make them especially tasty." He looked over the table. "None here. Pity. The bones make them too fiddly, I dare say. I can tempt you to something, surely. An ice, perhaps, with strawberries?" He nodded towards silver dishes sweating on a mountain of crushed ice.

"No." Augusta shook her head. "I find I've no appetite."

"Now, why would that be?" Rogue looked down at her. "Must be the excitement of your engagement. Bound to make any girl feel a little giddy."

"I'm not any girl." Augusta turned away from him. "And I don't feel the least bit giddy."

"No?" He took her chin between his fingers and turned her face to him. "You look pale to me, a little down in the mouth. Perhaps you're finding it all a little… overwhelming. Perhaps you need cheering? Lord Charles! Just the man! And Johnny Lockhart! They have your young friend with them." His tone was light, playful, but his expression was anything but. He looked surprised, annoyed, very put out. "I must leave you…"

"What's the hurry?" Johnny Lockhart stopped him.

"Urgent business elsewhere," Rogue muttered.

"Really? Perhaps you'd like to explain to Lady Augusta how her friend Tom ended up in your dungeons?"

"Dungeons!"

So that's where Tom had been. There was a cut on his lip, bruising to the side of his face. She turned to Rogue, hardly able to contain her fury. She felt like striking him.

"What have you done to him?"

Rogue sighed and shrugged. "An overzealous underling. No real harm done."

"Could have been." Tom rubbed his jaw. Before Johnny had turned up, harm had looked certain—and permanent.

"Best be careful where you venture. If such… misunderstandings… are to be avoided." Rogue's answer was more threat than apology. "Now I must go."

"Me, too," Lord Charles announced. "Time to join the throng."

"Just a minute." Johnny Lockhart held Wellesley's arm. "I have questions: how did Rogue's henchmen know about Tom? And how would they know he'd be at Bravey's?"

"I have no clue…" Lord Charles shook his head in denial but his ready colour gave him away.

"I think you do." Johnny's grip tightened.

"Well, I might have said *something*. To provoke a comment. Get a reaction. It makes a good story. For the

Young Men's Magazine, you know. I like to steal a march on my competitors."

"Is that all you care about? Getting a story? And if there isn't one, you'll make it happen? Is that the way of it? It's not good enough, Charles." He looked around and dropped his voice. "There's something going on. Something big. Rogue's rare lads are here, in the Palace, disguised as footmen outside every door. Go and look if you don't believe me. And they are armed. Who goes to a ball armed with pistol and sword? Everyone here is his prisoner. Rogue is poised to take Glass Town as his own. You can't stand on the sidelines, notebook in hand. If he wins, there will be no *Young Men's Magazine* by morning, no *Intelligencer*. The presses will have gone up in smoke, along with half Glass Town. Printers' Row will be the first to go."

Lord Charles blew out his cheeks, his bright hazel eyes weighing up the options. "Put like that…"

"I do put it like that. These are dangerous times. You have to choose a side. Which is it to be? Us, or Rogue?"

"You, of course. And Augusta. You have my pledge." Lord Charles put out a hand to both of them.

"Good man!" Johnny Lockhart took the proffered hand. He turned to Augusta. "You must leave the city. Once Rogue is in control, he will want you as his consort."

"He knows I hate him."

"All the more reason."

Augusta thought about how they'd danced, how he'd held her, how untroubled he'd been at her betrothal. She could hear the truth in what Johnny said.

"Augusta knows the secret ways of the palace. We used them enough as children." Lord Charles led them to the back of the dining room, to where servants were coming and going through concealed baize doors. "Remember the corridor to the Game Room, the one with the sporting prints?" Augusta nodded. "*Stag Hunt*, as I recall. You two go, and good luck. We'll find another way out."

Augusta took Tom's hand and they slipped out between hurrying servants too intent on fetching and carrying to notice them. They turned into a little-used corridor decorated with dusty hunting scenes. Augusta stopped at the third one on the right and pressed a hidden lever. The panel swung back, revealing a flight of steps.

"Careful. It's dark."

They felt their way down a circular stone staircase set into the walls of the palace. For a heart-stopping moment, the door at the base refused to open. Tom put his shoulder to it and they were out in the street.

From somewhere close came music and laughter.

"It's Fiesta!" Augusta squeezed Tom's hand, her dark eyes bright with hope and excitement. "We'll hide in plain sight. Join the Moorishco. I know them. They'll get us out of the city."

*   *   *

The streets and squares were full of people. An orange moon hung in the sky like a lantern; fireworks added great bursts of colour to the stars. The fountains were running with wine and the crowd was noisy and hectic. No one looked twice at them as they threaded their way through the throng towards the Moorishco musicians perched on their wagon at the centre of the square. The musicians wore brightly coloured turbans and long, flowing robes in red, saffron, indigo. A line of girls circled, holding hands, their blouses shimmering with coins, their wide, brilliantly patterned Turkish trousers glittering with glass and sequins.

When they finished one dance and before they began another, Augusta went up to their leader and whispered something to her. She listened, collected something from under the wagon and the two of them disappeared.

The leader of the Moorishco nodded to his musicians and they began to play on instruments strange to Tom. He had never heard music like it. He stood, entranced. The tune began softly, a single strand of sound thrummed on something that looked like a lute; this was picked up by another lute, held upright and bowed like a cello, and carried on by flutes and pipes, two boys beating time on small goblet-shaped drums. The girls tiptoed out on bare feet, unwinding into the heart of the square, slowly turning and turning, their wide, brightly striped trousers flaring, their blouses a-shimmer. They moved faster and faster as the music became more insistent and then subsided back to the slower pace with the lilt and tilt of the music. The pattern was repeated again and again. The effect was hypnotic. More and more couples joined them, whirling into the square, winding and twining around in intricate patterns, spinning off in each other's arms. Tom wasn't that great at dancing but he ached to join them. His feet would not keep still.

"Come!" One of the girls broke away and took his hand. "Dance!"

It was Augusta, dressed in the robes of the Moorishco. Tom laughed. He'd failed to recognize her. He found himself spun into the square, his arms round her. His feet seemed to know what to do, even if he didn't. They danced round in each other's arms, her hair silky against his cheek; he breathed her scent, of lemon and lavender, while the rest of the world receded, passing in a multicoloured blur, with the Moorishco girls laughing, clapping, shouting, "*Bravo!*"

Gradually, the music faded. The cart was on the move, the girls dancing alongside it, the musicians still playing, leaving their music to haunt the square.

Breathless, Tom and Augusta broke away from each other.

"Quick. We must follow them!"

Augusta took Tom's hand and they ran after the fading music, then she stumbled. Tom caught her and they were in each other's arms again. Tom kissed her and she kissed him back. Her hands went to his face, her fingers in his hair. Her mouth was warm; she tasted of cinnamon and summer. Somewhere, Tom could hear that tune playing over and over, weaving a pattern in his head that he knew would always be there.

A tocsin bell sounded and the music stopped. The steady beat of marching feet filled the space left by it.

"That's too early for curfew!" Augusta broke away.

She looked past Tom, her eyes widening. This wasn't the Watch. These weren't the Duke's soldiers. They wore blue jackets and tall bicorne hats pinned with tricolours. These were the Revolutionary Guard. Her hold on Tom tightened, but she was no match for the arms that tore him away from her, or for the circle of fixed bayonets.

Pigtail strolled up and seized Tom by the shoulder. "We bin looking for you, my lad."

CHAPTER TWENTY-FOUR

PITTER-POTTERING

*From all over the city, called by the
muffled tocsin bell, came the furtive
scuff of leather on stone, the swish of
sword, the click and snick of a gun
being cocked. Whispered orders...*

"'AST THA FINISHED YON SHIRT YET? Stop tha pitter-pottering. There's potatoes need peeling. Dinner won't mak itself."

The voice from the kitchen pulled her out of one world into quite another. Emily shook her head, as if to be rid of an annoying fly. Writing, reading, any activity that wasn't pegging out washing, mangling said washing, or ironing, or sewing and mending, or cleaning, or kneading bread and making puddings, or, yes, potato peeling, was "pitter-pottering" and thus wasting time. But she needed to get this down before it all vanished, the bubbles bursting and disappearing.

*The last strains of the Moorishco's haunting tune
faded as the band wound their way out of the city, tiny
figures pulling a tiny cart, like fleas in a circus...*

She was high up, standing on top of the Tower of All Nations. Higher than any other building, the darkened towers, domes and pinnacles of Glass Town spreading out and away like buildings in a toy town. There was no rail in front of her, no balustrade. She was standing on the very edge.

"Look down! Down!" The voice was close to her ear, full of glee and gloating. "Tell me what you see."

Augusta shifted her gaze to the Great Piazza. The shadows of buildings falling sharp across the moonlit square. Men with torches standing around a wooden platform. A cart coming slowly across the wide expanse of the square. Pulled by two big horses, its cargo too big for the bed of it. The cart was turning, the horses reversing. Men leapt up to lift; others stood braced to take the weight of the load. The great blade, set at an angle, caught the torchlight as it slid from the cart, flashing red as if already drenched in blood. The thin, tall structure was manhandled into the slots made for it. A man dressed in black busied himself with ropes and pulleys. He hauled the blade up inside its frame and then let it fall with a thud to the empty block at its base. He did this several times, adjusting the ropes and pulleys slightly, standing back, hands on hips as the blade rushed down at varying speeds.

"I sent for him from Paris." Rogue was speaking in her ear. "It was designed by a Frenchie, so it makes sense to have one to work it. I had it made especially and shipped over." His breath quickened. "Now to see what it can do…"

A watermelon had been placed on the block. At a signal from the Frenchman, the blade was hauled up. It fell quickly, splitting the watermelon. A slight squelch behind the chunk of the falling blade. One half tumbled into a basket; the other spilt pink pulp as it hit the platform. The mess was cleared, the blade hauled up and the procedure began again. A pumpkin this time. The blade fell and cut clean through orange flesh and rind. An assistant brought up a swede, about the size of a man's head; Augusta squinted—at least, it looked like a swede, but it was hard to tell at this distance. She hoped it was a swede; prayed it was. She closed her eyes as the blade fell.

Augusta opened her eyes to see Pigtail sluicing the platform. She turned away with a shudder. Since when did swedes have blood and brains?

"Perfect, perfect!" Rogue clapped his hands. His delight in this vile spectacle exposed the true viciousness of his nature. "The Frenchman is a genius. The balance is just right! No! Don't turn away!" He forced her head round. "You'll miss the best part!"

Below her, the man in black was stepping back, dusting his hands. The heavy blade was being hauled up.

"Quite the most efficient form of execution," Rogue was saying. "Modern and mechanical, and everyone meets death equally. No distinction between the axe and the hangman's noose. Quick and efficient, it can get through hundreds in a day, but it has to be adjusted correctly: too light, and the neck isn't severed cleanly; too heavy, and the edge is damaged." He held her head firmly. "Now we'll see what it can do to a living man—or a boy."

Two of Pigtail's rare lads were dragging a man across the platform, his feet trailing on the ground, hands bound, his shirt torn from his neck. They delivered him to Pigtail, who pushed him down under the hovering blade. Just as the blade was falling, the man moved. The blade sheared through the skull at the jaw.

Rogue shook his head, his lip curling with disgust as the bloody remnants of the man were dragged away; water was thrown to sluice the bubbling blood.

"I *told* Pigtail that wouldn't work. I've devised a *far* better system of delivery." He stared down, entranced by his hideous killing device. "In the morning you'll see just how efficient my new toy can be. Tomorrow, it will taste blood aplenty. I am merely giving the people what they want. They tire of tyranny."

"And what would they get under you?"

"Now is not the time for political debate. The Duke is my prisoner, as are you." Rogue gently swept her hair to the side. "Such a little neck," he mused, passing a fingernail across her skin, light but sharp.

Augusta raised a hand involuntarily to see if there was blood.

Rogue's fingers tightened and he forced her head forward. His breath quickened as two men approached the platform carrying a man strapped, face down, to a long board. This whole revolting display had been a kind of dreadful theatre, building towards this maximum horror for, when he turned his head to one side, Augusta saw that it was Tom...

"I'll do them later!" she shouted back to the kitchen, but it was too late.

She'd lost her grasp on the story. The fabric of the scene was disintegrating, disappearing as fast as silk in a flame. She threw down her pen in frustration. Ink splattered in a line of blots across the page. She joined them up, trying to doodle her way back to the line of her thinking but it was no good. It had gone.

She whistled Keeper to her. Time for a walk.

The rain had stopped, except for a few fine drops carried on the wind. She pulled up the hood of her cloak and set off. She'd changed into stout men's boots and had taken a strong blackthorn stick from the hallstand. She meant to take a long tramp. Keeper bounded in front of her, leading the way. She often did this if she was stuck somewhere in the story, had a knotty problem to tease out, or the world had to be reconjured, as now. Walls confine. Out here, the mind could go where it will.

She joined the broad path that led up behind the church and out of the village, head bent, eyes unseeing on the stone slabs beneath her feet, and let her mind range back to Glass Town. Was she in danger of writing herself into a corner? Of letting the excitement of the scene run over the edge of logic? And things did have to make sense—had to be within the range of what was possible—even in Glass Town.

The trick was to go back, to strip down; not to change things unless completely necessary, but to see what had to be put right to justify what was happening now. What *was* Rogue up to? What did he want?

Her wide, loping stride soon left track and village behind. Keeper had left her, bent on his own business; he was soon just a tail moving in the ferns. She followed her feet, taking the narrow crooked paths that branched between the bilberry bushes and low-growing heather. The rain had turned them into little rills and streams but she didn't mind that. Her aim was to get high, higher; to leave home, church, village behind; to get to a place where she couldn't even see them, to get to a place where she could think.

She was making for an outcrop of rock, one side sheer; the other, the more sheltered side, an uneven layering where the rock had split along natural faults and been further split for building stone, millstones, standing stones, like as not. The result was a stair leading to a natural chair, formed of great slabs of the coarse-grained stone. She was not the first to sit here; the stone was traced with faint cups and whorls marking other, older occupation. The place was protected from the weather and out of sight. Below her lay a place where streams met and pooled, spiked with reed and rush, bright with moss and fern. Beyond, the back of the moors spread away, only one distant building in sight, stone roofed and stone built, so huddled into the hills that it looked like part of the landscape. She settled herself, her arms resting, hands on the rough stone.

"No!" Rogue forced her head round, digging into the flesh between her skull and her neck, his fingers as strong as a metal clamp. "You *must* watch!"

"He's done nothing! He's an innocent!" Augusta could hardly get the words out. "Stop this now! Let him go!"

Rogue looked down to where Pigtail stood by the guillotine, the rope in his hands, awaiting his orders.

"On one condition. You have to promise yourself to me, Augusta."

Augusta stared down at Tom lying helpless. She was frozen with the horror of it. Paralysed with terror for him. Like in a dream or nightmare, her lips and limbs refused to move. Then, from somewhere very far away, she heard a voice, that didn't sound like her voice, saying: "What choice do I have?"

At a nod from Rogue, the rope was secured, and Tom dragged away from the hovering blade, released and hauled to his feet.

He looked up and Augusta knew he saw them far above him, standing together. He was shouting but she was too distant to hear him.

Tom began to struggle, fighting with his captors. Pigtail took something, the lead-weighted blackjack he always kept in his pocket, and dealt him a blow that sent him to his knees.

Rogue ignored the scene below.

"We are made for each other, Augusta," he was whispering. "You know it. Anyone else would be consumed by us, turned to smouldering ashes." Rogue looked over Glass Town laid out before them. "All this will be ours, ordered how we want it. We can create a republic, like the French."

"And that turned out so well," she whispered.

Rogue chose not to hear her.

"What is your man doing? You promised you'd release him!"

Since when did Rogue keep his promises? She blinked away tears of fear for Tom and fury at her own helplessness.

"I promised no such thing. I promised I wouldn't guillotine him. The two things are very different. Imagine it, Augusta," he went on, as if Tom and his fate were of no importance. "No more kings, no more dukes. No more noble families. We would rule together with the people. In a spirit of justice and fairness. Everybody equal. Isn't that what you've always wanted?"

Did he think that he could persuade her? He was both vicious *and* deluded. Augusta looked at the space falling away below her. There was no separation, nothing between her feet and the edge…

As if he sensed the slightest impulse, the anticipation, the first tremor of movement, he took her in his arms, his great cloak wrapping around her like black wings. He bent his mouth to hers and his kiss was savage, bruising; she tasted blood. She could feel the heat of him, the deep drum of his heart beating as he held her against him. She made no resistance, frozen by a thought more dreadful than any of the horrors she had been forced to witness. What if the emotion that she'd always taken for hatred had been love all along?

She was so still that she seemed carved from the very rock that held her. She stayed like this until the distant horizon reddened and the light began to fade.

At length, she rose, whistling for Keeper, who came bounding towards her through fern and heather.

"There's potatoes needing peeling," she said as she set off for home. "Best be getting back."

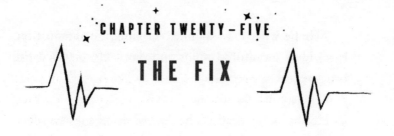

CHAPTER TWENTY-FIVE

THE FIX

"It's very strange. I don't know what to make of it."
Joe stood back from the bed, his genial face creased with
concern. "See here?"

Lucy went over to the bed. He pushed Tom's hair
gently; it was growing back thick and curly. She'd never
seen him like this. He always wore his hair cut short.
It made him look different, as if he could be in *Game
of Thrones*, or something. It was strange to think of his
hair growing, his nails. Joe had once said something
about Tom going somewhere. Travelling, he'd called it.
It was as though his body was waiting for him to come
back again.

"I don't know what it is," Joe said. "Or how it could
have happened." He held the dark curls back from the
left temple. The skin had a bluish tinge to it, yellow-
ing faintly at the edges. "It's very faint but it looks like
bruising."

She frowned. "How could that happen?"

He shrugged. "Search me."

She gazed down at Tom, inert and unmoving. "He
couldn't exactly do it himself. Could he have been
assaulted?"

"That's what it looks like, certainly, but I don't see how. He's monitored night and day." He brushed the hair back.

"Have you told anyone?"

He shook his head. "They'd just dismiss it as a slight discoloration, so faint as to be negligible. I noticed it this morning and it's already fading. I can't explain it. It's a strange thing."

She agreed. It was a very strange thing. The bluishness was disappearing. Even if Joe couldn't explain it, she knew someone who just might be able to shed some light.

"You still here?" he said from the door. "Like I said, don't know why you bother. How's the sleeping prince? Still sleeping, I see."

She put down her book. "What do you want, Milo?"

"To see my mate—what else? Check on how he's doing."

"That's exactly what I want to know." She got up from her chair. "How about we give him a bit of peace?"

Milo stared at Tom's sleeping form. "He gets enough of that, I'd have thought."

"Does he? See here."

"What? I don't see anything."

"Bruising. On his temple."

"So?" Milo shoved his hands in his pockets and hunched his narrow shoulders. "What are you saying? That I came in here and did that to him? You're crazy, you know that?" He shifted from foot to foot. "Everybody says so."

"Do they really? Like who? Your stupid girlfriend and her crew? What do I care what they think? Nice try, Milo, but back to the point."

"Which is?"

"No, I don't think you've been sneaking in here to assault Tom but I do think that you know something."

"Like what?"

"Like what is happening to him. Ever since you came in that time, he's been different."

"Oh, what?" Milo stared at Tom. "You can tell?"

"Well, yes, actually. And it's not just me. Joe thinks so, too."

"Who's Joe?"

"His nurse."

"The Latino?"

"Yes, if you want to put it like that. He's Guatemalan, actually. Time we had a chat. Let's go to the canteen, shall we?"

"Why would I do that?"

"Because, number one: if you don't, everyone in the whole world is going to know about you and Natalie—that she's cheating on *hashtag heroinacoma* with his 'best mate'. Number two: because I think you're worried."

"I remember," Lucy said. "Two sugars."

"And no sprinkles."

"Right."

Lucy went to the counter to get their coffees. The hospital had made an effort but no one would mistake the Four Seasons for a regular restaurant and coffee shop. Too many people in blue scrubs, staff on their breaks wearing lanyards, doctors with stethoscopes draped round their necks like scarves, not to mention patients in pyjamas and dressing gowns, men towing bags on stands, and the wheelchairs and Zimmer frames parked around.

She took their coffees to where Milo was sitting at a table near the window. It was a nice day. People were in the little garden outside enjoying the sunshine.

"I hate hospitals," he said. "They're full of sick people." He took the coffee without saying "thank you", shook the sachets and emptied them, stirring as the grains fell through the foam on his cappuccino. "So what do you want?"

"I want to know what've you done. What you've got him into and how you're going to get him out again."

"How do you know I've got him into anything?"

"Call it female intuition." Lucy stirred the chocolate sprinkles down into her coffee. "Stop messing, Milo. I know you're up to something. Why are you here?"

He took a small plastic box out of his pocket. The kind that contained SD camera cards. He held it between two fingers. "This came this morning. FedEx, no return address."

"What is it?"

"It's called a fish. Echeneis fish, in fact. It's a gaming gizmo. Very advanced."

"What does it do?"

"Sends the subject to a virtual world."

"Which one? Where?"

"Can't say exactly."

"And what are you supposed to do with it?"

"Put it in Tom's ear. This is the second I've had."

"So something comes through the post. You don't know who it's from, or what it does exactly, but you stuff it in the ear of your best mate who's lying in a coma?"

"I do know who it's from, actually," Milo countered.

"But not what it does?"

"Well." Milo shifted. "It's experimental."

"Oh, let me get this straight. You don't know what it does exactly but that's all right because it's *experimental*? How is that OK, Milo?"

Milo shrugged. "I thought it might help him. Stimulate him, you know?"

"That's the thing with you, Milo: you are all heart. Why did you really do it?"

Milo sighed and stirred another sachet of sugar into his coffee. "He isn't going anywhere, is he? Anyway, he wouldn't be like he is now, would he? In a *virtual* world, he'd be like he was before it happened. You know, like in *Avatar*. Imagine lying there like that, day after day. I see it as doing him a big favour."

He leant forward; thin hands clasped together, eyes magnified behind his glasses, full of virtual generosity. His default setting was lying. Even to himself.

"So, you stick this gaming gizmo in the ear of a boy in a coma. How's that even work? He can't tell you what's happening to him."

"He doesn't need to. We can track him. Except—"

"You don't know where he is."

"Not at the *moment*."

"I see. It wouldn't be the fact that he's in a coma, so if something happens to him, nobody'd know and it wouldn't matter?"

"Of course not. What do you take me for?"

"You don't want to know. So, just trying to get this straight—it's like some kind of game…"

"It's more than that. *Way* more. It's the next stage, the next level."

"Like virtual reality?"

"Beyond that, even." Milo was getting excited now. "It's a disruptor, you know—like Amazon and selling, or Uber and taxis. A game changer, in the true sense. You will be able to *live* in it. Experience it with all the senses. It'll be like you're really *there*…" He stopped talking for a moment, lost in contemplation of its wonder.

She stared at him. For someone with a brain the size of Yorkshire, he really was very stupid. She could see it immediately. Why couldn't he?

"OK, so when this thing launches," she spoke slowly,

as if speaking to a small child, "when it goes viral, every kid in the world is going to want one?"

"That's the idea."

"And they will enter some virtual world…"

"Of their own choosing," Milo supplied.

"Granted. Of their own choosing." She could see the faint pit in Tom's shoulder, the bruising to his head. "And live in it?"

"That's about the sum of it. Neat, eh?"

"So, if they can live there, can they die there?"

"Hell, no." He hesitated. "I don't think so…"

"But you don't know so…"

"Well, no. But that wouldn't make sense—"

"Wouldn't it? The world's children, young people, lost in cyberspace, living there and presumably dying there. What are you calling it? *Mindcraft Apocalypse?* Think of the *power*." She shook her head at the dawning enormity. "It would make cyberattacks look like *nothing*. Whoever's behind it would have the whole world by the balls."

"Put like that…" Milo looked uncertain, eyes darting, long, thin fingers playing with the sugar sachets, realization beginning to dawn.

"For someone who is supposed to be really, really brainy, you can be really, really dumb, Milo, you know that?"

"We thought we'd be able to track him, monitor how he was getting on. Except…"

"Except?"

"He disappeared entirely. We don't know where he's gone."

"So it's already going wrong."

"Not entirely. It's experimental, like I said." He held up the small plastic container. "This is the fix."

"How do you know?"

"It says on the box."

"A fix so he can carry on his virtual life, or come back to this one?"

"Well, can't say exactly…"

"Seems to be an awful lot you don't know. Stop lying to me, Milo. Why did you really do it? What's this really about?"

"It's like a syndicate." Milo studied his fingernails. "To be in it, you have to make a contribution. You have to give something to get something back. Not money. He's got plenty of that. Something to show your commitment."

"He? Who's he?"

Milo shook his head. "I can't tell you. It'd be more than my life's worth and I mean that in the literal sense."

"OK." She'd let that ride for now. "So you had to give him something and you chose Tom. Big of you, Milo. Why didn't you stick the thing in Natalie's ear?"

"Are you kidding?" He seemed genuinely shocked at the idea. "She'd be no good! She'd be blown away in a second. Tom would stand much more of a chance."

"Like I said," Lucy sighed. "All heart. You have to put a stop to this, Milo."

"I would if I could, babe." He shrugged, palms out. "I would if I could. But I can't."

"Get out of it, then. Get Tom out of it."

"Can't do that, either."

"Why not?"

"It's complicated."

Milo took off his glasses. Without them he looked different, vulnerable. Younger. He rubbed his eyes and when he looked back at her, she saw genuine fear.

"Once you're in it, you can't get out." He seemed to collect himself. "All I can do is put in the fix." He picked up the small plastic square, turning it around and around in his fingers. "See what it does. It's *all* I can do," he repeated.

He got up abruptly. Joe was coming towards their table. He stepped back, nearly spilling his tea as Milo dashed past.

"You going?" Joe asked.

Lucy shook her head and sat back down again. She'd been debating whether to stop Milo. Or tell Joe. Or get Joe to stop him, but she decided no. Let Milo do it. What else did they have?

"He's in a hurry." Joe took a sip of his tea. "Where's he off to so fast?" He put down his cup. His hand went to his pager. "Oh, what's happening now?"

"It wasn't a lie."

Milo was back, looking down at him. Agitated. More jittery than normal.

"Not completely. I really did think I'd be doing you a favour. I gotta do this. You wouldn't believe the pressure I'm under…" His voice faded, as if he was pacing away from the bed. "I have to do this," he repeated, but quietly, as if to himself this time. "I have to do this. I got no choice." He was close now. "You could see it as a kind of a fix."

Tom could hear the fear behind Milo's false brightness.

"I'd love to be there, bruv—you have to believe me—but it has to be you. You're the only one with access. You're all that stands between us and… what did she call it? *Mindcraft Apocalypse*. Good name for what could happen. It's up to you, bro."

He came near to the bed. Nearer. Tom felt something go into his ear.

"'S all right." Joe smiled. "Panic over. It was hairy for a little while but he's stable now."

Is he? She looked down the corridor, at Milo's black silhouette disappearing round the corner. Had he been hanging about, checking out his handiwork?

She set off after him. He was walking fast. She was running now.

Lucy caught him just as he was crossing the car park.

"That was you back there, wasn't it? That fix set all the machines off."

"He did that all by himself. He's very sick—don't you know that?"

"This thing you're doing—it's got to stop, Milo."

"Out of my hands, babe." He spread his own, to show how helpless he was. "I can't stop now. I told you. Maybe the fix will fix it."

"And what if it doesn't?"

He shrugged. "Like I told you, there's nothing else I can do."

"I don't believe that. You always know a way."

"Not this time." He put his hands in his pockets and kept on walking.

"Well, you better find one." She put a hand on his arm but he shrugged it off.

"Or what?"

"Or nothing." She put her hand out again. "Look at me, Milo. Look at me!"

This time he turned round.

"I can't threaten you, Milo. Just advise you. I'd advise you to do what you can because you know it's the right thing to do."

She watched Milo carry on across the car park and then stop. He stood for a moment, staring off, as though thinking of something. He half turned, as if to come back to her, then went on, head down, hands in pockets. Maybe he'd had that idea after all.

CHAPTER TWENTY-SIX

A VISITOR

THERE'D BEEN NO TIME TO WRITE. Potatoes waiting in their unpeeled state. The rest of the dinner to be prepared and eaten, mostly in silence. Nothing said, but eyes resting on his empty chair. Then Father retiring to his study and more stitching in the parlour, fancy work under Aunt's watchful eye. She'd had to wait for the time. The right time.

Emily heard Branwell come in when the rest of the house was abed. A stumble, a curse on the stair and his door slamming shut. She was in the Children's Study. She often slept in there but tonight it was too confined, too enclosing; the moonlight coming through the window unsettling. She needed to be out. Sometimes she left the house, walking through the night with Keeper by her side, especially on nights like this, when the moon was full and bright as a new shilling, but that was for thinking. Tonight, her fingers were itching to hold a pen between them.

She sat at the turn of the stairs. She often positioned herself here. At night, when she wouldn't be questioned or disturbed. She liked it here: neither up nor down, off solid ground, between one state and another. She felt safe, melting back into the shadows, knees up to her chin, notebook on her thighs, inkwell by her side. They knew she wrote but they didn't know what, although Charlotte wasn't above spying. She didn't want them to know. It wasn't so much secret as private. For her alone. To share was to give away too much; to leach away the power.

The moon's light, casting through the window, washed bluish as she bent to the inviting blankness of the page. She dipped her pen, loading it, ready to make a mark, but a sound held her hand suspended between inkwell and paper. She glanced up. Her eyes were on a level with the upstairs floor. There was a light coming from under his door. It was bright—brighter than lamp or candlelight flicker. There was a harsh, violet aspect to it, like the fierce glow of lightning striking. The light faded and intensified as if someone was pacing in front of the door. She could hear voices. *Is he talking to himself?* That was quite possible, but there was a difference in timbre and tone between the voices: one low and mumbling; the other jeering and imperious, veering from scorn to anger and back again. The second voice sounded very like Rogue. Could he have broken through somehow? Had he been brought to life, manifested by the obsessive power of the imagination, as they say? Could obsession, imagination be enough to manifest from the world of their imaginations to actually *be* there, in that room? She gathered her writing things and crept up the stairs. Suddenly, she wanted very much to be elsewhere.

*   *   *

In the morning, she went into his room. He was lying fully clothed across the bed, one arm dangling on the floor. She eased his boots off and spread the cover over him. Pale as milk, not stirring. Not dead—she checked that he was breathing—but dead to the world. On the chair he used as a bedside table was a bottle of brandy and next to it an unstoppered bottle of Black Drop, the laudanum he got from Betty Hardacre at the druggist's. The reddish brown liquid was trickling down the ribbed glass, staining the label, adding its sweetish sickly smell to the room. *How much has he taken?* Not enough to kill him, but enough.

He'd begun to take laudanum to dampen what Father termed his "nervous excitability", but he'd discovered its other qualities through his heroes Coleridge and De Quincy and often took it along with strong spirits to set free his imagination, to allow his mind to escape the bounds of everyday life and go where it would—and she knew where that would be. Now, she thought he took it to escape from the haunting obsession that threatened to possess him body and soul.

She looked around the room at the screwed-up bits of paper, hatched and cross-hatched with minuscule writing, with tiny sketches in the margins. A careful and complex drawing of a tall, many-windowed building, towered and turreted, rendered as precisely as an architectural drawing, surrounded and overlaid with letters and words. Pinned to the wall, a larger drawing, so heavily shaded the ink was still wet, soaking and buckling the cheap paper. Not a bad likeness. A man in profile: high-domed forehead, dark, curling hair falling on to his collar and brushed forward on to his temples, deep-set eyes, thin nose, mouth curving downwards in haughty disapproval. Another, more fanciful—the same man dressed as a pirate, standing with a swagger, sword dangling at his side. *Alexander Percy. Duke of Northangerland.* Rogue's name and title.

The other two have escaped in their own fashion: one distancing herself into the intricate minuet of Glass Town romance and social dalliance; the other into making maps and plans, elaborating hairstyles and dresses for Gondal. But Emily felt it as powerfully as Branwell: the pull of a world so much more exciting, so much more seductive, than everyday, humdrum existence. It was there all the time. She could go there without the need of stimulants, slipping into it as easily as she slipped her arms into the sleeves of her coat. It was part of the weave of her waking life.

She stared at the curling portrait pinned above the desk. Beyond the cloying laudanum, she thought she caught the sharpish, metallic tang of electricity—as if he had been there, in this room.

CHAPTER TWENTY – SEVEN

FLIGHTS FROM GLASS TOWN

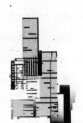

THE NOISE GREW AND GREW. A great wind enveloped them; dust and sand swirled around in a gritty cloud. The noise was so loud, the sudden wind so strong, Augusta thought that they were in the grip of the Jinn.

"Grab hold!" a voice boomed from above, and Augusta looked up to see a harness falling down towards her. "Grab hold! Put your arms through it. That's it. Hold tight."

She put her head and chest through the padded loops and was whirled into the air. She saw Rogue staring up at her, his arms outstretched, as if to draw her back to him, but it was too late. She was being hauled up towards the craft hovering above. A small, squat machine, like an enormous mosquito, blades whirling above the body of it, like sycamore wings.

"Put your foot on the bar." Tom's voice came through the shatter of noise. "That's it. See those handles? Grab hold and haul yourself in. That's it! That's it."

Augusta pulled herself into the flying machine and fell on to the floor. She lay there for a moment or two, gasping like a fish on the shore. Then she inched towards the open door. The machine was rising with incredible speed. Rogue beneath her, getting smaller and smaller, still staring up, his arms reaching, his cloak-like wings; he looked like the dark angel he longed to be.

As they rose higher and higher, she saw Glass Town as she'd never seen it before. The towers and turrets, the enclosing walls, the spider span of the bridge, the dark-glass gleam of river and harbour and the sea beyond. Lights showed here and there. Torches moved like lines of fireflies along the darkened streets, converging on the Great Piazza.

"There's a clasp at the front of the harness," Tom said without looking round. "It unclips. Come up here and sit by me."

Some unseen mechanism slid the open door shut behind her and Augusta crawled forward cautiously, not trusting the shifting movement of the frail-looking craft, a mere skin of metal and glass between them and the empty air. She took the narrow seat next to Tom.

"Now it's payback time," he said. "Let's see how Pigtail likes this."

The craft wheeled around. They were diving down with an angry hornet's whine. She could see the slender frame of the guillotine in the Great Piazza, the faces around it upturned in awe and wonder. Augusta cowered back, fearing that they were going to crash. Tom pressed a button with his gloved thumb and the piazza disappeared in a staccato blast of cannon fire.

The craft swooped up again, like a hawk in flight. The only sound was the *thump*, *thump* of the rotating blades.

Tom turned to dive again, this time with the Duke's Palace in his sights.

"No!" Augusta shouted and reached to cover over his gloved hand. "Annie's down there and Keeper, Isaac, Amos and lots of innocent people. They don't deserve to die. Go there—in the bay!"

The craft dipped and veered away, heading towards the sea where ships showed dark against the glint of the water. Tom pressed a button and missiles flew down, stitching their way across the harbour, targeting one ship after another, ending with the black freighter, which disappeared in a series of explosions, billowing smoke and flame.

They both stared, awed, their faces illuminated by the flickering red glow from the burning ships.

"That was carrying some serious ordinance."

"What is this thing?"

Augusta looked around in wonder. In front of Tom and above his head were switches, buttons and dials, glowing green and red; small glass windows showing moving maps, bright and lit up; a compass, the dial white against black. They were flying almost due west, the dial registering even the slightest change of direction. She automatically reached out her hand.

"Don't touch anything! It's called a helicopter. A flying machine," he tried to explain. "The blades on the top turn very fast, creating an updraught which keeps us in the air. The blades in the tail keep the craft stable."

A flying machine. Why not? Men had always envied the birds and dreamt of such a thing. Didn't Leonardo da Vinci sketch a machine that turned and turned like sycamore wings? Augusta savoured the word. Helic-o-pter. From the Greek, she guessed, *helix* and *pteron*—"spiral wing".

She twisted round. Glass Town was slipping from view, a smudge in the distance. They were flying over water, the land a dark band receding all the time.

"We have to go back!" Augusta was filled with sudden panic. "We can't leave now!"

"That's the only thing we can do."

"When will we be back again?"

"I don't know."

"Where are we going?"

"I don't know that, either."

That was the truth. Tom had no idea as he flew the helicopter out over the open sea. They were in another kind of game now, one where he could fly helicopters like a Navy Seal—Milo's "fix", no doubt, but one where Tom had no influence over where they were going. None of the controls responded to him. They were being taken on a predetermined trajectory, as if caught in a tractor beam. He didn't have a clue where they were heading or how it would play out.

They were flying over water, the restless black glitter of the sea far below them. They were heading west, into a constantly setting sun. Augusta sat quietly, taking in all this strangeness.

"What are all those little lights in front of you?" she asked. "The switches and dials?"

"This shows how high we're flying; this shows how fast. This is for..." Tom paused. "Not sure what that's for, or that, or that. Oh, I think that one's fuel. This is a gyro, keeping us steady; these are maps, showing where we are and where we're heading; and this is a compass."

All Augusta really understood was compass.

"We're travelling north-west," she said.

"Looks like it."

She was intensely curious, wanting to know how the machine worked, asking all sorts of questions that Tom couldn't answer. Amazing how much you took for granted. This was a helicopter. They just *were*.

"Are there more machines like this?" she asked when she'd exhausted his scanty knowledge of the craft. "That can fly?"

"Yes," he answered. "Many. Bigger than this, more powerful. Flying higher and faster—much faster. Rockets, even, that can travel to the moon and out to the planets."

"With men in them?"

"To the moon, yes. The planets are much further, so not yet."

Augusta was silent. She didn't seem fazed by any of this. Not at all. She was just absorbing it as an interesting new thing. Men had always yearned to fly. Such things only existed in stories but there was no limit to the imagination. It wasn't that strange that they would one day find a way to do it…

"The Fairish Lady *said* you were from the future…"

"About two hundred years in the future—at a rough guess."

"To live in a world where such wonders are real." Augusta's grey eyes were wide with wonder. "I envy you."

"Some things are better." Tom leant back, arms folded. No point in keeping hold of the joystick—the thing was flying itself. "Life is much easier for most people. We can cure many diseases. Machines do much of the work for us and we can travel any distance. Speak to people on the other side of the world. Some things haven't changed, though. We can't cure every disease and we still have wars and fighting, and the weapons we've invented mean there's killing on a scale you wouldn't believe."

Augusta nodded at the logic of that. Just as men have always wanted to fly, they'd always want to find more efficient ways to kill. Even so…

"I'd love to see it," she said.

"Something tells me that your wish is about to be granted."

The helicopter banked and changed its trajectory. The compass on the dashboard swung north-north-west. On the digital map, Tom could see the southern seaboard of the United States approaching. They were over the Gulf of Mexico. Tom could see ships beneath them, small as matchboxes, and oil rigs lit up like Christmas trees. They were crossing the coastal highway, following a necklace of lights. Then they were turning inland. In between the blackness of less populated areas, cities and towns showed in grids and starbursts connected by snaking strings of white and gold.

"What are those lights?" Augusta asked. "It's like looking down on the stars."

"Houses, roads, streets. Where people live."

"How are they lit so bright?"

"Electricity."

"Mr Faraday's invention?"

"Yes, I guess. It kind of took off."

Augusta fell silent, staring out of the window, fascinated by the carpet of sparks below her. They were flying over more and more darkness, the lights strung out and sporadic.

Tom was flying higher, faster, further—way beyond the capability of a craft like this. He wasn't flying it at all—somebody else was, he knew that, but who that could be he had no idea.

The craft was rising, going over mountains. High mountains. There was snow on the peaks below them. Tom thought he knew where they were and where they might be heading.

He took a sideways look at Augusta. Her face was set and serious, grey eyes taking in everything. She looked different. Younger. Also more ordinary. Her beauty had lost that edge that made you catch your breath, but Tom preferred her like this. She looked real. Like a real girl.

"You're not Augusta any more, are you?" Tom stared ahead.

"No," she replied simply. "I'm Emily."

CHAPTER TWENTY-EIGHT

GREAT GLASS TOWN

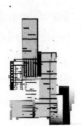

THEY WERE COMING TO HIM. They had no choice in that. He was calling them. At a touch he could make the craft crash, blow apart in mid-air, but he didn't want that. The cargo was too valuable, too precious.

The image he was seeing filled the screen in front of him. He pulled out from the intimacy of the cockpit to watch the helicopter fly down from the Rockies and out across a darkened California. At a touch, it disappeared into a corner to become just one of many small screens, showing a thousand, thousand worlds that made up an image of himself.

The terrain flattened out. The darkness below was spangled with light again. Freeways snaked between grid after grid, town after town. They were descending into a basin, a webbing, a skein of lights spreading from the eastern horizon to the blackness of the sea. Lines of red and white streaked in twisting rivers that ran like veins, like arteries, merging and splitting apart. Nowhere was completely dark below them. An orange and yellow glow spread along the ground, bursting out here and there like brushwood fire. Tom recognized it from any number of films, games and

TV shows. Excitement tightened and bubbled up inside him. He wanted to laugh. He'd always wanted to do this. They were flying over Los Angeles, into one dazzling golden glow.

Downtown rose up like an island in the centre, in obelisks and oblongs, soaring towers set at angles to each other, a many-storeyed glitter of glass in the darkness, lit against the night sky, illuminated from within. Emily caught her breath and held it; she had never seen or imagined anything like it. This truly was Great Glass Town. Huge images played: women's smiling faces and almost naked bodies many feet high. Their mouths moved but no words came out of them. She had no name for the dazzling bright hues—the pinks, violets, greens and blues—that filled the spaces, then disappeared again, like liquid decanted from a bottle.

They were flying through downtown LA now. The helicopter was manoeuvred down the canyons, between the towers, the *chock-chock* sound the blades made amplified by the narrow walls they passed. Emily watched the mosquito shape and turning blades appear and disappear in the glass on either side. In the silver streets below, the traffic's ceaseless flow marked paths like sparks from a blacksmith's hearth.

"This is your world?" She craned forward to see more. Her voice was full of amazement and wonder.

"It is a real place. And it is in my world. But not my world, exactly. I mean, Glass Town isn't your world, is it?

Not the place you live in all the time, eat, sleep and do ordinary things. My real world is like yours. Changed a bit since your time but you'd recognize most of it. I've never been here, not in real life, and this isn't real life—it's like Glass Town, a fantasy, a made-up place."

"So how are we in it?"

"I don't know. I guess we'll be finding out."

They were through the canyons and out the other side. Below the wide, empty gash of the LA River. They were following the line of a multi-lane highway, heading north, out of the city, sea on the left, mountains on the right, their peaks pink and saffron with the coming dawn. Behind them, the buildings were turning to burnished bronze in the rising sun.

"Where are we going?" she asked.

"I still don't know." Tom shook his head. "North. Probably San Francisco."

She guessed it was the name of a place, although it meant nothing to her beyond being that of a saint who founded a monastic order.

They were higher now. The sky was deep blue, the land beneath them a milky brown, with wide valleys and riverbeds, pale, wrinkling hills patched with forest and fissured with canyons.

Tom thought they might be heading for Silicon Valley. The craft was flying low and fast, its shadow flitting over gridded streets lined with trees, the grey roofs of houses, bare backyards and bright turquoise swimming pools and bigger, low-rise buildings, surrounded by car parks. It was hard to tell if they were offices or shopping malls. Screening trees and black windows made him think the former.

The helicopter circled and circled, making a noise like an angry wasp, spiralling down towards a flat, one-storey, matt graphite-black building clad in some non-reflective material. Then they were on solid ground; the blades wound down. Not solid ground exactly: the roof of a building.

Before they could open their doors, before they could do anything, they were descending, helicopter and all, into the centre of the huge building.

CHAPTER TWENTY-NINE

WELCOME TO MY WORLD

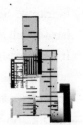

He was standing in front of a wide desk, dressed in a black T-shirt and black jeans. Young. He could be anyone. Except he wasn't anyone and he wasn't even what they were looking at. The bank of screens filled the entire wall. Up there many, many games were playing, making up an ever-changing mosaic of little coloured tiles, all carefully shaded and arranged to make up a face. The face of the man coming to meet them. A face they both knew. Dark hair, swept back from a deep widow's peak, straight black brows, blue-black eyes, long nose, full mouth with the lips curving between a sneer or a smile. They were curving upwards now.

He came towards them. His arms were tanned and muscular, as though he worked out. The long side whiskers had been shaped and cut close to his cheeks; his short beard sculpted to chin and upper lip. He wore a chunky watch, an expensive one; leather bands circled his other wrist, braided and embossed, which went with the black jeans and black tee. Very twenty-first century but Rogue nonetheless.

"I see you recognize me. I go under different names—as you do, my dear—but you can call me Rogue for old times' sake."

Emily. She was Emily now. Her true self in a world beyond anything she, or any of them, could have imagined. It was strange to see him the same but so different. Her mind was full to overflowing with wonders. And questions. But what was the point in asking questions? Logic and proportion had disappeared a long time ago.

"Have you no questions?" he asked. Disappointed. Disconcerted. As though he could guess what she was thinking. "Don't you want to know why I brought you here?"

She stared back at him, anticipating his sigh of impatience. He'd answer them anyway.

"I wanted to see you again, my dear. Tom was my Gulliver, voyaging to unknown lands. He found you there. Not something I foresaw. A happy accident, you might say. Now, he has brought you to me. Welcome to my world. Sit." He indicated two deep chairs with a wave of his hand. "I've arranged a little tour and you might as well be comfortable."

He took a seat next to them. The chairs were arranged in a semicircle facing the bank of screens that flickered with a myriad of games all playing at the same time.

One of the windows began to grow and expand until it filled the whole screen. Then it got bigger, until the room they were sitting in disappeared altogether.

CHAPTER THIRTY

ZOMBIE APOCALYPSE

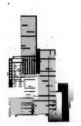

Tom and Emily were alone, standing together on a high ridge, a lookout. A hot dry wind whined in their ears and tugged at their clothes. They instinctively reached for each other's hand and moved closer together.

The landscape was familiar. It was like the country they'd been flown over in the helicopter. Why waste good graphics? A plain stretched out before them, its distance lost in a brown haze. In the foreground was a town of red and grey roofs, a main street running through it, with traffic lights swinging in the wind, still changing from red to green, but nothing was moving; no traffic and no one to be seen. It had a deserted, empty look about it. The sky had an unhealthy aspect, the clouds bulging down, purple as a bruise, yellowish at the edges. A bad sky was a bad sign. Tom focused on the far distance, squinting his eyes. The remains of a city, towers and tall buildings, black and broken, like tree stumps after a forest fire, windows empty, fretted against the sky.

Tom felt the first spots of rain on his arm. It stung. Acid, no doubt. Had that caused this apocalyptic devastation, or was it caused by it? *Who knows? Who cares?* That was not how these games worked. You were just *there*.

Something had caused it, that's what mattered. That—and the stinging rain.

He looked around. There were woods behind them. They could find shelter there. Although maybe it was a kind of survivalist scenario. Heavily armed groups making a life, fighting it out for scarce resources. They seldom welcomed newcomers, unless as a source of food. It could be some kind of cannibal game—where they'd be hunted, captured, kept in a hut, fattened for the barbecue. He didn't fancy that. They'd have to be careful. Use their wits. Find weapons from somewhere...

"Rogue sent us here?" Emily found that she was whispering, as if he could hear.

"It's not him," Tom whispered back. "It's an avatar."

She frowned. "The manifestation of a god in human form?"

"Not exactly." Although the original definition might be accurate in this case. Tom tried to explain. "In my world it means something a bit different. It's the graphical representation of a person. In a game, you take on a character—it becomes your avatar. Like in Glass Town, Augusta is your avatar. Rogue is—"

"My brother's."

"Exactly."

"Lord Charles is Charlotte's, so is Zenobia. Johnny Lockhart is me. Well, not me precisely. A version of me."

"So, you can be more than one person. It's the same here. There's someone behind this. The Game Master.

That's who we met. He's taken on Rogue as his avatar. We have to figure out what he's about—"

Tom broke off what he was saying, nostrils flaring, picking up the vile stench of rotting human flesh.

"There are people. Down there."

She put her hand over her mouth as the smell grew stronger.

Tom gave out a groan. Zombies. He hated zombies worst of all.

They were labouring up the slope, a whole lot of them, probably the population from the deserted township below. Dressed in suits and regular clothes. Zombies were always in collar and tie; Tom never knew why. They had the usual chunks knocked off them; grey skin, or black and peeling; empty sockets; bits of skull showing, along with half a jawbone and a line of teeth. They always walked with that lurching gait, and nothing stopped them—not guns nor any kind of weapon; it just knocked off more chunks, removed a limb or two—they always came lurching on.

"What *are* they?" Emily stared, caught between horror and fascination.

"Dead people walking."

"But, how?"

Tom shook his head. "Don't ask for reasons. There are no reasons."

"What are we going to do?"

"Run!" He held her hand tighter. "Find shelter. Somewhere they can't get to us. Zombies are really stupid, literally mindless, but it's best not to get caught out in the open."

They found a hut, deep in the woods. It was falling apart and wouldn't hold for long, but it would give them some kind of breathing space—as long as it wasn't a cannibal lair. Tom looked around. No sign of any other occupation. Not for a long time, anyway. The hut appeared to be long abandoned, with paper peeling off the walls, only a few sticks of furniture. Tom broke a piece up: a chair leg was better than nothing.

Soon enough, the rotting flesh smell heralded their presence.

Fire. *Zombies don't like fire.* There was an old lighter on the mantelpiece. Tom prayed it would work. He tried it, spun the wheel once, twice.

They were prowling round now, making groaning zombie noises. It would have been funny if this wasn't for real—if they couldn't hurt you, and turn you into a zombie. But that could happen. That was the game's USP. Then you'd be lurching around here for ever with the rest of the rotting crew.

Tom spun the lighter again. His hands were shaking, which wasn't helping, but this time it worked. He looked around. A lamp on the table. *It might hold kerosene.*

The thing about zombies was that they were really dumb. They depended on numbers and the fact that they were dead already so they couldn't be killed. They were all trying to get in at once, pushing at the door with their zombie numbers, ripping at the flimsy wood with their zombie strength. Blackened, bony fingers curling round gaps in the wood.

The smell was getting worse. Tom grimaced; he really hated zombies.

See how they like this.

He threw the lamp like a petrol bomb. It exploded in front of the door, flames shooting up the dry wood, catching all those reaching arms and groping fingers.

There was a chorus of zombie howls, shrieks and yelps. They certainly didn't like fire.

"Quick—out the back."

He grabbed Emily's hand. Zombies never thought to check for other ways out. They were all out at the front, dancing about, suits on fire, the remains of their flesh burning like candle wax. They would come back as blackened burnt things, but not for a while.

Tom and Emily ran up the slope behind the house, creating distance. There was a building up there, through the trees.

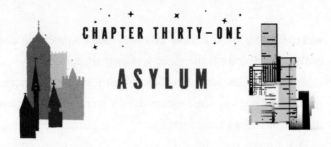

CHAPTER THIRTY-ONE

ASYLUM

THE DOOR CREAKED OPEN on an abandoned asylum or hospital, or something. Of course. It would be. Big, high ceilings, ancient signage, long corridors with rooms going off, beds rusting in halls. Plenty of places to hide. Plenty of places for other things to hide, too.

"I don't like it here." Emily shivered.

"I don't think you're supposed to."

Tom sniffed. The place smelt of nothing worse than damp and decay. No one had been here for a long time; there were trees growing through the floor. He checked the downstairs rooms to be sure, though. Long wards with more rusting bedsteads, tiled wet rooms, basins bearded with stains from dripping taps. The house was a trap in itself, with rotten floorboards and crumbling brickwork. The stairs were a no go. He cocked an ear. Something was up there, stirring, rustling. There always was.

They couldn't stay here. Tom pulled back mildewed curtains. A fragment of glass left in the frame jabbed into his hand as he made a gap in the rotten plyboarded windows. This room must have been a staff lounge, with its high ceilings, leather armchairs, heavy wooden furnishings. Looked like the rats had been at the chairs and the panelling was springing off the walls. No sign of the zombie hoards, but the creaking on the stairs was getting louder.

"Not my best idea," he said. "Let's get out of here."

The heavy wooden outer doors were closed against them. Of course they were.

Tom went back into the room they'd just left, picked up a chair and threw it through the window. The boarding gave way under the impact but it just meant easy access for the zombies who were now massing, blackened and still smouldering, in what must have been the car park, and were lowing and groaning in the way they do when they sense warm flesh.

"Wow! They got a move on!"

He grabbed Emily's hand. They would have to make a break for it.

Out in the hall, weird white creatures were leaning over the banisters, long hair wisped round faces with empty sockets, withered skin, black holes and skeletal grins; long arms reaching, bony hands with yellow nails, long and sharp, like claws. They were keening and moaning, like ghosts do. It was such an old-school cliché it would even have been funny, except that Tom could smell their long-dead graveyard smell, musty and mouldy; not the ripe and rotten, spoilt meat stench of the zombies, but the smell of ancient decay.

The cut on his hand hurt and it was bleeding. This was the same as Glass Town. You could die here. There were a whole lot of the ghost things and those yellow clawlike nails would do damage. And that wasn't the worst that could happen. He could hear the zombies tearing at the woodwork. Ghost or zombie? He didn't want to end up part of the game.

Basements weren't always a good idea, but this time it was inspired. Tom had noticed the little door when he was making his inspection of the ground-floor rooms. He jammed a handy mop against the door to deter followers. The stairs were pretty rickety but held their weight. The basement was a mess of abandoned furniture, pipes and old plumbing. At least there were no coffins that he could see. That would rule vampires out. Tom broke off a length of lead, testing the weight of it on his hand. It might be a handy weapon.

There was a smeary light coming through small windows set above ground level. He wondered how long it would be before they saw zombie faces peering down at them. Pipes, hung with rotten lagging and cobwebs, ran down tunnels under the building. It looked dark down there. Tom could see pinpoints of red and hear ominous squeaking. Rats. Tom flicked the lighter and wondered how long it would last but it looked like their best bet.

"Come on."

He took Emily's hand and led her on down. Soon all light was gone apart from the flicker of the lighter. The red points were growing, the squeaking becoming louder; the rats were getting bolder.

It was wet underfoot. They were soon splashing through water. The pipes had gone. The tunnel was brick lined. They were in a culvert of some kind. The flame of the lighter was getting smaller; just when it was about to give out altogether, Emily caught his arm.

"Look! Up ahead!"

They waded on, sloshing towards a greying of the darkness. Faint but there nevertheless. They came to a turn in the tunnel; from there they could see a distant semicircle of daylight. Tom glanced back. Nothing seemed to be following them.

They walked on, hand in hand, and finally came to the brick-rimmed exit of a culvert. The stream gleamed in the sunlight, chuckling over stones, through overhanging willows. They followed the stream past a children's play area until they came to a low bridge.

Tom helped Emily up on to the road and looked about, trying to figure out where they were now. The road was narrow, no kerbs, and tarmacked. The sky was blue above them, but he couldn't see any sun. The air was warm, still; there was the noise of humming insects, but otherwise no sounds. No birds, no animals, no children on the swings and roundabouts, no people anywhere that he could see, although there were houses set back from the road with cars in the driveways. He thought maybe they were in one of those American suburbs that they had recently been flying over: ranch-style houses, double garages, all with their own yards. A country where space wasn't a problem.

They began to walk along the road. There was a bus stop up ahead and a bench with a backpack on it. Right around the corner, a bike lay abandoned in the road. A bit further on, a car had slewed into the verge. Strangeness on strangeness. A shopping trolley on its side outside a minimart, groceries spilling on the ground. Shop door open; nobody inside.

"Did you see that?" Emily asked. "Little golden lights dancing like fireflies, but when you look again, they vanish."

Tom nodded—he'd seen them, too. "Could mark where something happened. Someone disappeared. Or could be a guide to a place that holds clues, or a warning—a place to be avoided."

They went on walking. There was no sense of immediate threat, but the silence made the everyday ordinariness sinister.

Another bicycle, lying on the pavement, the wheels turning, as though a kid had just left it.

They walked past a deserted garage and auto shop. Doors wide open, cars up on ramps, but no mechanics in sight.

"Hello?" Tom called. "Anyone home?"

No answer.

"Let's try one of the houses," Emily suggested.

Same thing: doors open but empty. Kids' toys strewn about, breakfast things on the table. Tom put his hand on the kettle. Still warm. Like whoever lived here had just popped out, but the whole town was like that…

Tom looked round warily. *Is this part of the old game? Are they all going to lurch into view as zombies? Or is this some new thing?*

"Maybe it's some kind of Rapture," he said.

"What's that?"

"An end-of-the-world scenario. All the Faithful are whipped up to Heaven."

"What happens to the rest of them?"

"Apocalypse. Like we've just seen. Once the Believers are safe out of the way, the world is destroyed by war, fire and famine."

Emily nodded. She knew the scripture. She'd seen the etchings of John Martin's paintings.

"And they make a game of this?"

"Why not?" Tom shrugged. "You can make a game out of anything. We don't know if that is what's going on here. Sometimes there's clues as to what's happened, like those little lights dancing. In the game you go round collecting them to find out."

"So why don't we do that?"

"We don't have time for it." Tom spread his hands. "We don't know what they are, or even how the game works. It could take for ever…"

"We do know how the game works," Emily said. "If you know who made it, you know how it works. There's a mind behind the Avatar Rogue. I don't know him, but I do know Rogue. He's driven by two things: vanity and viciousness, in almost equal measure."

"Avatar Rogue—I like that." Tom smiled his appreciation. "He's got us running around in these games like rats in a maze."

"'Game' is a good name for it. He'll keep moving us around like pieces on a board until we're exhausted."

"Or dead."

Emily shook her head. "I don't think so. I don't think he'll want that to happen. Frightened, yes. Petrified. Terrorized, certainly, but I don't think dead. That could play to our advantage. It may be the only one we have."

"So what do we do?"

"The unexpected. It's always best to do the unexpected."

"Which is?"

"Nothing. We do nothing. Stay here." She went to the taps and turned them on and off. "The water's hot! I'm going to have a bath. Find different clothes. There must be some here."

"How do you know?"

"There's a picture of a boy and girl on the wall over there. They look like us."

Tom went over and picked it up. So they did. It was like Avatar Rogue had made a home for them in this deserted place where nobody lived. There was something creepy about that.

"Maybe he wants to keep us here." Tom felt goosebumps travel up his arms. "Like pets."

"Maybe. We don't know what he wants, do we? But I know I want a bath."

"There must be a bathroom upstairs," Tom said. "You go first."

The shower worked. Tom showed Emily how to use it and the shower gel and shampoo. She was in there a long time.

There was a girl's room, clothes laid out ready, as if she'd been expected. There was a guy's room down the corridor. He looked around. It was a replica of his room at home. The clothes were his clothes. Not *his* clothes exactly, but in his size and makes and labels he favoured. The weirdness made the goosebumps spread from his arms to the hairs on the back of his neck.

He heard her leave the bathroom then he went for a shower. There was a first aid kit in the cabinet with antiseptic cream and plasters. He put a dressing on his hand, changed into jeans and a sweatshirt and went downstairs. He sat on the sofa and picked up the remote. Maybe what was playing on the TV would give him a clue.

A blue light glowed on the DVD player. The disc drawer came out and went back in again. A home movie came on the screen. Him and Emily, walking by the little river, holding hands, laughing together. He turned it off quickly.

"What was that?"

Emily was standing by the door. She looked completely different. Like a modern girl, in jeans and a sweater, her hair tied back in a ponytail.

"A…" Tom searched for the right word to explain it. "A moving picture. Of us. Here."

"Let me see." She sat down next to him.

He played the DVD. It was them—or it looked like them—walking by the river, playing on the swings, sitting on the bench by the bus stop, walking hand in hand up to this house. Like they lived here, or had always lived here, or always would live here…

"What's it doing?" Emily frowned as the DVD player began to whir.

"It's on a loop. It's starting again." Tom turned it off.

"What is it for?" Emily looked around. "What does it mean?"

"Maybe it's meant to spook us."

"Spook? A ghost?"

Tom shook his head. "Frighten, disturb."

"Oh, I see." Emily smiled. "Like seeing a ghost, you mean?"

"Exactly."

"What do you do if you see a ghost?"

"Run away."

"Well, that's what we are not going to do. Rogue was never known for his patience. If we stop playing, we change the game. What else can you see on the moving-picture machine?"

"I don't know." Tom picked up the remote.

"You know how it works, though?" Emily stretched out her legs. "Make it work for me."

CHAPTER THIRTY-TWO

THE GAME MASTER

HE WENT TO OTHER PLACES, but this was his favourite. Coffee-opolis. Corny name but he liked it. A little independent, fair-trade place, with red and white decor, wooden tables and counters, big, bright murals, vines growing up the far wall. Cookie jars on the counter, gluten-free brownies and muffins, cupcakes and granola bars. Coffee made any way you want it, herb teas, juices and smoothies served by pretty young baristas wearing T-shirts with slogans like *But first, coffee*, *Life begins with coffee* and *Coffee: always a good idea*. He came here often, laptop in his backpack, no different from a hundred other guys in a hundred other coffee shops all over the town, all tapping away, dreaming of their start-ups, the big break, the money they were going to make. He either worked here, or in the sleepy little branch library around the corner from his apartment. It was quieter there—the librarian was strict about no disturbances— but sometimes he liked people around him; liked the anonymity.

He was the Game Master aka Sinbad, founder and owner of Magic Carpet, the darknet empire, but nobody here knew that. He was hiding in plain sight, known only by his choice of coffee, which changed from coffee shop to coffee shop, chain to chain.

He took his usual spot in the corner, back to the wall, and had a look around, like he always did. Being careful had become second nature, but no one stood out. A few guys like him, lost in their laptops, a table of hockey moms fresh from the gym, drinking herb teas.

There was a trainee barista, but the usual girl made his coffee. She knew him, knew his order: decaf soy latte in his keep cup. He liked her—she was pretty, with brown eyes and a shiny ponytail, and she always smiled at him. She was smiling now as she brought his coffee over and stamped his loyalty card.

He powered up his laptop. He sipped his soy latte. Time to check what was happening. There were many sides to his business but only one interested him right now.

He clicked through the files. *Zombie Apocalypse, Asylum, Deserted Village*. Nothing special about the games. Standard. Generic, even. Tom would've recognized them, in type if not specifics. Innovation wasn't the name of *this* game. He wanted gamers to choose their favourites from what was familiar to them.

Spooked by the *Lost Village* video, Tom and Emily should have reached *Terrorist Train*. He clicked on the file. It was still in the *Lost Village* station. Blood seeping down on to the track. Nice detail, that. Perhaps they'd already boarded. He took a view down through the carriages.

Corpses in place, sprawled across the seats and into the aisle, blood pooling and running across the floor. Flies buzzing. He couldn't access it here, but there would be the smell: the slightest hint of decay under the metallic reek of fresh blood mixed with cordite.

He took his view into the next carriage. Two men standing in the aisle, AK-47s pointing up, balanced on their hips. All in black, faces scarfed, heads swathed, webbing over their combats, sewn with pouches and all wired up. Ready to go. Except the game hadn't been triggered. Neither had *Grand Theft Auto*—there were always two ways to go. That was a shame. He almost felt sorry that Tom hadn't had a chance to test himself there. He had a feeling the boy would have been good.

He sat back. His latte was cold, so he ordered another. He clicked back. They were still in the village playing happy families. Their reluctance to engage was frustrating. He'd have to send in special forces to extract them. He was tempted to dump them in a war zone; he had plenty of scenarios to choose from, anything from Roman Legions to World War Three. Something with modern battlefield action: tanks and gunships. See how they liked that. But there had been some suspicious traffic on the site lately.

He looked around again. The hockey moms had been replaced by a younger crew with strollers. A boy and a girl who looked like college students were setting themselves up to work together. The girl smiled, so he smiled back.

Best to be sociable. Nothing exceptional. No one out of the ordinary.

He relaxed and turned back to his laptop. He began to click keys. Time to collect them and have them brought to his own favourite place to be.

CHAPTER THIRTY-THREE

GOTHAM CITY

THEY WERE FLYING OVER a crowded cityscape fretted against a dark and stormy sky; the setting sun gleamed sulphur yellow through clouds of gunmetal grey. Crooked lines of lightning cast a lurid glow over a sprawl of tall buildings, monolithic structures stepped like ziggurats, row houses, factory chimneys, warehouses and storage facilities, long canyons between skyscrapers, twisting alleys leading to the docks. Rain spread and streaked across the windscreen in front of them. Rain and darkness; the vintage look of it, art deco with noirish touches.

A powerful searchlight intermittently swept the sky. To Emily it looked like an inverted "W", but Tom recognized it as the Bat Signal. This was Gotham City.

The craft landed and they stepped out on to a wide-roofed terrace. Carved gargoyles: devils, dragons and mythical beasts jutted out from the corners of the building, their scaly stone wings spread, claws and teeth bared at the city streets that ran far, far below.

"Welcome back."

Avatar Rogue stepped out from the open doors of a glass dome set into the roof. Rogue in a sharp suit, channelling Bruce Wayne rather than the Caped Crusader.

"I hope you enjoyed my little tour. You were in no real danger, of course." He looked at Tom. "You acquitted yourself well. I had more treats in store, but time grows short. I'm almost ready to put my plans into action. Soon I will be welcoming many more to join me. Gotham City will be a popular destination. The gamers who come here can be part of this world. They will be in the game. Part of it." He stared out at the darkened cityscape. "Isn't that what people have always wanted? Since the first shadow plays on cave walls? Haven't we always wanted to be *in* the story, from listening to the storyteller sitting by the fire, to reading a novel, watching a film or box set, playing a game? Isn't it all the same desire to escape from the everyday, the mundane? Not just as a spectator, as part of the action. The all-round experience. No screens, no barriers. To be able to smell and feel as well as hear and see. What if you could live in the story for ever? What if it *became* your world?"

Tom felt a deep chill. He remembered the screens playing in Avatar Rogue's Silicon Valley headquarters. It wasn't just zombies and superheroes. Some of the games he'd seen up there were for much younger players: *Zoo World*, *Sally's Farm*, *Izzy Bizzy*—his little cousin played those and she was three years old.

Tom shook his head. "This is crazy. This has to stop."

Rogue ignored Tom, addressing Emily, his eyes intense, burning. "You must understand, if anybody can."

"Oh, I understand." Emily stared back at him. "And I agree with Tom."

"Crazy or not, it is going to happen. I'm going to change the world as we know it. Roll this out to the gaming population. I have amassed millions of contacts, names, addresses—"

"Amassed?" Tom laughed. "You mean hacked."

"How I came by them is no matter. Soon, everyone on my database will be getting one of these through the post." He held up a small plastic box. "It contains the Echeneis strip, just like the one you have, Tom. Its use will spread like wildfire via social media. Millions upon millions, the youth of the world and older, will be checking out of this life and into another."

"Will they be able to escape?" Tom thought of his own predicament, the helplessness he felt.

"Why would they want to escape? Would you not rather be here than in your hospital bed?"

"And if they are hurt—die, even?" Tom felt the throb of the cut on his hand, the ache of the bullet wound in his shoulder.

Avatar Rogue's voice became cold. "That's the choice they make."

"Why are you doing it? To hold the world to ransom?"

"For money, you mean?" He laughed. "I don't need money. I have more money than I could spend in a lifetime. Several lifetimes."

"So why then?"

"Because I can. I'll be doing mankind a favour. Providing an escape from everyday boredom. People are spending more than nine hours a day online. Well, now they can live there. A virtual life—so much more exciting. Wouldn't you agree, Tom? Or would you rather be back in that bed? Do you have nothing to say?"

What is the use of arguing? Tom felt all the strength leach from him, as if he really was back in hospital, unable to move.

"Your silence speaks for you. No power on earth can stop me! Least of all you. You brought Emily to me, so you are of no more use to me. I could send you off to battle through one world after another, or down to the streets below to be perpetually hunted, but I will be merciful. I'm deactivating the Echeneis that my associate inserted and sending you back to your own world. Such as it is." He turned to Emily. "You and I will work here together. With your mind, your *imagination*, there is nothing we can't do."

Before Avatar Rogue could touch her, Emily took Tom's hand and ran to the very edge of the roof. She steadied herself on the stone back of the rearing, fork-tongued gryphon, his stone face soot-stained and streaked as if his red eye was weeping for the city below. She looked out for a moment. It was like Glass Town but greater and more decayed. Dark and dirty, with a perpetual rain falling, all shades of black and grey. Stay here? With him?

She stepped out, taking Tom with her, and they began to fall into the shadow.

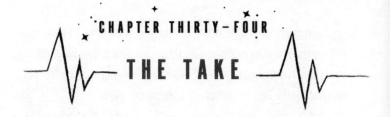

No!

The scene he'd been viewing had disappeared. The screen was black. He stared at the blankness, uncomprehending. Hit keys.

Nothing doing.

Then two letters appeared inside an oval, black on white:

M ♦ M
This site has been shut down.
Enquiries will be redirected.
Nice working with you.
Milo

Before he had time to react, before he had time to take in what he was seeing, or even register that the message was in Greek, one of the young moms leapt over to grab his laptop, and the trainee barista and the smiley student girl were cuffing him.

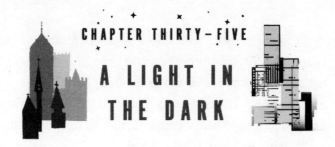

CHAPTER THIRTY-FIVE

A LIGHT IN THE DARK

THEY NEVER HIT THE GROUND. No dark glitter of glass, no sidewalk rushing up to meet them. The gothic streetscape—the soaring skyscrapers and narrow canyons, dark towers and monoliths, monuments, mansions and civic buildings—had disappeared. They were in a darkness so absolute it seemed physical. Solid. Like they were falling through soot, or Indian ink.

Tom didn't know where Avatar Rogue was. He might have been flying next to them, batwings extended, but he didn't think so. He was pretty sure they were completely alone. As alone as it is possible to be in this world or any other. His grip on Emily's hand tightened. At least they had each other.

The blackness went on and on. There was no light. No light anywhere. A total eclipse, like all the light in the world had gone out. A blackness so complete you couldn't tell whether your eyes were shut or open. Tom felt fear close around him like the darkness. This was how he'd felt after his accident. But he could touch. He could feel. And he was not alone. Emily's hand in his was warm and clutching on so hard that her nails were making him wince. He was glad of the pain.

"I'm frightened," she said, not an emotion he'd ever heard her express before. She spoke in a whisper, as though the admission had been dragged out of her.

"Me, too," Tom whispered back and put his arm round her. Whatever was happening here, they were in it together.

"What's happened?" she asked.

"I... I really don't know," he answered.

He thought he knew, but had no idea how to explain it to her. All the places they'd been, ever since Glass Town (and how real was that?)—none of it had been real. It had all been computer generated. He suspected that the system had crashed.

"Wait. There's a light." Emily looked down at the bracelet she wore. On the inside of her wrist, the stone was giving off a faint, greenish glow. As they watched, it grew stronger. "Perhaps we can use it to see our way out of here?"

"The light's not strong enough for that."

Tom shook his head. He didn't want to say it, but even a battery of klieg lights wouldn't be strong enough. He didn't think there *was* a way out of here. They were trapped in some kind of cyber limbo. The darkness that engulfed them could go on for ever.

EVIL TECHIE GENIUS TAKEN DOWN
Dark Web Empire Uncovered

MILO SCROLLED THROUGH the headlines with satisfaction and pride. It didn't matter that he'd been deeply involved, up to his neck in it—he'd done the correct thing, right? Gone to the Feds, helped with their investigation, shopped Sinbad, the guy behind it all, the one he'd been working for, and earned immunity from prosecution, which was something, since pretty much all he'd worked for had gone pear-shaped and he'd been hit where it hurt—in his pocket.

So he might have merited a *Well done, Milo. You did the right thing there, Milo. Saved the day*, but no. She was still looking at him like something unpleasant she'd found in the tread of her trainer.

"What were you expecting?" Lucy said as she stirred the chocolate into her cappuccino.

They were in the hospital cafeteria. Milo was here most days now and they'd taken to having coffee together.

"You only did what any decent human being would do." She gave a half-smile. "Given what you were before, that is some sort of achievement, I guess."

"What do you mean?" Milo sat up in his seat. "I saved the world from *Mindcraft Apocalypse* and all that other dark-web stuff he was operating. I'm a hero! A lot of people were seriously upset. I've had death threats. All sorts. Well," he said, stirring sugar into his coffee, "I would have if they knew who I was."

He'd stolen a goodly amount of data from Magic Carpet, and M & M Enterprises was about to go global with Magic Carpet Reloaded, but he wasn't going to tell her that.

"How did you do it? Correction: how did you get away with it?"

"You wouldn't understand."

"Try me."

"OK. I knew the Feds were after Magic Carpet—it's not just this world domination gaming thing. Magic Carpet would supply anything: drugs, guns, people, you name it. My job was to keep them out—the Feds, I mean, or any other hostiles sniffing about. I was a trusted employee, a trusted lieutenant, one of Sinbad's merry voyagers."

"Sinbad?"

"Yeah. He's the guy behind it. That's his username. I knew how the whole thing worked. Sinbad's personal tag was Asmo. All I had to do was find out who he *really* was. A techie living in San Francisco, it turns out. I passed that on to the Feds. They caught him in a coffee shop, machine open—Fed speak for red-handed."

"So, you saved the world. What about Tom? Can you save him, too?"

"That's trickier…"

"How?"

"Well, there never was a way to bring people *back* again." Milo sipped his coffee. "That was Asmo's vision. His whole idea, good or bad. You're there for ever." Milo pushed his chair back and looked round. "I'm starving. Fancy some chips? They do good ones here."

"God, Milo!" Lucy rolled her eyes. "You really don't care!"

"I do care, as it happens, or I wouldn't be here."

She left Milo dipping his chips in ketchup and mayo. The two got mixed together. He really was a disgusting individual. He'd got Tom into this thing with no way to get him out of it again—even less so now that Evil Techie Genius, who presumably *might* know, was behind bars.

"He's not going to be any help," she said to Joe when she got back to the ward. "No help at all."

"Go home." Joe smiled at her. "You look tired. Nothing more you can do here. Give me your number. I'll text you if there's any change."

Joe stayed, looking down at Tom. There was no alteration in the boy's condition and he wasn't expecting one any time soon. He was further away if anything. He didn't know what Milo had done to him, but this was the nearest he'd seen to a spirit journey and Tom was travelling far. *How long has he been like this?* Joe did a quick calculation. Soon he would be beyond reach.

CHAPTER THIRTY-SEVEN
THE LIGHT WEB

Tom and Emily held hands. The only small, faint light was from Emily's wrist. She held it up. The glow seemed to strengthen. Glowing like that, it really did look like some kind of smartwatch or Fitbit. *But how can that be? The Fairish woman had given it to her—where would she have got hold of that kind of technology?*

"The light's getting stronger," Emily was saying. "Don't you think?"

He nodded. "Seems to be."

Tom blinked. He didn't want to believe it, didn't want to cling on to straws, but it was definitely brightening, the green light washing over Emily's face, giving her an eerie, otherworldly beauty. He frowned. It was like it was some kind of face recognition software...

The stone was changing from pale jade to piercing emerald. Emily dropped her wrist and luminous green lines ran out across the darkness, marking a path, like the emergency lights on the floor of an aeroplane cabin.

They looked at each other. Tom shrugged. There was nothing to do but to follow.

They kept their eyes on the glowing green path. Their heads were filled with white noise, a kind of roaring, as if of the sea, although they could see nothing. Either side was a black void.

Time did not exist, so they couldn't be sure how long they went on like this—it could have been days, minutes, a lifetime. At last, some way in front of them, they could see a luminous, nebulous cloud. As they moved nearer, the mist began to separate into strands, each made up of many tiny lights like strings of jewels: ruby, carnelian, topaz, emerald, sapphire, amethyst. They were being led into a great, intricately woven, three-dimensional web, like some celestial dreamcatcher extending all around them, as deep as they could see beneath them and way above their heads, going on and on, all around and outwards in all directions, turning with distance to bright, shining white light. They were cradled by infinity.

The web felt strange under their feet, strong but insubstantial. Both of them staggered slightly, struggling to find their balance. It was like walking a safety net over the void.

"It takes a little getting used to," a voice behind them said.

They turned to see the Fairish Lady gliding towards them. She held up her wrist. The bracelet she wore there gave off a light of its own.

"It brought you to me. True Thomas. Emily." She reached out as the net of light swayed under them. "It is quite safe. You grow accustomed to it."

"What is this?" Tom asked. "Where are we?"

"Between Heaven and Earth." She took their hands and led them across the pulsating, radiating lines of light. "This is the Light Web. We've found our place. Our space. There was nowhere left for us in the lower world: humankind has filled all the wild places, our glens and valleys; our rings, mounds and knolls bulldozed and built over; our green paths turned into motorways. So we have made our home here, in what you call cyberspace, between Heaven and Earth. It extends far further than you know. There are no limits. It attracted us from its very beginnings. It has grown and grown and will go on growing. You have created it, so it reflects your collective mind. Wild and undisciplined, full of good things and bad things in almost equal measure. Good and evil, constantly duelling with each other, as they have for time out of mind."

"Did you free us?" Tom asked.

The Lady shook her head. "Someone else did that. Someone from your world. I can find no trace of your enemy. He seems to have disappeared, along with most of the sites he controlled. We rarely act directly. The Light Web acts like a dream snare, holding on to the bad, letting through the good. Do you see the larger lights where the lines meet? Each of those is a site, or a person, we support in one way or another—though they don't know it, of course. They think that it is Providence, or the Universe, or synchronicity, but we help those who are helping to spread goodness, wisdom, light. Healers, teachers, shamans, believers—young, some of them, very young; others old—all ancient souls who have come to recognize the power for good that this thing you call the internet contains. It is strange: the more material your world becomes, the more people seek for something 'other'. These wise ones provide just that. We help to connect, that's all—allow the word to be spread, give guidance, help to light the way."

"How do you do that?" Tom asked.

"We monitor social media, looking for likely causes and candidates. That's what this is partly about." She indicated the intricate web of light around them. "When we find someone, they receive help with their project. Always anonymously, but no one turns down money." She laughed. "Or at least, they haven't yet. We also help with crowdfunding. We have a charitable foundation in your world that supports many, many causes. Some of our number are among you, passing as rich, philanthropic individuals who are happy to invest, to lend a helping hand. My brother is there now."

"How do you fund all that?"

"Anything to do with the Fair Folk is very popular," she said. "Our sites do very well."

Tom looked at Emily and wondered what those wide grey eyes were making of all this. He was finding it hard to take in, but at least he knew what the Lady was talking about when it came to the internet. He needn't have worried. Emily was treating it a little like the helicopter and all the other strange things that had come after, one following another. With interest and not a little wonder, but with acceptance, too. That is how things are.

The Lady smiled as she saw the look that passed between them.

"Don't worry," she said, as though she could read Tom's mind. "Emily's imagination is so wide, she can take anything in her stride."

Emily smiled back. This was no stranger than any of the places that Tom had shown her. She didn't fully understand what they were talking about—didn't need to; her eyes were fixed on the weave of colours pulsing across the web of light. Her capacity for unquestioning wonder was as wide as her imagination, and that was infinite. It made no difference whether she was out on the moors at night, looking at the stars, or here, wherever this place was. Looking for meaning, explanation, would only dull the shining, pulsing brilliance around her, consign it to the ditch of ordinariness. But the Light Web was surrounded by darkness, just like the stars in the night sky. "*Good and evil*," the Lady had said, "*constantly duelling with each other.*" Rogue would always be somewhere...

Glass Town. How little she'd thought about it, so caught up had she been in what had been happening—and with no way clear way back to it, there had been little point. Now that things had changed, anything could have happened there, but she wouldn't know.

"We have to get back to Glass Town," she said. "Can you help us?"

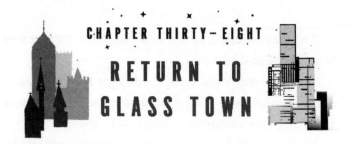

CHAPTER THIRTY-EIGHT

RETURN TO GLASS TOWN

"Where have you been?" Annie's brown eyes grew wide with wonder. There were tears there, joy and relief mixed together. "We've heard that many rumours. That you was tack off by Rogue. *He's* disappeared wi' that Zenobia, looks like. That you run away wi' that soldier lad, Tom. Even took by the Fairish—imagine…" Annie sniffed and dashed a hand at her cheeks. "Here's me tacking on. Are you safe, my lady? Are you sound?"

"Quite safe, Annie." Augusta took her hands. "Quite sound."

"And you, milad?" she said to Tom.

"I'm fine, too," he replied.

At the sound of their voices, the yelping and whining at the door became a deep-throated roaring; scratching turned to a battering attack.

"He's pined summat chronic," Annie said. "Wouldn't eat. Howling all day, all night, piteous to hear. Wouldn't let no one near him. We had to lock him up, he were that wild."

Tom opened the door and Keeper bounded in, swinging his big head from side to side, his jaws clamped by an iron muzzle.

"Douro's orders," Annie explained. "It was either that or he'd have had him shot."

His skin hung loose on the bones of his huge frame and he whined like a pup when Augusta knelt to remove the muzzle. She cast the ugly thing aside and put her arms round the dog. He whined softly, nuzzling at her, licking her face with his rough tongue, then he gave the same greeting to Tom, nearly knocking him over, planting his big paws on Tom's shoulders.

"Whoa!" Tom laughed and put his arms round the dog. "Let's get you down to the kitchen—find you something proper to eat that's not me."

"'Appen they'll have plenty there," Annie said as they went to the kitchen. "The Duke were due to hold a state banquet. Now he's gone back to 'is estate, and wi' that Mina Laury… 'looking after him'… well, that's what they're calling it. Douro's gone off to found a whole new country—going to call it Angria, so they say. Good riddance, I say."

"So if the Duke and Douro have gone and Rogue's disappeared…" Augusta frowned. "Who's in charge?"

Before Annie could answer, Lord Charles Wellesley came sweeping into the kitchen.

"Speak of the devil," she said quietly.

"What's that, Annie?"

"Nowt, milord." Annie sketched a very small curtsey. "I were just about to mention your name."

Lord Charles ignored her, his bright hazel eyes on Augusta.

"Augusta! My dear girl! Where have you been?"

"Well, I…" Augusta was at a complete loss as to how to explain the extraordinary set of adventures that had befallen her.

Luckily, Lord Charles didn't wait for an answer.

"You missed *all* the excitement. Rogue disappeared. We've put it about that he was banished by the Duke, but really we have no idea where he went and could not care less. He appears to have taken Zenobia with him." He gave a mock shudder. "A relief to everyone. Without him, his 'revolution' collapsed like a paper bag. Johnny Lockhart rallied the troops. Those ruffian bully boys Rogue calls his 'rare lads' beat a hasty retreat back to their kennels, the men they 'recruited' melting away by the second. Simplicity itself for Johnny to go in with some loyal troops and mop them up. It was all over in no time—hardly a shot fired. That Frenchie was sent packing back to Frenchiland with his hideous machine. The Duke caught wind and left for his country estate at first light, and Douro's decided he's had enough of Glass Town and has gone off somewhere to set up the New State of Angria. Leaving me and Johnny and a few others to run things here. We had a meeting in Bravey's: me, Johnny, Bud, Tree, the doctor, even Young Soult. Glass Town is to be a true democracy. The Tower of All Nations is to be renamed the Tower of the People and every citizen allowed a vote. Representatives of your Dark Lantern Men were there and some of the Original Twelve—Parry, Ross. It's all here in this morning's edition."

He gave Augusta a copy of the *Young Men's Magazine*. The story filled the front page under the headline *A Full Account of the Recent Momentous Events by Lord Charles Wellesley*.

"Parry and Ross, you said?" Augusta looked up from the paper.

"Yes, they're back." Lord Charles went on. "They've been back for a while, it seems. Rogue's black freighter was stopping them getting into the harbour. Then it was destroyed in a mysterious explosion, along with the rest of his pirate fleet. Parry and Ross and their sailors helped mop up elements of resistance down by the harbour before coming up here to lend a hand. All peaceful now."

Parry and Ross meant escape from Glass Town. Parry and Ross meant taking the North-west Passage through to the Pacific. That had been her dream, for weeks, months, years. All she'd wanted was to leave this place and establish a kingdom, a queendom, of her own. Gondal.

"They'll be sailing on the morning tide."

"So soon?"

"They are only waiting on your return." Lord Charles hesitated. "I know that to go with them was all you've wanted. All you've wished for. We would dearly like you to stay and help us build the new Glass Town Republic but I know it's not where your heart lies. It was never me who desired to stop you. Never me who didn't want you to go."

In her mind, she could see the ships moving slightly with the ebb and flow of the water; hear the lapping, the creak of rope and timber. What had seemed impossible for so long was here. A short walk away. All she had to do was take the steep slope down to the harbour. *Why would it be so hard to do?* Because of Tom. She looked up at him. He was thinking the same thing; she could see it in that slight creasing frown of his. He could come, too. Of course. It was so simple. She felt a great lightness and excitement as the idea caught her. They need never be apart. He would love it there. So much to find, so much to discover. Together. Always together. Pictures and plans tumbled after each other. A whole new world. Theirs alone.

From outside came the haunting refrain of the Moorishco. Obviously. She smiled as she took Tom's hands in hers. They would go out now and celebrate, then take ship on the morning tide.

"Don't mind me." Lord Charles strolled to the window, thumbs lodged in waistcoat pockets. "Moorishco are back for Fiesta, I see. The *People's* Fiesta." He peered out pointedly. "I'm blowed how they know…"

When he turned, he was alone apart from Keeper, gnawing on a great ox bone.

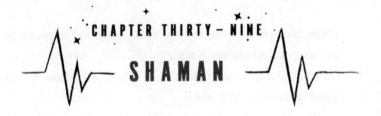

CHAPTER THIRTY-NINE

SHAMAN

JOE WAS IN THE HABIT of coming into Tom's room as often as he could. Not always because he had anything to do. Sometimes, he would just stand by the bed and watch him. He was not aware of any particular time passing.

When he looked up on this occasion, Lucy was in her usual place in the corner. She moved quieter than a spotted cat. She reminded him of the margay, his favourite among the jungle cats of his country: shy, solitary, clever and the prettiest of all.

He turned up his watch. "I'm due a break. Do you fancy a coffee?"

"Yes." She smiled. "OK."

"I'll meet you down there."

Lucy took the lift to the ground floor. The hospital was a bit of a maze but Lucy was used to negotiating the hubs and corridors. A woman rushed past her in tears, obviously the recipient of bad news; then a young couple, both heads bent towards a very small baby that they held between them in a carrycot. *That's what this place is about*, Lucy thought, as she walked past the little shops selling snacks, books and magazines, gifts and accessories. *Strip everything else away and it's about life and death, going on all the time, in the same place.*

Lucy got her soy latte and found a quiet corner in the Four Seasons coffee bar.

Soon Joe came over with his Americano. He took a sip and put his mug down again. "They always make coffee too hot," he said after a moment. "I want to try something, with Tom. Will you help me?"

"Of course. Anything," she said. "I'll do anything. What are you going to do?"

He didn't reply to that.

"I am a shaman," he said, stirring his coffee with a stick, making the black liquid swirl this way and that. He looked around. "I don't tell anybody here. They wouldn't understand."

Lucy looked down at her coffee, pleased that he would think that she did.

"In my country, among my people, we are born, not chosen. The women who delivered me knew as soon as I came into the world; my mother says she knew even before that. It's not an easy road, not one that parents wish for their child. You are respected, yes—treated with awe, even. But feared also, even hated." He laughed. "That's heavy for a little kid. Those who cure can kill; those who heal can harm. Isn't that what was said here about your own wise women, the ones that people called witches?"

Lucy nodded. She'd heard that.

"I come from a tiny village many miles from any city," he went on. "As I got older, I became restless. I wanted to see more of the world and I wanted to learn Western medicine. I went to Mexico City. I couldn't afford to become a doctor, so I enrolled to train as a nurse. The shaman can't cure everything." He laughed. "Sometimes vaccines, antibiotics work better."

"How did you end up here?"

"A girl." He smiled, his face lit with memory. "British, a doctor, working with an NGO. When she came back to the UK, I came with her."

"Are you still together?"

He shook his head and laughed again, but there was hurt there this time, a shine about his black eyes. "Nah. I travelled around a bit after we split but wound up back here."

"You said you want to try something with Tom?"

"Yes, I do. But I need you to be there. To keep watch. To make sure no one comes in. I can time it so's it won't coincide with doctors' rounds, and I'm in charge of his other care, but I need you to be there to stop anyone else."

"When will you do it?" she asked.

"I need time to prepare but it has to be soon. Evening visiting. Just before I go off shift. Tomorrow."

CHAPTER FORTY

THE PEOPLE'S FIESTA

THE LIGHT OF THE SETTING SUN was on the buildings, rose red and honey gold. The air was warm. Here and there, lights were showing, brightening in the gloaming. Fireflies danced in the corner of the square.

As the music started, she took his hand and held it high, then she slipped her arm round his waist and held him.

"Do you remember?"

"I remember," he said.

Whatever was happening in the morning, wherever she was going, he was going with her. What was the point in returning to real life? What real life? Lying in a hospital bed, tethered to machines that were doing the living for him? That was no life. He'd rather be dead...

He didn't have to say anything. He knew that she wanted what he wanted from the way she was looking at him, holding him, the closeness of her. She'd gone off with one of the Moorishco girls and came back dressed like her, the skirt beaded and embroidered, the blouse sewn with coins that shimmered as she moved. Her hair was down, snaking round her shoulders. There was a wildness about her; he couldn't keep up with her. She spun away to dance alone, whirling to the music, like the Moorishco.

They were playing for her, playing her even, the music getting higher and higher, wilder and wilder. One of the Moorishco girls was dancing with her now, matching her movements; everyone was clapping and stamping, as they danced faster and faster.

She came back and threw her arms around him. He felt the heat from her, the sheen on her skin, hair damp under his fingers. She shivered as the night air cooled her and he held her tighter. He bent his face to hers and they kissed. He felt drunk, even though he hadn't tasted a thing. She broke from him and was away again, grabbing a passing cup and drinking it off before dancing off after the Moorishco as they left the square. He grabbed a bottle of wine from a table and went in pursuit.

Above them the moon was huge, hanging in the sky, its seas and craters showing like tarnish on its burnished surface. Its bright light took colour away, rendering the world silver and grey with inky deep shadows. Tom plunged into a narrow street, the worn paving shining in the bluish light, the high walls casting sharp shadows across the stones. He'd lost her.

He followed the twists and turns from one street to another. Finally, he stood, hands on knees, out of breath and panting, wondering which way to go, trying to locate the sound of the Moorishco, which seemed to come from all around, everywhere and nowhere at once. Then he heard a piercing whistle and a low laugh.

"Over here. What took yer so long?"

He heard the creak of a garden door and followed her into the shadows.

Inside, the garden glimmered in the blue and white light, the moon picking up the white of the flowers in dark foliage, the flutter of the moths gathered about them. The air was soft, heavy with the scent of jasmine and oleander. They wandered, hand in hand, down a winding path set in patterns of black and white stones. It led them past a pomegranate tree, laden with heavy red fruit, to the glitter and trickle of water. A fountain playing into a pool starred with water lily and lotus, the moon reflected in the rippling surface. Carp rose and disappeared like green-gold shadows moving in and out of the lily pads.

Beyond lay a pavilion roofed with vines, the floor thick with carpets and scattered with cushions. *It's like the perfect chill-out area*, Tom thought—there was even a hookah in the corner. They sat down and shared the wine and talked of Gondal.

"It will be ours, love," she said. "All ours, to do what we like with, peopled how we wish. There could be armies, fighting…"

Tom shook his head. "No armies. No fighting."

"But you are a soldier." She frowned. "I thought you'd like that."

"No armies, no fighting." Tom shook his head again. "And no other people." He traced a finger over her silvered skin. "Just us," he whispered. "Just us."

*   *   *

"Are you sure this boy is what you want? Are you really sure?"

The voice made her start. It was accompanied by that sardonic laugh, clear and loud. Was he here, somewhere in the garden, watching from the shadows, smiling, waiting for her under the pomegranate tree? She sat up, suddenly alert, as if she could see him, but there was no one. It must have been a trick of light and shadow. The sound, just an owl hooting. There was one perched on the corner of the pavilion. It was looking down at her. A big bird with tufts of feathers like horns and something odd about its eyes—and there were words in his call, words she recognized. She rose to come closer and it was gone with a quiet soughing of its huge wings.

Tom stood up, stretching and yawning. "It must be nearly morning. Hadn't we better go?"

"Are you sure you'll be OK?"

Lucy nodded.

"No one is to come in, remember. No one. Any interruption could be dangerous."

Lucy nodded again. "What if someone does? Want to come in, I mean."

"They won't. Doctors' rounds were ages ago and I'm in charge of Tom's care, remember? So no one, none of the other nurses, needs to come in. Tell them I'm in there, giving him a flannel bath—need a bit of privacy. You'll think of something."

With that he slipped into Tom's room. He put his old monkey-skin bag down on the chair and just stood for a while, listening to the sounds all around him: the machines doing Tom's breathing, the monitor beeping and, further away, traffic, an ambulance siren mixed into the hum of the huge building, alive and active, like a great hive, twenty-four hours a day.

Time to get started. The girl was right: he would not have all night. He'd made most of the preparations before coming here, fasting and purifying himself. He opened his bag and took out a small bottle, emptying the black liquid contents into a small bark cup. He drank it off in one, grimacing at the bitter taste. He waited for the herbal draught to take effect. That was why he'd arranged to do this thing after he came off shift and why he would be going home on the bus. He lit a sage smudge stick, blowing on the end until it was glowing, being careful, keeping it well away from the smoke alarms. It was a risk but it was important to cleanse the space of bad energy. This was a hospital: people suffered here, died here—who knew what bad stuff, what negative chi, might be trapped in this room, unable to move on to another place? He then turned and bowed to the four directions—South, West, North, East—muttering a prayer to honour each one and to ask for the help of the guardian spirits who lived there; he held his hands in prayer to reverence Mother Earth and opened his arms wide to Father Sky. Once he'd done that, he was about set.

Some shamans used all kinds of other stuff—special stones, pipes, crystals and such—but for Joe it was pretty much him and his drum. He took it out now, an oval wooden hoop covered in stretched skin painted with pictograms and symbols. To Joe it was a living thing. It spoke to him. It had been given to him by a *noaidi*, a shaman of the Sámi peoples. Joe had travelled far in his search for knowledge.

He began to walk slowly round the bed, tapping the drum softly, singing his song. He was a soul catcher, a natural, marked out as such from childhood. He'd worked with all kinds of lost and damaged souls, but coma patients were tricky. No knowing how far the soul had wandered, whether it wanted to return at all, or was getting ready to transcend, leave for good.

As he drummed and chanted, he began to get a sense of things. Tom was with another, in the Middle World, the World of Dream. He was happy there. Didn't want to come back. So he would not, could not return on his own. Joe would have to go get him. Joe was descending inside himself, going deeper and deeper, but his senses stayed alert, waiting for a guide. A white shape, broad wings outstretched, heading straight for the window, its sclerotic eyes blinded by the light. Joe flinched back, anticipating the impact, but the bird landed on the sill. An owl, a barn owl. It looked at him for a long moment with its sad, black eyes. It swivelled its big, round head, winding to look behind it, then it was gone, its silent wings shining in the moonlight as if sewn with pearls.

Joe pulled his cloak tighter around him. The tugging wind hinted at rain. Britain, he guessed. He was in Britain. He should have been used to the climate by now. North. High moorland, few trees in the rocky ground, and he could feel the cold breath of the Old Ones on his face. He was in an ancient landscape. Very ancient. He could feel the age of the stones. They held inside them all knowledge: of what had been; what is; what is yet to be. He could hear the run of trickling water, see it pooled in hollows thick with fern and spiked with rushes. He put his hand down to touch the rough, wiry bushes that grew low about him. He was unfamiliar with the flora but he guessed heather as he bent closer to see the colour and taste the scent of the tiny bell-like flowers.

He stood as still as the rocks about him and listened, searching for a suitable spirit animal. He sensed a hare near, asleep in its form, but there was plenty of other life about. The place was busy with it. All around, he could hear the snuffling, scuffling and scurrying of animals— mice, weasels, badgers going about their business—but most were too small or slow for his purpose. A handsome fox stopped to look at him. He stood quite still on delicate black legs, his fur a blaze in the moonlight, and stared with yellow eyes. He twitched one black-tipped ear then the other. Joe kept the fox's eyes on him and was just about to merge when he heard a cry like tearing silk and an owl flew by, crossing the moon as it did so. That was the one.

She wasn't hard to find, seated in a chair made from slabs of stone. He landed on a bush not far distant and settled to watch. Perhaps the rocks had naturally formed that way but Joe didn't think so. This was a seers' chair made for the ones who wander to be kept safe on their journeying and on their return. Made by those who had lived here a long, long time ago. Their trackways still criss-crossed the land; the stones that they had placed still bore the marks that they had made and whispered of their presence here.

She sat straight-backed, her feet firmly planted on the ground; hands resting lightly on the two slabs of stone that made the arms of the chair. She was travelling now, her eyes open but unseeing. She was a natural—he knew straight away. One who could slip out of her skin, step from this world to another as easily as she might leave the house. *How had she learnt?* he wondered. *From whom?* With his people, the apprenticeship was long and hard. Maybe there were folk hereabouts who lived by the old ways, kept the ancient wisdom alive. Maybe she didn't need a teacher. Maybe the land itself had taught her. All that did not matter. He'd found her, and through her he'd find Tom.

He spread his wide wings and swooped, landing on her knee. The grip of his talons made Emily glance down. She was looking at the owl with human eyes. There were words in his purring call. Words she knew.

CHAPTER FORTY-TWO

DEPARTURE

THE AIR WAS COOL as they took the steep road down to the harbour. The cockerels were only just beginning to crow. The sun had yet to clear the hills; there was still an orange glow behind Glass Town.

"The tide is turning." She stopped.

"How do you know that?"

"I just do."

"Well, shouldn't we hurry?"

She didn't answer that. "I... I had a dream. Well, I think it was a dream. I heard a voice in the garden."

"Whose voice?"

"Rogue's voice."

"He's gone. You heard them say so."

"What if he hasn't? What if he's here somewhere, waiting?"

"He can't have you. Not if I'm around." Tom took her hand. "Anyway, you're leaving, going to the other side of the world, to a place where he will never find you."

"I know. But what if I go there..." her voice dropped to a whisper, "and lose you?"

"But why would you?" He frowned. "I'm coming with you."

"After I heard Rogue," she said, shivering, "I saw an owl, as close as you are now. It was there to tell me something. Owls rarely bring good news."

They were above the harbour now. Annie was waiting, her bundle on one side, Keeper on the other. The last of the supplies were being loaded, great nets swinging across to the decks. The gangplank was still down, but there was urgency about the orders being given. A ripple in the surface of the water, a slight shimmer in the perfect reflection of the ship, a movement in the houses and buildings of the town mirrored there. Glass Town: mutable, changeable, nothing permanent about it. In the outer harbour the mirror water was taking on colour, turning from steel blue to bright, burnished copper. The tide was on the ebb, going out, and it would take the ships with it.

She found her feet dragging, held by a sudden reluctance to take the steep, worn steps down to the docks.

"It was only dreaming. Come on." Tom put his arm round her. "We have to go. *You* have to go and I'm coming with you—I promised, didn't I?"

"There you are!" Annie was looking out anxiously from the hood of her cloak. "Where have you been? All yer boxes are stowed." She looked up at the net swinging above their heads. "That's the last of them now. You were supposed to be here last night. Commander Parry's been that mithered—" She broke off and looked at Augusta and Tom, standing close, hands clasped. "So that's the way of it, is it? Well, you," she addressed Tom, "think on. Owt happens, you answer to me. Do you understand?"

"Yes, ma'am," Tom said.

"Don't ma'am me. I'm plain Annie."

"Yes, Annie."

The dog gave a growl and half bark, as if adding his own warning.

"Hush, Keeper. It's all right now." Annie put her hand on the dog's head. "I had to put the muzzle back on," she said by way of apology. "He don't like sailors."

The shout went out. "All aboard who's coming!"

Annie hurried for the companionway, Keeper following reluctantly, tail between his legs; he didn't like water, either.

Parry and Ross were up on the quarterdeck, beckoning impatiently. Men in naval uniforms and Lord Nelson hats. Tom didn't know one from the other but he guessed he would soon find out.

"Come on, then." He turned to Augusta. "We better go."

She didn't reply. She was looking past him, her eyes huge and wide, her hand to her mouth. A man was coming towards them at a steady, easy pace, neither dawdling nor hurrying. Dark-skinned, with his long, dark hair braided, a bright patterned blanket wrapped around him, bag over his back, a hat pulled down over his eyes. He could have been a lascar, from the Indies, from South America. Sailors came from everywhere. The docks were full of them looking to take ship. But she knew that wasn't his purpose.

He looked up at her, his large, dark eyes unusually round and brightly glittering under the hat's broad brim. She'd seen those eyes before. He was going to take Tom from her. He had to go home—that was the meaning of the words behind the owl's call.

Tom frowned. There was something about the man that looked familiar. He knew those broad features; knew there would be a gap between his front teeth even before he smiled.

"Come, Tom." The voice was deep and gentle with a lilting accent, a voice Tom recognized even though he couldn't quite place it. "Say your farewells. It's time."

CHAPTER FORTY-THREE

RETURN

LUCY HAD STATIONED HERSELF outside Tom's door, not quite sure what she would do if anyone wanted to go in there. "You'll think of something," Joe had said. She scanned the corridor for signs of activity. Everything was quiet. Visiting time was over, but they were used to her being here at odd times. She'd become part of the ward, part of the furniture. They didn't even notice her any more.

She glanced at the closed door and wondered what Joe was doing in there. He hadn't explained; just went in with a leather bag over his shoulder and shut the door. There were sounds coming from inside, just audible. Drumming and a deep humming, maybe singing. It was pretty faint but she looked up and down the corridor, in case someone else heard it and demanded to know what was going on. She had her story ready. Sound was supposed to help coma patients and people played them all sorts: music, talking, even football chants.

She looked at her watch. Time seemed to be passing very slowly. It actually wasn't that long since Joe had gone in but it seemed like ages. She jumped as the ward bell buzzed. A nurse walked past to open the door. Lucy busied herself with the hand-sanitizer dispenser.

What if someone did want to go into Tom's room? Whatever Joe was doing in there would probably be unorthodox enough to get him sacked. Even worse than that: to interrupt him might harm Tom, and mean he was lost for ever. Lucy realized with an uncomfortable jarring to her heart just how much she wanted him to come back. But what then? How could he possibly feel the same thing? He hardly knew her. She was in no way important to him. Besides, he already had a girlfriend. True, she hadn't been here lately but she'd be back with a vengeance if he came round: *#miraclerecovery, #goodbyeloserlucy.*

Lucy sniffed and searched for a tissue. This was stupid, crying over heartbreak that hadn't even happened yet.

At last, the doors opened and Joe came out. His face was greyish, clay coloured and he looked at least ten years older. His dark hair was plastered to his forehead and stood in spikes on the back of his neck; his scrubs were patched a darker blue under the armpits, down his back. He carried his bag as if he was transporting ten-kilo kettlebells.

She moved towards him but he waved her back.

"No." He shook his head. "I'm all sweaty. I need to shower. Go in to him. Stay with him as long as you can."

"Is he…" she began. "Have you—"

He shook his head again. "Too soon to tell. But if he wakes, he'll need to see a friendly face."

Joe went off down the corridor and Lucy went into the room.

"*If he wakes…*"

Suddenly, it seemed as if after all this time lying like a sleeping prince in a fairy tale Tom might actually wake up.

She went over to the bed. He looked just the same.

Lucy bit back her disappointment. "It can take time," Joe had said. She'd just have to be patient.

CHAPTER FORTY-FOUR
"THAT QUIET EARTH"

LUCY LOOKED AT HER WATCH. It was getting late. She'd have to go soon or they would throw her out. There was still no change in Tom. The only sound was the electric pump attached to the ventilator.

She was nearly at the end of the novel she'd been reading. Just one more paragraph to go. Had he heard any of it? Had it all been a big fat waste of time, like Natalie said? Did it even matter? She forced her focus back to her book. Might as well finish it now.

"*I lingered round them, under that benign sky; watched the moths fluttering among the heath, and hare-bells; listened to the soft wind breathing through the grass; and wondered how any-one could ever imagine unquiet slumbers, for the sleepers in that quiet earth.*"

As she spoke the last words, she was aware of a new sound. A choking sob coming from the bed. The book slid from her lap on to the floor. She was over there in less than a heartbeat, her hand on the red emergency button.

Tom was coming round and he was crying. His cheeks were wet with tears and he was sobbing, struggling against the machines that were giving him life.

*   *   *

The crash team were there in seconds and Lucy was hustled out. She retrieved her book from the floor and left the hospital, not sure when she'd be back. Would he want to see her again? There were more important people in his life. He didn't even really know her. He'd been unconscious the whole time. If she turned up, he'd wonder who she was and what she was doing there. It would be awkward, difficult. She'd just be taking up space. If she'd helped him just a little bit, she was glad of it, but it was time to step away, melt into the background again. She was nothing to him.

Tears caught in her throat as she walked down corridors that she had come to know, breathed the familiar hospital smell: disinfectant and hand gel. She probably wouldn't be here again. The smell would always remind her of him. The quiet time in his room. Just the two of them. She swiped the tears from her eyes and she told herself not to be so stupid. People would think she'd lost someone when the opposite was true. He'd come back to the world, but his world did not contain her. She was nothing to him, she reminded herself again. Nothing.

CHAPTER FORTY-FIVE

THE MARGAY—
THE PRETTY ONE

"Hi. Is that Lucy?"

"Yes. Who's this?"

But she knew it was Joe: the accent, the deep voice on the edge of laughter.

"It's Joe. I still have your number. Tom's come round. He's out of the coma."

"I know," she said, sharper than she intended. "I was there."

"Course you were. Course you were. Doctors are amazed. Busy explaining it: locked-in syndrome; spontaneous recovery. It happens. Rarely, but it happens. Let them think that. I'm just glad he's back. I'm sure you are, too." There was a pause. "Anyway, thought you'd like to know he's doing well. Coming on in leaps and bounds." There was another pause, longer this time. He cleared his throat. "You haven't been around. Just wondered if there was a reason for that?"

"Oh, you know…" She was tempted to say, *I've been busy*, but that sounded trite, cheesy, like bad dialogue from a movie. Besides, she couldn't lie to Joe: he'd see straight through it. "I, um, didn't want to be in the way. He doesn't really know me. There are other—more important—people in his life."

"He wants to see you. He keeps asking, 'Where is the girl who was reading?'"

"Why?" It was all she could think of to say.

Joe laughed. "Maybe he wants to discuss the book with you. All I know is he asked me to ring you."

"What about Natalie? Milo?"

"Unh-hn." She could hear the shake of his head. "Won't see them. Not allowed within a mile of the place. Only his family. And you. Nobody else."

Lucy had wondered. Nothing about Tom on Natalie's social media, or Milo's. No #boyfriendsback or #bestmateoutofcoma. She hadn't seen or heard from either of them, but it was the holidays and their social worlds did not coincide.

"OK," she said. "When does he want to see me?"

"Now would be a good time."

Tom was sitting up in bed. He smiled when she came in.

"At last! I've been waiting for you. Where have you been?"

"Uh, nowhere really." She was tempted to take the "busy" line again but lying to him would be like lying to Joe. "I didn't know if you'd want to see me," she said.

"Why wouldn't I? You were the only one who was there for me day in, day out—except for Joe."

"And your parents."

"They didn't have a choice so they don't count. Come—come here." He patted a place next to him. "Sit on the bed."

She went over and perched awkwardly.

"I do remember, you know," he went on, as if he was the one who should put her at her ease. "I used to like you coming, you reading. I'd look forward to it. You have a nice voice, you know that?"

Lucy could feel herself blushing. "Yeah, well…"

"Don't say anyone would have done it cos they wouldn't and didn't. My sister? Too busy getting her nails done—important stuff like that. Natalie? Too busy being Natalie and posting selfies. What were you reading, if you don't mind me asking?"

"*Wuthering Heights.* Emily Brontë. Didn't you recognize it?"

He shook his head. "I've heard of her, of course. Just never read the book. Strictly science and maths, me."

"Are you OK?"

He was trying to make a joke about it but his voice was weak and all the colour had drained from his face.

"Maybe I'm tiring you. I better leave…"

"Oh, no, no. Don't go. I'm OK. Just low blood pressure, probably. Something like that…"

He lay back. *How can I explain?* Just her name had sent a deep, jolting pain to the region of his heart. But what could he say? How could he tell her? Tell anybody? He'd met a world-famous writer and she was just an ordinary girl. No. Not ordinary. Never that.

"Will you lend it to me? The book?"

"Sure."

"I should get out of bed. Move about. Will you take a walk with me? Nowhere too exciting. End of the corridor and back is about all I can do. I'm supposed to take exercise. Left me weak as a kitten. Legs are a bit wobbly. Can you grab that dressing gown for me and the slippers?" He gave a wry grin. "They're my dad's. Feel like an old man in more ways than one. I might have to lean on you."

"That's OK."

"Awkward, huh?" He leant into her. He was taller and she thought he'd be heavier. He'd lost weight, lying there on the bed. "What do you reckon on our chances in the three-legged race?"

"At the moment? Nil."

"High as that?"

"We might get better with practice."

"Practice? I'd like that. Same place, same time?" He stopped at the turn of the corridor. "We could build it up. Go further. I don't even know what's round the corner. We could explore! It gets boring in here," he said as they started off again. "And I miss you reading."

"You can read yourself now."

"I guess. Tell you what I won't be doing—playing video games. Milo was here just now. Desperate to tell me how he'd saved me, what a hero he was. Then he offered to let me try out his latest 'gaming concept'—still at development stage, he says. Can you believe that?"

"Of Milo? Yes. Totally. I thought you didn't want to see him?"

"I relented. I guess I owe him." He couldn't explain just how much. If it wasn't for Milo, he never would have met her... "Emily," he said as they came back to his door. "What else did she write, besides *Wuthering Heights*?"

"Nothing." Lucy shrugged. "No more novels, anyway. Poetry. I can bring you some in to read."

"I'd like that."

"She died before she could write another novel."

"How old was she?"

"She was thirty."

"That's not very old." His eyes suddenly filled. "Sorry." He sniffed. "I get emotional for no reason."

"That's OK." She handed him a tissue from the box on the stand by the bed. "Understandable after what you've been through." She helped him up on to the bed. "A lot of her writing was destroyed."

He frowned. "How was that?"

"Who knows?" Lucy sat on the side of the bed. "Maybe she did it herself. Or maybe it was her sister, Charlotte." There was a pause. Lucy took a deep breath. What the hell—she had nothing to lose. "Tell you what. I'm planning a trip to Haworth, to the Parsonage, where they lived. Would you like to come with me? When you're better, I mean. When you're stronger, obviously. And only if you're interested, that is. I've passed my test. I can drive us there." It all came out in a rush, too fast and too much. "Of course, you don't have to," she added quickly. "Really. I don't know why I thought... We're doing *Wuthering Heights* for A level and… and I've developed a bit of an obsession—with Emily. I was going to go with my mum, but I just thought… You don't have to, honestly. Forget—"

"Sssh!"

Tom laughed and shook his head. He laughed because it felt good to laugh; because he could; because he was so glad to see her, and she was funny, even when she didn't mean to be—especially when she didn't mean to be; and he liked the way she blushed and the way she caught the tip of her tongue between her teeth. Joe called her the margay, the pretty one. Tom could see what he meant.

"I'd love to," he said. "I really would."

CHAPTER FORTY-SIX

HAWORTH

Tom was outside the Parsonage, leaning on the grit-stone wall. He couldn't be inside any longer, going from room to room, up and down the narrow stairs, the guide's voice droning in his ears. This was a special year and she was everywhere, her face on boards six foot high, the image taken from Branwell's famous portrait of the sisters. Photographs of the actresses who'd played her in various films. Some pretty close likenesses; others nowhere near.

He'd suddenly felt faint and had to go out. It felt better outside. The weak autumn sun appeared from behind the running clouds, casting a golden light over everything. The wind, tugging in his hair, dried the sweat from his skin. He closed his eyes and took a few deep breaths, as Joe had told him to do, and then focused on the rough stone under his fingers, the grey and yellow frills of lichen, the bright green of the moss growing on the wall.

"Just breathe," Joe had told him. "Take your attention to something outside yourself."

If ever he felt like this, if ever any kind of panic threatened to overtake him. And it did. He had to admit.

He wasn't over it yet. Not fully. It would take a long while.

He breathed deep, nostrils flaring, and caught the tang of woodsmoke in the air, with a sharper note of burning leaves. Someone having a bonfire. There was an allotment behind him. Probably coming from there. He looked round—actually, the smoke was coming from up behind the house. Tom boosted himself off the wall. He hadn't noticed anything there before.

He crossed to the wall opposite and looked over. Up a slight slope, next to rows of bean sticks, a bonfire was burning. A girl stood next to it, a girl in a long chequered dress with a grey woollen shawl wrapped tightly around her. She was feeding small ink-marked pages, like leaves, into the fire. Tom looked around. Was this a re-enactment, a workshop, or what? But the wall he'd been leaning on just now had disappeared, along with half the buildings and all of the trees. He looked up at the girl as he opened the gate into the garden.

She looked older than he remembered, thinner, taller. Keeper was by her side, wearing the big brass collar Tom had just seen in the museum. The dog got to his feet slowly as Tom approached. He was older, too. The growl growing in his throat turned to a yelping yawn as Tom held out his hand. The big dog reared up, paws on Tom's shoulders, nearly knocking him over.

"Hey, boy." Tom stroked the big head. "Good to see you, too."

Emily looked up at the sound of his voice. She tucked a lock of straying dark hair behind her ear and shaded her eyes against the dazzle from the fleeting sun.

"Oh, it's you." She smiled, her grey eyes pale as the clouds scudding over the moors behind her. "What took yer so long?"

She tore up the last of the little books and dropped the leaves into the fire.

"Come, lad." She held her hand out to him, so thin and white it was almost transparent. "Come wi' me."

She led him out of the little garden and up on to the moors that lay beyond it.

"There you are! I wondered where you'd got to!" Her voice changed to concern as she saw his face. "Are you OK? You look very pale."

Tom turned, and the world turned with him. Woodsmoke drifted from the allotments. An old man was raking leaves. The modern world came crashing back. Tom was outside the Parsonage as it was now, surrounded by trees, swollen with extensions and the extra buildings tacked on to the back of it, beleaguered by groups of visitors who had come from everywhere: Malaysian girls in hijabs; Japanese students taking selfies; Chinese tourists taking a group photograph, making rabbit ears above each other's heads.

Lucy was looking up at him, a Brontë Parsonage Museum bag swinging from her arm. The group of

Japanese students was forming up outside the entrance, the air full of their excited chatter. Another lot were in the garden, taking more photographs, swarming everywhere. Still more were issuing from the gift shop's exit, toting bags like Lucy's.

"Yeah," he said. "Yeah. I'm good. Felt a bit strange in there, that's all. Claustrophobic. Too many people. Just needed to come outside. Get some fresh air."

"Are you sure you're all right? You're not supposed to overdo it."

Tom's strength was coming back, but recovery was a slow process and it was going to take some time before he was back to normal.

"Yeah, yeah." Tom boosted himself off the wall. "What now?"

"I want to go into the church. See where Emily's buried."

Tom looked up at the grey stone building and frowned.

"It's not the original church," Lucy said. "Not the one they knew. It was rebuilt in 1879."

"What's the point, then?"

"They're still buried there."

"It doesn't seem right." Tom shook his head. "She should be out here, not in some mouldy old vault."

"Please, Tom. I'd really like to see her final resting place."

"OK. Tell you what. Why don't we go up on the moor, pick some heather for her? If she can't be out here, we can take the moor in to her."

"What a good idea. Are you sure you're up to it, though?"

"We don't have to go far. Don't fuss. You're my girl-friend, not my mother."

"OK."

They linked arms and set off, following a worn track up on to the moors.

"Let's go a bit further—away from the tourists taking selfies."

They walked on until they'd lost the crowd. Tom stopped next to a little dell. Above it stood a formation of rocks that looked very much like a chair.

"Oh, I know this," Lucy said. "I read about it." She took a photograph with her phone. "Ellen Nussey mentions it in her biography of Charlotte."

Tom wasn't listening. He was staring off at the sky-line, at two figures silhouetted there, turning away from him—always turning away from him. Emily and a version of himself.

"Tom? The heather?"

"Oh, yeah. Right." Tom took out a penknife and cut some sprigs, bound them into a bunch with a few spikes of rush.

They walked back to the squat, grey church, making their way through the crowded gravestone slabs and going in at a side door.

It wasn't hard to find the Brontë Chapel. They were all buried together—apart from Anne, Lucy explained, who had died in Scarborough and was buried there.

THE
BRONTË FAMILY
VAULT
IS SITUATED BELOW
THIS PILLAR,
NEAR TO THE PLACE WHERE
THE BRONTËS' PEW STOOD
IN THE OLD CHURCH.
THE FOLLOWING MEMBERS
OF THE FAMILY
WERE BURIED HERE
MARIA AND PATRICK.
MARIA, ELIZABETH,
BRANWELL,
EMILY JANE, CHARLOTTE.

"Why are they buried under a pillar?" Tom objected. "That's a bit weird."

"I don't know. Maybe it happened when the church was rebuilt."

"But why would they do that?" Tom went on. "I mean, these are the most famous people to be buried here and they stick them under a pillar!"

"I don't know, Tom. Does it matter?"

"Suppose not," he muttered, but somehow it did. It mattered a lot. He could feel the anger rising inside him and fought to control it, taking deep breaths. That was one of the things he'd been left with: mood swings.

He looked around for somewhere to place the heather. He didn't want to put it at the bottom of the pillar. He had no sense of her there.

Nearby was a brass plaque set into the floor. Again, it seemed really arbitrary—vaguely positioned between a pillar and a wall.

IN MEMORY OF
EMILY JANE BRONTË
WHO DIED DEC. 19TH 1848,
AGED 30 YEARS.

Tom placed the little bunch of heather next to offerings laid by other people. He stood, hands clasped, head bowed, but he wasn't praying for her because she wasn't here. She was out there, somewhere, out on the moors, and some part of him would always be with her.

"Come, lad." He heard her voice whisper. "Come wi' me."

"We Wove a Web in Childhood"

In June 1826, Branwell Brontë was given a box of wooden soldiers by his father, Patrick. He shared the gift with his sisters: ten-year-old Charlotte; Emily, who was eight; and Anne, the youngest, who was six. Each child seized a soldier and named him. Branwell called his Buonaparte, Charlotte chose the Duke of Wellington, Emily and Anne called theirs Gravey and Waiting Boy, later to be changed to the explorers Parry and Ross. These became the Young Men. The children immediately began to make up stories. They sent the Young Men off on an epic voyage of exploration and conquest that would take them to the west coast of Africa, where they would found their own country and build a new city, Glass Town, at the mouth of the Niger River.

The adventures of the Young Men were first explored as plays but soon they were written down in minuscule writing in tiny books no bigger than the palm of a child's hand. The little books were stitched together and bound in sugar bags and wrapping paper—anything that the children could find about the Parsonage. The books contained stories, poems, articles produced for, about and by the inhabitants of Glass Town. They were handwritten, handmade versions of adult books and magazines with author, editor and publisher carefully printed out on the title page. The miniature books were for their toy soldier readers but their diminutive size also kept them away from the prying eyes of adults. The Brontë children wrote for themselves, for each other, the early stories reflecting their interest in violent battle scenes, bodysnatching and hauntings, magic and the supernatural. Their focus on the whole book, not just what was inside it, suggests that, even as children, they wrote to be published.

The siblings had plenty of material; they were very well informed. They studied current affairs in magazines and newspapers: the history of the Napoleonic Wars, the military leaders Wellington and Napoleon, exploration and emigration, national politics, local events like the riots and strikes in rapidly industrializing Haworth and nearby Halifax. They read widely and they absorbed everything: natural history and geography, the novels of Sir Walter Scott, *The Arabian Nights* (from where they borrowed the Genii), folk stories of fairies and ghosts on the moors. All that they read, all they were told, all that they learned fed into their writing and into the creation of the intense, complex fantasy worlds that were Glass Town, Angria and Gondal.

Over time, the writing became an increasingly sophisticated, fully realized world that was constantly evolving, added to and changing. They were creating a continually shifting social and political scene, which they illustrated with maps, drawings and paintings. The characters they had first created acquired stories and personalities of their own. Branwell's Napoleon became Alexander Augustus Percy, Duke of Northangerland, also known as Rogue. Charlotte replaced the Duke with his sons, Arthur Wellesley, Marquis of Douro, and Lord Charles Wellesley. They peopled Glass Town with many other characters, high born and low: Branwell's "rare lads", the resurrectionist Dr Bady. Charlotte provided various wives, lovers and mistresses: Lady Zenobia Ellrington, Mina Laury, Marian Hume. Many of these characters appear in *Glass Town Wars*. Charlotte and Branwell wrote extensively about their characters, adding others and involving them all in a dizzying catalogue of wars, feuds, and a complex web of relationships. Ross and Parry remained Emily and Anne's preferred characters, along with Johnny Lockhart. I confess to borrowing Augusta (Augusta Geraldine Almeida) from their later fantasy of Gondal.

At the beginning, all the siblings were involved in Glass Town and Angria, but nothing written by Emily or Anne survives. All of the little books in existence now are the work of Branwell or Charlotte. An intense rivalry developed between these two. Maybe Emily and Anne tired of this exclusion, or the society as imagined by Charlotte and Branwell was not to their liking. In 1831, the two younger sisters went off to found Gondal, an island in the Pacific Ocean ruled by a passionate, powerful queen, in contrast to the male heroes of Angria and Glass Town. Unfortunately, all we have left of Gondal are a few poems. The worlds that they created had a powerful hold on all the siblings well into adult life. Charlotte bade farewell to Angria when she was twenty-three, but Branwell and Emily continued to be absorbed by their imaginary worlds right up to their untimely deaths in 1848.

In 1847, Charlotte, Emily and Anne Brontë published their first adult novels, *Jane Eyre*, *Wuthering Heights* and *Agnes Grey*, under the pseudonyms of Currer, Ellis and Acton Bell. When contemporary readers and critics discovered the true identity of the authors, they were astonished that these novels were the work of three daughters of a parson with a living in a village on the edge of the Yorkshire Moors. These were writers of rare talent, even genius, but their achievement was not sudden or spontaneous. They were already experienced authors of Gothic fictions, romances, historical sagas, magazine and newspaper articles, and poetry. They had served a long apprenticeship.

Acknowledgements

I would like to thank my husband, Terence Rees, and my daughter, Catrin, for their help and encouragement during the writing of this book. I would also like to thank fellow writers Linda Newbery, Adèle Geras, Julia Jarman, Cindy Jeffries, Yvonne Coppard and Helena Pielichaty for their writerly companionship. I am grateful to the staff at the Brontë Parsonage Museum Library, Haworth, Yorkshire, and particularly Amy Rowbottom, for allowing me to view their collection of the Brontë juvenilia. And to Debra Collinge for advice on things medical, and to Faye Reason and Lucy Coats for telling me something about shamanism.

I would also like to thank my editor at Pushkin Press, Sarah Odedina, for her support and enthusiasm for this project, and Madeleine Stevens for her careful copy-editing.

Find out more about my inspiration and research on my website: www.celiarees.com.

TEEN AND YA FICTION FROM PUSHKIN PRESS

THE RED ABBEY CHRONICLES

MARESI

NAONDEL

MARESI RED MANTLE

Maria Turtschaninoff

Translated by Annie Prime

'Combines a flavour of *The Handmaid's Tale* with bursts of
excitement reminiscent of Harry Potter's magic duels'

Observer

THE BEGINNING WOODS

Malcolm McNeill

'I loved every word and was envious of quite a few…
A modern classic – rich, funny and terrifying'

Eoin Colfer

THE RECKLESS SERIES

I. THE PETRIFIED FLESH

2. LIVING SHADOWS

3. THE GOLDEN YARN

Cornelia Funke

'A wonderful storyteller'

Sunday Times

PIGLETTES

Clémentine Beauvais

Translated by Clémentine Beauvais

'A triumph of a book; so funny, so original, so sharp, so warm'
Katherine Rundell, author of *Rooftoppers*

THE DISAPPEARANCES

Emily Bain Murphy

'*The Disappearances* is a wonder of a book. I lost
myself in this world where reflections, scents and
stars go missing, and revelled in its reveal'
Kiran Millwood Hargrave, author of *The Girl of Ink & Stars*

THE WILDINGS

Nilanjana Roy

'A stylish, bloody, literary addition, set in India and
already a considerable critical success there. Rich
in cat telepathy and shuddery feral madness'
Guardian

THE OKSA POLLOCK SERIES

1. THE LAST HOPE
2. THE FOREST OF LOST SOULS
3. THE HEART OF TWO WORLDS
4. TAINTED BONDS

Anne Plichota and Cendrine Wolf

Translated by Sue Rose

'A feisty heroine, lots of sparky tricks and evil opponents
could fill a gap left by the end of the Harry Potter series'
Daily Mail